→ RISE OF THE ←
KNIGHT SHADES

BOOK ONE:
THE DJINN

J. KENT HOLLOWAY

CHARADE
MEDIA

Rise of the Knightshades: The Djinn
Originally published as The Djinn

ISBN: 979-8-9876847-8-8

Charade Media, LLC
www.charadebooks.com

Cover art and design by Kirk Douponce
www.fictionartist.com

PROLOGUE

Jerusalem
946 BCE

Screams echoed down the corridor as swords clanged from just a few chambers away. The weary king's brow furrowed; his uncertainty betrayed by dull, pained eyes.

"My lord," one of his advisors said. "Are you certain this will work?"

King Solomon shook his head. "I'm about as certain as I am of anything, Yosef. Truth be told, the magicks employed by Rakeesha to create these abominations are still rather new to me. I've no way of knowing how strong it will be."

The mighty king glanced down at the clay human-like figure resting unnaturally upon the stone dais and sighed. Such a tremendous waste. He should have known better, but his thirst for knowledge had grown almost as insatiable as his hunger for power.

Yahweh, forgive me, he thought as more of his soldiers were torn apart at the hands of the twelve abominations created by his wife. *When will I ever learn?*

For someone renowned to have great wisdom, the revered monarch had made his fair share of mistakes. Chief among them was his own love for the fairer sex. His fascination with women after all had compelled him to take on nearly a thousand wives and concubines. A full nine-hundred and ninety-nine more women than any man—no matter how brave, wise, or noble—could possibly handle. And more than one of them had caused a tremendous amount of grief for his kingdom and his God.

But Rakeesha had been different. Or so he'd thought. More beautiful than the painted sky over Cairo, the ebon beauty had been given to him as a gift from her father—a chieftain of a warrior tribe that now guarded one of Solomon's many diamond mines near the untamed lands of Cush. The spirited girl had never forgiven her father for the cruel way in which she'd been handed over to a king of a foreign land. Nor had she ever fully warmed up to the significantly older Solomon. That is, until about a year earlier.

"My lord, I'm not sure how much longer my men will be able to keep them in the Vault," Meneniah, the captain of the guard, shouted. Fear and desperation etched on his face.

The king looked around the antechamber to the Vault…a place his servants had simply called the Hub. Torches burned within their wall sconces illuminating the intricately carved gold trellises that hugged each corner of the room. Several piles of gold, gems, and trinkets of all kinds lay scattered along the floor. The treasure was all that could be rescued from the inner sanctum of the Vault before the creatures had overtaken it. The rest, Solomon knew, would soon be sealed inside forever.

A mere trifle in the scheme of things. He had much more where that came from. The important thing was to stop these monsters from doing any further damage to his people.

More shouts arose from the Vault's interior, followed immediately by some inhuman roar. Meneniah was right. They were running out of time.

Looking over at the high priest, Azariah, he nodded and held out his right hand. The priest placed a strange, cylindrical device in it before bowing and backing away. The king then turned his attention once more to the clay statue resting in front of him. Muttering a silent prayer, he gripped the cylindrical implement and began carving away at the clay along the figure's forehead. He worked at it until a strange script was visible, then took his signet ring and pressed down upon the marking. His prayer escalated in volume as the pressure of his ring increased and he quickly felt heat building from around his ring finger. After three complete minutes of this, he withdrew his hand, backed away, and took in a deep breath.

It had not been the first time he'd done this. Nor was it the first time he'd waited anxiously to see if the ritual would succeed —whether or not the ring, believed by many to hold *magical* properties, would imbue his creation with "the breath of life." On the contrary, he'd practiced this same ritual many times within the last year. Ever since catching his wife, Rakeesha, practicing her witchcraft on a warm, mid-summer night.

He'd been transfixed...spellbound...as he'd watched her sculpt a small feline animal from a pool of wet clay. So near perfect the facsimile had been. Even the striations she'd carved to simulate fur seemed so real. So lifelike.

Imagine his surprise when he'd seen her carve a strange word, utter a string of imperceptible words, and breathe upon the figurine—only to watch as its paws began to move of their own volition. Of course, the cat facsimile had not survived long. The energy that had animated it dissipated within mere minutes of its own quickening.

When questioned, Rakeesha, who knew intimately of her husband's insatiable lust for knowledge, had explained that these clay beings needed one of two things to maintain their animation. They required either the blood sacrifice of a young, healthy human or they needed the divine gift of life itself.

Something, she hinted in the most subtle of ways, that Solomon alone was best suited to provide.

He'd spent the better part of the next three months pondering what she'd told him. Imagining the implications that such a thing provided. After all, with an entire army of these automatons, there would be no force on earth that could ever threaten Israel as there had been in the past. He would never have to risk a mother's son or a wife's husband in battle again.

And with this in mind, he'd approached Rakeesha and she'd agreed to teach him the secret, if not forbidden, art. He'd watched her sculpt the first three creatures with rapt fascination. Then, when he felt confident enough, he'd joined her in molding and fleshing out the next nine. Several painstaking days went by as their humanoid creations took shape.

Solomon shuddered at the memory. Twelve creatures. Each nearly nine feet tall. Their clay frames kept moist in the humid confines of the subterranean Vault in which they were constructed. Once animated, these monstrosities would be living, moving stone walls that no army would be able to vanquish.

"Sire!" Meneniah's pleas broke him from his train of thought and he was once more in the present. "Nothing is happening. Why isn't it working?"

Solomon looked again at the figure. It had not so much as twitched. There was no sign of life in it at all. Which was not altogether surprising. It had taken nearly ten full minutes the last time. Ten full minutes before he realized that his wife had completely betrayed him.

Of course, he should have known as much when she'd insisted that she be the one to quicken them to life. Oh, her reasoning was solid enough. The king had never attempted such powerful sorcery before. One mistake could have devastating consequences for everyone involved. No, it just made sense to let his witch of a wife breathe life into their twelve clay soldiers by using his very own signet ring.

What he'd not anticipated was her complete and seething hatred for her husband. What he'd not been told by her was that the creatures would be enslaved to the person who brought them to life and no one else. So, after the ritual was finished, she'd merely stood there for those excruciatingly long ten minutes and watched mirthlessly until the creatures she'd called *golems* began to move away from the walls that had seemed to birth them.

That's when she began to laugh. A deep-throated, malicious cackle that sent ice through his veins. As the golems moved forward, Rakeesha turned to face her husband...her king...and she continued to laugh for several seconds before speaking.

"For such a wise man, my lord, you are an utter and complete fool," she'd hissed between clenched teeth. "For the crime of taking me against my will...for the cruelties you've shown my people...you and your kingdom will now suffer beyond your wildest imagination, and I will be free of you once and for all."

She then turned her attention back to her creations and hurled a string of curses in a foreign tongue in their direction. Once done, she turned back to Solomon and let out one final laugh before pulling a dagger and dragging its razor edge across her own throat.

Her plan had been ruefully ingenious. Her commands had been given. The golems were now set on their path and with her death, any hope of forcing her to call her monsters off was lost forever.

That had been two days ago, and her golems had dealt a devastating blow. Countless innocents lay dead or severely injured from their berserkers' rage. Soldiers had been torn asunder with simple flicks of the golems' wrists. No weapon within Jerusalem's arsenal could do them any harm. And Solomon had all but given up hope—until just a few hours before, when he'd conceived a way to end Rakeesha's curse as best he could.

Though they did not have the means with which to destroy

the creatures (his wife had omitted that in her lessons to him), they could still be restrained. And there was no more secure place within all Jerusalem than the subterranean tunnels of his own personal treasure vault. But merely luring them into the Vault was the easiest part—they would simply follow the soldiers of Solomon anywhere they moved. The difficulty would be containing them once inside the Vault's interior. Because of the way in which it had been constructed, to attempt to seal them inside would be in vain. The Vault was designed, after all, to keep people out, not in. The only way possible to contain the monsters within would be to destroy the Vault itself.

Which meant he would need someone on the inside. Someone with strength enough to bring the ceiling down on top of everyone in the main Vault. And that, he surmised, would require another golem. So, he'd constructed one. Larger by a full two cubits in height than the others. More massive...more powerful... than anything Rakeesha could have anticipated. This golem would act as Warden to the others. It would keep them in check for all eternity and the people of Israel would never have to fear the clay creatures' wrath again.

"My king! It moves!" Azariah shouted. "It moves!"

Solomon watched as his own creation moved a single finger. Then another. A smile formed slowly across the king's face as he watched the golem sit up from the dais.

Good, Solomon thought. *Now, by the grace of Yahweh, let us end this.*

He moved over to the clay figure and mumbled a string of unintelligible words, then pointed toward the doorway of the Vault's main chamber. Immediately, the creature turned and moved inside and into the mayhem beyond. The clash of swords and screams of his men still resonated from beyond, but there was nothing that could be done for them. They too would be trapped inside once the Warden accomplished its mission.

The king, captain of the guard, high priest, and handful of

advisors stood in grieved silence as the battle raged beyond the door. Gradually, after several minutes, the screams of Meneniah's guards dwindled away. Smoke roiled from the Vault's interior, wafting over those watching in safety. Then, as suddenly as it had started, all fighting inside ceased. Solomon could make out nothing through the murky haze.

One heartbeat. Two. Three. Nothing happened. Four. Five.

Was that the sound of a foot shuffling against the rocky floor? Six. Seven.

Yes, he was sure of it now. Something was definitely moving on the other side. Coming toward them.

Eight. Nine. Ten. Elev—

Without warning, the earth beneath the king's feet rumbled. The subterranean depths of the Vault shook violently as dust and debris exploded from the portico in front of them. Then, with the sound of thunder, the entire ceiling from the Vault's interior collapsed in front of them, sealing it off forever.

Solomon exhaled deeply as he struggled to steady his shaking limbs. It was finally over. The consequences of his own sin were now buried along with tons of stone, mortar, and blood.

After several long, silent moments, he turned to the high priest and handed him his ring. "Take this. Protect it with your life," Solomon said gravely. "See to it that no one unworthy ever wields it again...including myself."

And the last thing Solomon did before turning and walking away was to utter a brief prayer for those who fell to the thirteen abominations now resting quietly within the collapsed vault, followed immediately with another for God's forgiveness.

1

Jerusalem
AD 1184

Thick rivulets of sweat clung to Horatio's tunic as he clambered up the stone walkway toward the Jaffa Gate. The arid heat burned pitilessly through his tired lungs which heaved for breath with each exhausted stride. It was nearly midnight and the cool relief of the nighttime desert had failed to drift toward the City of David.

Horatio could not remember a time he was more miserable, or how many times he and his dimwitted cousin, Samuel, had already walked along the same path this evening.

Too many times, he thought, and nothing to show for their labors or discomfort. If he kept it up, his chain mail would surely rust from perspiration—or he'd die of dehydration. Either way, his skills and talents were being wasted here. Countless battles won on behalf of Lord Gregory, and this was the gratitude the pompous braggart showed him. He was a knight, after all. A knight of low birth, surely, but a *knight*, nevertheless. It was simply unthinkable. Reduced to sentry duty—securing the gate until the caravan escorting a group of soon-to-be slaves for Gregory's excavations arrived. Which was ridiculous when one considered it. The Jaffa Gate was unique among all the gates of Jerusalem for being built at a right angle—a natural defense against attackers and brigands coming up from the Jaffa Road. The architecture was the reason the baron had chosen this gate to receive his newest commodities.

Gregory had insisted the caravan arrive during the night with little to no pomp or ceremony. To keep the slave transaction as clandestine as possible, he'd opted to utilize only one of his knights as opposed to a full company as he would have if the mission was truly as important as he'd told Horatio.

No, the knight was beginning to believe the baron was having his fun with him. Teaching him a lesson from ever speaking out against the baron's methods again. And what better way to teach an errant knight a bit of humility than by placing him on menial guard duty?

But the sentry work wasn't what bothered him the most. It was the object he was forced to protect. Slavers. The very thing he'd questioned Gregory about. No, this assignment was all about a lesson in blind obedience.

Of course, he had been told the assignment was one of utmost importance. He'd been led to believe he'd been chosen for his valor...the last defense against a ghost, a myth, a...

"What was that?" asked Horatio.

"What was what?" asked his squire, Samuel.

"Shut up and listen!"

"Listen to what?"

The knight didn't answer. Clamping one gloved hand over Samuel's mouth, Horatio cocked his head to the left, straining to identify the strange noise that jolted him from his sour reflections. But he could hear very little in the shell-like confines of the helmet.

He didn't have time for this. The slave caravan would be

advancing the hill any moment. Now was not the time to allow anything to slip through the perimeter.

Placing a finger to his lips, the young knight removed the headgear, struggling to keep the mesh neck protector from clinking the stillness from the night.

"What, pray tell, are we listening for?" Samuel's hoarse whisper grated against the silence.

"If I knew that, then I wouldn't have to be listening, now would I?"

"I dunno 'bout that."

"Do be quiet," commanded Horatio, increasingly irritated with his wife for insisting he make Samuel his squire as he took up the *Holy Cross*, as the crusaders called the great quest to the *Outremer*, 'the Land Beyond the Sea.' "Just stand still and listen. I heard a strange noise, so just keep quiet for a few more seconds." He paused and glared at his cousin. "Please," he added.

Samuel merely nodded before becoming distracted by some unseen object within his own nose. His finger dug furiously to dislodge the nuisance. The sight disgusted Horatio, but at least it kept his squire occupied, and more importantly, kept the idiot quiet.

Tensing, Horatio peered into the darkness beyond, carefully listening for any signs of an intruder. The silence devoured all sounds, as if the very city of Jerusalem had been swallowed by the sweltering night. A few palm fronds swayed in a hot breeze coming up from the valley while the gentle song of locusts pulsed rhythmically all around them. But the noise the knight had originally heard was no more.

Horatio strained to place the sound—a gentle rustle of canvas in the wind, a flurry of light footsteps from wall's walkway above. He just couldn't put his finger on what it had been. Nor could he exorcize the uncomfortable sensation that the sound had elicited upon him. It was an irrational feeling, he was sure. Fear without merit. There simply was nothing out there. All was still.

"Oh!" cried Samuel, shattering the silence. "You're listening for the Hob!"

Horatio's throat squeezed up toward his skull as he jumped involuntarily at the sudden outburst from his cousin. He felt one of his knees give slightly as he mustered enough strength to refrain from leaping out of his own boots.

"Quiet, you fool!" Horatio hissed, smacking the simpleton on the backside of the head. "You'll give someone a heart attack! And no, I'm not listening for the *Hob*, as you put it. There's no such thing as goblins or ghosts or anything of the sort."

Horatio wished he was as confident of that fact as he sounded. With all the talk about the hobgoblin that was terrorizing the Christians now occupying the Holy City, even he was beginning to believe it might be true. This, of course, was unthinkable. Horatio was educated. He had no time, nor inclination, to entertain the tales of old wives. He just wished he could convince his own nerves of that.

"But I thought that's why we were out here tonight."

"No, we're out here tonight as lookouts against any possible brigands or heathen that would try to take what belongs to Baron Gregory," said Horatio, willing himself to overcome the nagging fear that was creeping up his spine.

But who could really blame him? All this talk about a spectral creature made of smoke and mist, shadow and nightmare, stalking the Holy Soldiers of God in the dead of night would have most anyone rattled. The Saracens were calling the creature a *djinn*, some dark spirit sent by Allah to protect them from the Christian occupation. Horatio had called it hogwash when he first heard about the attacks. Now, he wasn't so sure. At least thirteen knights and foot soldiers had disappeared without a trace since the Djinn's attacks had begun six months ago. What if he was wrong? What if the Hob was real? What if Gregory's excavations of the tunnels below Jerusalem had somehow awakened some ancient spirit that even now sought vengeance upon them?

Yes, even the great knight known as Horatio was having his doubts. But he wasn't about to let anyone know it.

"But Lord Gregory said…"

"I don't care what Gregory said. There's no such thing as hobgoblins, I'm telling you. Especially not here."

"That's not what gram said, Horatio. She told me stories. Those hobs are bad business, I tell you."

Horatio sighed. There simply was no reasoning with the buffoon, so he continued walking.

"She said that the hobs would visit the unwary sinner in his sleep and carry them back to their holes and do all sorts of unspeakable things," continued Samuel, straining to keep up with Horatio's long strides. "No one ever returned from a hob hole, it's said. And Horatio, the very same thing is happening here."

"If no one ever returned then how on earth do we know such things exist?"

"Well, they say there are some…those with learnin' in sorcery and such who can speak with them," Samuel was persistent. "That's how we know such things."

Horatio could do nothing but continue walking into the darkness, shaking his head. There really was no convincing the youngster and Horatio wasn't even sure he should try. All the signs pointed to Samuel's conclusion. It all seemed so supernatural. The attacks. The disappearances. And in each encounter, it was said that the very shadows around the Djinn's victims came alive and swallowed them whole. A shiver rattled involuntarily down Horatio's sweat drenched body.

The torchlight from the city streets no longer reached them out on the outer edge of the walls of Jerusalem. Horatio's sharp eyes searched the path ahead, looking for any movement in the murk before them. For one brief second, he could have sworn that an amorphous shadow slithered against the stone wall, but it was gone as quickly as it appeared.

This is crazy, thought Horatio. *The boy's rattling my nerves. It's just superstitious nonsense, after all.*

"Lord Gregory says this djinn is nothing more than a good ol' English hobgoblin," droned Samuel. "And there's plenty of ways to deal with the likes of him, he says. But I'm not so sure. I think that maybe...urk!"

The prattling rant of his squire ceased with a yelp, spinning Horatio around, sword drawn in one swift motion. Samuel was nowhere to be seen. In the place where he had stood was nothing but a plume of smoke, reeking of brimstone. Horatio spun around again, scanning every nook and shadow that lined Jerusalem's wall.

The Hob had struck. It had taken poor Samuel in a flash of hellfire and Horatio had been unable to do anything against it. Panic welled up in the knight's chest. He knew the creature still lurked somewhere nearby and unseen.

"Come out!" Horatio cried, angered that his voice had squeaked like a drunken barmaid.

The knight spun left, then right, his sword extended out from his body, ready to strike at anything that moved against him. The reek of brimstone burned his nostrils, and he struggled not to retch. The stench was ghastly. *Nothing can smell as bad as this*, Horatio thought, as he tried to compose himself.

"I say come out, coward!"

A soft breeze blew across his face, the beads of sweat rolled over his brow like icy fingertips. Horatio placed his helmet on top of his head once more and stepped toward the spot where Samuel had only seconds ago stood.

The wary knight looked down to examine the ground. A weird black powder scorched the earth near his squire's footprints.

"Odd," Horatio said aloud.

Crouching down, the knight dipped his finger into the powder. Bringing the residue to his face, his nose wrinkled in disgust. There was no doubt about it. *Brimstone*. The nausea washed over the knight's senses again. He felt dizzy.

"Foul odor," he muttered. "The vestiges of hell itself."

"Not exactly," said a cold muffled voice from somewhere behind Horatio.

The knight spun around. A sharp hiss shot out from the darkness and Horatio felt the frigid bite of unseen tendrils snaking around his ankle. A jerk from above, and the knight's foot flew up into the sky pulling the rest of his body with it. His sword slipped from his grasp, clanging as it struck the hard, dry earth and Horatio found himself hanging upside down, five feet off the ground.

A gleefully malicious cackle resonated from somewhere in the darkness.

The Hob.

Twisting his head around to look for the source of his sudden misfortune, Horatio let out a single whimper. Sheer, unadulterated terror wrapped around his body like spiny tentacles, threatening to squeeze the air from his lungs.

Standing mere inches from the upended knight stood a creature as dark as the night itself. Its black turban—what the Saracens called a *tagelmust*—flapped in the warm breeze, blending itself perfectly into the darkness. Horatio reckoned it stood a full ten feet tall if it stood an inch and hid its horrible features behind a shroud of black cloth. Long leather boots reached above its knees and the ebony-hued scimitar clutched in the creature's clawed hand glistened in the light of the moon. Its other hand clutched at a strange cord that stretched up and around a wooden awning that jutted from the city's wall and descended again around Horatio's ankle.

The Hob leaned forward. Horatio struggled against the bindings around his ankle, trying desperately to free himself...to flee...but it was no use. The dark spirit had cast its accursed spell against him, and the knight hung helplessly in midair, frozen with dread.

The Hob glided over; its outstretched claw caressing the frightened knight's face, pulling his head up to look Horatio square in the eyes.

Those eyes. Horatio could not recall ever seeing such horribly dark eyes. Eyes of vengeance. Eyes of malice. Eyes that glowed with green ethereal fire as though reflecting the very flames of Hell itself.

"Nay, not quite from hell," the Hob said as if reading his mind. "But I've been there."

Horatio wasn't quite sure what the creature meant. He wasn't quite sure of anything, actually, except for the suffocating horror that coursed through his blood at that moment.

"Wh-what do you want with me?" Horatio managed with a great deal of effort. "What do you want?"

The creature paused for several seconds in thought. Its head tilted slightly, looking up into the night sky. It turned to face the knight again.

"It's simple. I've come to free the prisoners your lord uses as slave labor to dig his tunnels. You know...the ones you are standing sentry for."

"Prisoners? I have no idea what you're talking about?"

A snarl from the creature told Horatio he wasn't buying the lie.

"All right, all right," said Horatio, a voice squeaking. "I do know, but it'll do you no bit of good. They're heavily guarded. You'll not be getting close enough to even glance at them, much less free them."

Another chuckle erupted from the creature's bowels.

"You misunderstand, sir knight," it hissed. "The deed is already done. They have already been freed and the few guards that survived have been taken as my *own* prisoners."

Horatio's throat seemed to whither at the news.

"Taken?" he asked. "Like the others?"

The Djinn merely nodded.

"So, d-do you plan to take me as well? Did...did you take my squire too?"

The creature stared at his captive for several long seconds. He seemed to be savoring the knight's ordeal. Horatio felt the sudden urge to vomit but willed himself against it.

"Have no fear, sir knight," said the creature. "You will better serve me in other ways. I want to give you a message to relay to your lord."

"A...a message?" Horatio could hardly control his voice. "What message?"

"It's simple. I want Gregory's mad quest to end. I want him and those who follow him to leave this land. But most importantly, I want Gregory's personal quest to cease."

That confirmed it. Only a creature in league with the devil would desire God's holy army to withdraw from their noble mission. The baron and his knights had been sanctioned by the Pope himself...sent to Jerusalem for a very special task. They had the blessing of God Himself. Any creature who sought to undermine such a sacred endeavor could only come from the Evil One.

Horatio felt his fear waning. Righteous indignation burned in his breast and contempt for the demonic beast before him outweighed any dread he had once harbored.

"Never, foul creature!" said Horatio. "We will never surrender to the devil or his henchmen. I'm not sure what Baron Gregory is searching for, but I'm sure it is to honor the Most High God!"

The Hob glared at the upside-down knight. To the knight's surprise, a roar of laughter erupted from the creature's throat—not a menacing evil laugh as the Hob had released before, but one of genuine mirth. Horatio wasn't sure he liked this laughter any better. It was completely unexpected, and it unnerved the beleaguered knight beyond what he would have thought possible.

The creature sheathed its sword in a leather scabbard, stretched his arm back and brought it swiftly across Horatio's backside. It wasn't a brutal hit at all, but one that comrades in arms might land when goading the other in jest.

"I like you, sir knight!" the creature said. "Aye, I like you a great deal. You have a spine after all. It's something your fellow crusaders should endeavor to emulate."

The Hob's other hand suddenly released the cord and Horatio fell helplessly to the ground in a blur of motion. The knight wasn't sure he was better off having been released from his aerial prison. Upon standing up from the dirt, he found himself surrounded by a maelstrom of smoke and brimstone, cutting off all light and breathable air. Horatio gagged on the rancid fumes as he tried desperately to retrieve his fallen sword.

But the creature was gone. Terror gripped Horatio's heart once more. Would the Hob strike now that his guard was down? Would he finally be carried away to the dark recesses of the earth that hobs were known to dwell?

"Tell Gregory this," said the Hob's strange and distant voice. Horatio couldn't make out where it was coming from. It sounded as if it was coming from inside his own head. "Tell him that the Djinn has marked him for his treacheries. Tell him that I know of his plans and will not allow him to carry them out. Tell him to leave now or he will face me soon enough."

Horatio could only hack at the sulfurous smoke now burning a path to his lungs.

"And dear Horatio," said the voice, "remain steadfast, young knight, and you may one day see the truth for what it is...not what you wish it to be."

With a flurry of wind, the presence of the Hob was gone—the lingering plumes of brimstone the only evidence that it had ever been there at all. Horatio had survived. He had encountered the grim spirit and lived to tell the tale. He could think of nothing but to fall to his knees and thank the Lord for his deliverance.

His praises were soon interrupted by a strange murmuring from behind a large boulder to Horatio's right. The knight stood, drew his blade once more and carefully tread around the stone—cautious of an ambush.

But a smile quickly replaced the scowl he'd been wearing since first encountering the Djinn at the sight of Samuel, trussed up by ropes and gagged with a cloth strip and laying prone on the ground. Despite a few bumps and abrasions, his poor squire appeared to be fine. Just one more thing for the knight to be grateful for. Despite the boy's irritating ways, Horatio truly cared for Samuel. He was pleased to find him safe and not stuffed waste deep in some dank hob hole.

TWENTY-THREE MINUTES LATER, he and his dazed squire found themselves stumbling into Lord Gregory's palace.

He's definitely not going to like this, was all that Horatio could think as he made his way through the vast hallway toward his master's study. *He's not going to like this one bit.*

aron Gregory De L'Ombre hated Palestine. He hated the unbearable heat. He hated the stench and beasts of burden that spewed their foul odor wherever one might breath. He despised the people—whether the few remaining Jews that still resided in the land or Muslim; or even Christians for that matter. He loathed its history and the ridiculous fanaticism that came with it.

Though he would never say it aloud, the truth was, Gregory longed to see the wet, cool shores of home once again…to be rid of this God-forsaken place forever. His beautiful and loving daughter, Isabella, had never seen the land of her fathers. She had been born here in *Outremer* and had never known the pleasures of truly civilized country. It was his single greatest regret since the death of her mother—attempting to raise such a precious child in so horrid a place. He could not wait to return home and introduce her to the land where God—if such a being even existed—truly dwelt. France.

But that simply wasn't to be. At least, not yet. The baron still had things to accomplish, and he could not move forward with his plans until he found the secret that would secure the

Christians' position in Jerusalem forever. And once he had it...
now *that* would change everything. The world would be a vastly
different place and he, for his part in the discovery, would be
made nothing less than an emperor.

He'd long ago given up on the Pope's promise to him. His
Holiness had sent him here personally, along with his traitorous
brother William, for the most trivial of matters and for the most
ridiculous of rewards. But Gregory was no simpleton. He would
not be made a fool by the Holy See as so many before him had.
He had plans of his own that would not be denied.

Still, the papal commission itself came with immense benefits.
Benefits that Gregory intended to use to his full advantage. But
his own machinations could not be realized until he found what
he'd been searching for. Found the two items that would give him
almost limitless power. Quite literally, power as limitless as the
very sands of the *Outremer*.

But apparently, now was not the time to reflect on his
mission. No. Now was the time for inane superstitions and
bumbling fools.

This Djinn was truly becoming a nuisance. At first, Gregory
had found the very notion rather quaint. He had toyed with the
gullible minds of his knights with tales of goblins from back
home and had even encouraged them to seek out the vile spirit
for the sake of God's kingdom. In hindsight, perhaps, not the best
of ideas. But he had felt that such a supernatural enemy would
keep the men sharp and more alert than they had been of late.
After all, Saladin, the Sultan of Egypt, was amassing power and
had his eyes fixed on the Holy City. Already, a handful of Muslim
tribes aligned with the Saracen war-chief had begun sacking
minor villages throughout the kingdom. Gregory's knights had
to be prepared for anything until he'd succeeded in his quest and
an evil specter was just the thing to keep the men vigilant.

But the legend was growing out of control, and nothing
seemed to stop it. The Djinn seemed to be everywhere now.

Waylaying a traveling textile merchant from Antioch. Viciously attacking a squad of weary foot soldiers trudging through the desert from Damascus. And now this attack on one of his most trusted knights and the caravan transporting his recently acquired slaves.

Thankfully, he'd had the foresight to transfer the Essene monk by different route. If the Djinn had managed to free him, Gregory's plans would have been sorely hindered. After all, it were the Essenes that guarded the secret he'd been seeking for so long now. Guardians of an ancient knowledge that would completely decimate his enemies. And it was the baron's hope that this particular monk would, with no little *persuasion* from his mercenary Gerard, reveal those same secrets to him.

But if this Djinn continued with its own personal crusade, all his planning and hard work would be for naught.

The baron sighed as he looked up from his writing desk at the cowering knight before him. "Let me get this straight," Gregory said to Horatio, who was standing at attention in the center of his great hall. "You are telling me that this evil spirit swooped down from the sky, levitated you six feet in the air, and told you to warn me away from my post? Is that what you're saying?"

"No, m'lord...I mean, yes, m'lord," he squirmed under Gregory's gaze. The knight's squire, Samuel, fidgeted behind him, never looking up from the stone floor. "That's exactly what happened. I would have never believed it myself, but not that I saw it with my own eyes!"

Gregory stood quietly from his chair—not quite a throne, but he imagined it might be some day—and walked toward the cabinet that contained his wine.

"And you say this creature, this 'djinn' as the locals call it, was not human?" Gregory poured the dark crimson liquid into a silver mug. It was perhaps one the best things about this place... the wine. He savored a small portion of the drink in his mouth as he watched the knight from the corner of his eyes. A stream of the liquid snaked through the rumpled course hairs of his salt and peppered beard, dripping onto his light blue tunic.

"Well, I can't say for sure, m'lord," Horatio said. "All I can say is that he seemed to be made of nothing more than smoke and darkness. The shadows themselves, they came alive around him, and his voice was like the sound of some wild beast from the dark country."

Gregory whirled around, glowering at his knight. Swallowing the wine that had been swishing around his mouth, a cold smile spread across his face. His right eye, pupil grayed over and completely sightless, twitched. This was perhaps the most preposterous thing he'd ever heard. He couldn't believe he was wasting his valuable time on such fables.

"Horatio, my dear friend," said Lord Gregory, walking over to the knight and placing an arm around his shoulder to lead him toward the door. "Here is my suggestion to you: the next time you so nobly go out on your patrol and the creature sees fit to pounce upon you and you do nothing at all to stop him..." Gregory paused for effect. "Go ahead and beg him to kill you, because you will find no more mercy from me."

With that, Gregory removed his arm from Horatio's shoulder and shoved him out the door. He then spun around and nearly slammed into the still, but trembling form of Samuel.

"I caught a glimpse of the dark beastie m'self," said Samuel. "Although I was unconscious most of the time. Want my report too, m'lord?"

The baron glanced at one of the large bodyguards at the door and nodded to the squire. Without a word, the guard grabbed Samuel by the arms and tossed him out the door. Gregory sauntered to his chair, where he ceremoniously plunged himself in a huff.

This was beyond all so beyond the pale. He had too many preparations to make to divide his time with ghost stories. Whatever was going on out there, Gregory knew that something needed to be done. It was simply a matter of pure good fortune that the creature had not removed his one advantage from his grasp—the Essene. He might not be so lucky next time. No, this dark spirit had to be dealt with.

But as in any strategy, it was imperative that sound intelligence of one's foe must be gathered and there was no one within Gregory's own court that could provide the necessary information. There was only one person who might be able to shed light on the subject, though he was loath to approach him.

The baron's younger brother, William, was considered a traitor by all the nobles of the Kingdom. And rightly so. Being the second born in the family, William had no choice but to follow one of two paths—knighthood or priesthood. He had nobly chosen the path of the warrior and had fought bravely in many battles. That is, until fifteen years ago when he was defeated attempting to quell a rebel uprising.

William had suffered severe injuries and was taken prisoner by a band of nomadic Saracens. They had demanded ransom for him, but Gregory, having no desire to share his aspirations with his brother, refused to pay.

Rumor had it that when William's injuries failed to heal properly, a well-respected sheik in the area took him in and nursed him back to health. It was discovered soon afterwards that William suffered from leprosy—an ailment that many people attributed to God as an act of punishment. For William was soon adopted by the sheik as his own son, an offense to both Christians and Muslims alike. William had accepted the adoption and had, in that single moment, renounced his Christian heritage in the eyes of his family and the Church.

Of course, Gregory could care less about his religion. In his eyes, religion was merely a magnificent tool to gain enumerable wealth and power. And he had wielded that tool skillfully—unlike his brother, who sought after more arcane pursuits such as philosophy, science, and rhetoric.

Still, despite his shortcomings, Gregory's brother had developed a deep knowledge and understanding of the customs and beliefs of the infidels. If anyone knew anything about this creature the Saracens called the Djinn, it would be William. And despite his misgivings, Gregory prepared himself for a trip to his brother's palace.

illiam's physician, Tufic, was as insufferable as ever when Gregory announced himself at the entrance. His thin, wiry frame barred the way into the palace doorway as he glared at the baron.

"I'm sorry, my lord," the Saracen doctor said. "But Sir William cannot be disturbed. He is feeling rather frail this morning and needs his rest. I'm truly sorry, but you will need to come back another time."

"Nonsense! My brother may play the part of an invalid to gain sympathy from the others, but he'll get no such quarter from me."

"But I really must insist…"

Before Tufic could muster another protest, Gregory and his two bodyguards pushed past and stormed through the cavernous vestibule that greeted the few who visited William's palace.

Palace. What a joke, thought Gregory as he made his way to his brother's bedchambers. It was little more than a large tent erected in the desert nearly ten miles north of Jerusalem. It was opulent, to be sure, and contained numerous large rooms. But Gregory would hardly consider it palatial.

The walls of the tent were tall, running nearly twenty feet into the air. Made of pure crimson silk, they were inlaid with Moslem symbols and letters embroidered from golden thread. Large Persian rugs lined the wooden floors while expensive furnishings from the Far East littered every room with decadent abandon.

His brother certainly knew how to live well, despite his circumstances. Since William, being the youngest, had been unable to inherit Gregory's title of Baron, his brother had made do and had become a sheik instead. It would have been impressive indeed if the title carried any weight with the people from the region. But no Muslim could honestly bow down to a Westerner playing at sheik. And no Westerner would waste his breath on a Christian who became an infidel.

Complicating matters further, William's leprosy was in its advanced stages now, and well, his life really meant very little to anyone of importance. He was doubly cursed, and Gregory found an odd satisfaction in that.

The baron could smell his brother before he saw him. The disease that plagued William elicited a most foul stench from his bedchambers. It smelled of rotten, decomposing flesh...an odor that the baron had become all too familiar with since coming to the *Outremer*.

Gregory quietly slid a velvet curtain aside and stepped into William's chambers. The baron wasn't surprised at all to find his brother bent over an altar in prayer. William had always been the more devout of the two brothers...whether to a Christian or Muslim god.

The older brother stood in the doorway; arms folded over his tunic. After a few moments, he cleared his throat, prompting William to turn his head. The baron gasped involuntarily at the grotesque visage that stared back at him. The younger man's face was grossly deformed with snow white skin resembling a corpse pulled from the Jordan, with wisps of hair just as pallid and sickly. Nodules of puss and boils layered over his features, completely distorting the handsome qualities he once had. His nose had long since been surgically removed from his face to allow for clearer breathing and the flesh of his lips had all but disappeared, giving him the impression of a skull grinning back at him. William truly was as repulsive as his stench suggested.

"Forgive me," William said as he arose, walked over to a night table, and began wrapping his head with linen bandages. Gregory noted that his brother appeared more stooped than the last time they had spoken. "I wasn't expecting company. Had I but known, I would surely have prepared myself to avoid bringing any discomfort to you, my brother."

Gregory waited impatiently as his brother worked shakily to cover his face. He walked over to the center of the room and plopped down amid the pile of plush silk pillows that were used for lounging in such domiciles.

"Really William," said Gregory. "When will you bring some civilization to these rags you call a home and purchase some real furniture? No wonder you are stooping. I could hardly imagine having to climb in and out of these pillows every time I wanted to sit."

His brother ignored the comment, merely waving Gregory over to sit across from him on the other side of a small table that was used primarily for dining.

"May I offer you something? Wine? Food? *Absolution?*"

"No thank you," Gregory replied with a dry smirk. "I have no need of *any* of those things."

"Well, then, what do I owe the pleasure of this most unexpected visit?" William said as he clapped his hands together in quick succession. Immediately three veiled, but undoubtedly lovely maidservants entered the chamber, each bearing oversized palm fronds. Once in place at different corners of the room, the trio began fanning the room to provide much needed air circulation.

Tufic, also, with two rather formidable looking guards, walked in at that moment, but remained silent. They stood at the doorway, devoted sentries committed to protecting their charge at all costs. Gregory could not help noticing that the two men appeared to be of Western descent and bore little resemblance to the Palestinians who populated the region. They also seemed particularly familiar, though he couldn't fathom from where he'd ever seen them before. Of course, it was really of no importance. He was here for information about the Djinn...not where William acquired his staff. Once he had what he sought, he would leave this filthy place and be on his way.

"I need some help with a rather small problem, brother. It seems that I'm having a bit of difficulty with a local myth from these parts."

"You mean the totems you've been so obsessed about for the last nine years?" asked William. "Really, Gregory when will you give up? They're merely the things of legend. I truly doubt there is any truth to those old stories. I mean, really...men made of clay that..."

"It's not that," the baron interrupted. "It's something... something entirely different."

"Then what, pray tell, are you talking about? What myth? What kind of trouble?" William said as he dipped a grape into a chilled cream made from goat's milk and popped the delicacy into his mouth through an almost imperceptible slit cut into the linen wrappings around his face.

Gregory knew that his brother was feigning indifference. Of course, William would revel in any misfortune that befell him, and he obviously wanted to savor the moment as best he could.

"Well, as I said, it is merely a trifle. I just require a little of your exquisite knowledge of Saracen lore."

William's eyes looked up from the dish of fruit on the table before him. Although Gregory was unable to see past the bandages wrapped around his brother's disfigured face, he was sure there was an amused smile there. And it infuriated him.

Still, if it would help him deal with the nuisance of this silly superstition plaguing his camp, the baron was willing to play the game.

"I'm referring to anything you know about a mythological creature known as a..." Gregory's tongue stumbled over the word. He couldn't believe he was actually going to say it. After all, to do so gives credence to such outlandish fables. "...a djinn."

The servant girls stopped their fanning. The silence in the room grew deafening. No one moved, except for Tufic who immediately slipped from the room, unnoticed by all save Gregory.

"A djinn, you say?" said William, whose countenance had instantly shifted from delight to mortified seriousness. "What do you know of the djinni?"

"Nothing! Nothing at all. That's why I've come to you."

The baron's brother reclined against an oversized pillow. One gloved finger absently pushed the fruit bowl away from the edge of the table, as the leper looked up into the folds of the tent in a taciturn glare.

"You've seen one?" William finally broke the silence. "You've actually seen one?"

"Of course not! Such a thing would have to exist for one to see it," said Gregory. "However, my men are being troubled. They are being hunted...hounded by someone...the local Moslems around Jerusalem have given him a name. The Djinn."

The baron told his brother all that happened to his men, the merchants, and townspeople since the Djinn had first appeared. He explained how the men were growing irrational over these encounters despite Gregory's own protests over the validity of any supernatural explanations that had been espoused. He even found the nerve to speak of the creature's attack on Horatio and his idiot cousin, though he left out how the Djinn had missed the Essene monk. There was no point in his brother discovering how close he truly was to finally fulfilling his...obsession, as William had called it.

The leper burst out in boisterous laughter at the account of Horatio.

"Oh, poor Horatio!" William said between guffaws. "He must truly have been beside himself. Doubly so afterward, I'd imagine."

"He was," the baron couldn't help but find the humor in it. "He tried so hard to put on airs of bravery, but from all accounts, he was completely useless during the entire ordeal. Imagine, being terrified of a ghost story!"

The two men shared laughter that was rarely heard in William's home. Suddenly, the younger man's countenance grew somber.

"But why dismiss Horatio's account so quickly? He's never been prone to irrational fancies, and he only *rarely* drinks while on duty."

"Because the very idea is ludicrous. It is merely a myth concocted by infidel dogs!"

"And how do you know this creature isn't what the locals claim it to be?"

Gregory's brother had always been prone to believe those tales of a more spiritual nature, but he never would have imagined him falling for something so...so absurd.

"Surely, you jest!" the baron asked. "You might as well tell me you believe in the old hobgoblin stories our parents told us when we were growing up."

"I'm serious, brother."

"So am I!" Gregory exploded from his cushion. "I can't believe I'm hearing this. I mean, I realize that your faculties must be suffering a great deal from this...this filthy disease." He waved a hand at his brother, indicating his entire decayed body. "They would have to be for you to turn from your God to follow after a heathen one..."

"Wait just a minute, *brother*!" William spat as he jumped up from his own seat. "You listen to me now. I have never renounced my faith in Christ! Never! And I have had it up to here with those who suggest otherwise."

Gregory was speechless at the leper's outburst. He could hardly move. He'd never seen his brother so angry—at least not in a long while.

"What I renounced was my faith in the Roman Church...a Church that would wage war on people of a different religion for the sole purpose of bolstering their land holdings and fiefs for their knights." William glared at the baron; the stoop of his shoulders replaced with fiery defiance. "I renounced my faith in a Church that required murder for the remission of sins. But Christ still reigns in my heart and don't you ever forget it! I suppose the other nobles can believe whatever they want, but you of all people should know better."

Gregory knew he needed to calm his brother down. He had not yet required the intelligence he had sought, and William's illness would not allow him to continue this tirade for long without draining him completely.

"I'm sorry dear brother," Gregory said, holding his palms out in show of peaceful supplication. "I meant no offense. Please forgive me."

One of the servant girls moved toward her master, ready to catch him in case he fainted. The movement wasn't necessary. William gently collapsed onto the cushions again and absently tossed a date into his mouth.

"All right, Gregory," William finally said. "You want to know about the djinn. Here's what I know. You cannot win against such a thing. The legends go back for centuries...even before the time of Mohammed. The Quran speaks of them as spirits made entirely of smokeless flame. Like humans, they are said to have free will and can be a force for good or a creature of unimaginable evil. They are often considered guardian spirits and sorcerers have sought for centuries for ways to bind them to their will."

William took a sip of wine from his jewel encrusted goblet and smiled.

"King Solomon supposedly learned the secret to this, actually," he said as his eyes drifted up to the rafters of his tent. "At least that's what the Quran says. He apparently learned to bind the djinni to various objects...lamps, bottles, even walking sticks. Then he would force them to do his bidding..."

"Wait." Gregory suddenly became excited. "What did you just say?"

"About what?"

"About Solomon. About him having the power to bind the spirits and force them to do his will. How, pray tell, was he able to accomplish this?"

William sat quietly; his eyes closed as if trying to recollect some memory from long ago. A few seconds later, they opened once more, and he nodded. "I believe legends say he used a ring. Supposedly a magic ring known as the Ring of Aandaleeb, but more commonly referred to as the Seal of Solomon."

Gregory could hardly contain the smile that threatened to break out across his haggard face.

"Aandaleeb?"

William shrugged. "I think that's what it's called. Why?"

This time, the baron didn't bother to contain his own amusement. "Why, dear brother...that's one of the very objects I've been searching for all these long years. For the *totems*, as you call them. You're essentially telling me that if I find it, I will be able to kill two birds with a single stone."

"But you've been looking for this thing for nearly seven long years," William said. "What makes you think you're any closer to locating it?"

Gregory simply waved a hand away at the question. "Never you mind. The point is…once I've obtained the ring, I will be able to use it to rid me of the burden of this Djinn once and for all."

"I don't think you quite understand," William continued, a look of confusion in his eyes. "The djinni are creatures of immense power. The Moslims believe that they are below the angels, but above human beings…but live lives very much like humans. They marry. They grow old…though they live for thousands of years. But they eventually die. They have strong magic that no human is capable of defending against. I'm not quite sure that you'd be able to contain this djinn that haunts you even if you were able to find Solomon's ring."

Gregory shook his head. "Dear brother, you're missing the point. The power the ring has in overcoming the Djinn doesn't come from magic. It comes from man. My men believe he is a spirit. But they also believe in the magic of Solomon's Seal. So, if it fails to subdue my nemesis with its power, the knights under my charge will see him for exactly what he is…a mortal man. His power will be stripped from him in an instant. His reign of fear will end, and my men will end his life as easily as they would a mongrel on the street."

William shrugged. "It's possible. But you still must find it and that will be the difficult part."

The baron smiled as he strode casually toward the bedchamber door. "Have no fear of that, brother. Even now, I'm closing in on the location of the ring…as well as the secrets of raising the golems of Solomon. Have no fear of that at all." He walked out of the room without so much as a goodbye to his brother. He had a great deal to think about and he had little patience for familial niceties.

As he made his way out of the palatial tent, he couldn't help but wonder where his brother's physician had gotten off to. It didn't matter much. The only thing he was now concerned with was getting home before sunset. Gregory wanted to spend time with his daughter, Isabella, before the night fell and the spirit of uncertainty edged its way back into his world.

4

T ufic watched silently as the baron and his heavily armed
entourage rode away from the palatial estate, his hands
absently clutched into two tight fists. Though he would
admit it to no one, he feared for Gregory. William's brother was
headed down a dangerous path...one that would not easily be
remedied if allowed to continue. One that would end in disaster
for himself...or worse, his daughter Isabella.

Turning from the doorway, the weary physician of a hunched
and dishonored leper strode through the tent's many rooms until
he came to the library. Taking a deep breath, he moved to the
center of the room, bent down, and pulled open the small trap
door carved into the wooden floor. He then climbed cautiously
down the narrow staircase into the vast cavern system nestled
beneath William's estate. Tufic negotiated the labyrinthine
tunnels without aid of any light, as if he'd been born of the
darkness, and stopped as he entered a large chamber.

"We're running out of time," a voice said from the shadows.
The clicking of flint in the darkness sent a blossom of sparks
onto a torch and the Djinn's hooded face was revealed.

The chamber lit by the single torch was roughly fifty yards in diameter and twice as high. Jagged stalagmites hung from the ceiling like the fangs of some long-dead and buried dragon. Save for a single worktable with a variety of scientific accoutrements, two chairs, and a medicine cabinet, the room was completely bare. Dozens of hibernating bats hung precariously over their heads, oblivious to the outsiders intruding in their domain.

"First things first," Tufic said, his face grim. "You need your regimen."

Though he couldn't see through the Djinn's hood, Tufic knew he was smiling. He knew further even, what the thing of shadow standing before him was thinking: *For such a young man, you worry like an old woman.* Or at least, that's what had been said in the past when the physician pressed him like this. "I'll be fine," the Djinn said. "We have much larger problems to worry about at the moment."

Tufic nodded and then walked over to the table where an assortment of strange medical apparatuses rested meticulously in their place. Taking a dagger from the implements, he moved to a nearby patch of damp earth and began digging without looking up.

"Gregory's getting closer to the Ring of Solomon," Tufic said. "If that happens, all will be lost."

"Please don't call the ring by that name, my friend," rebuked the Djinn. "It was Aandaleeb's long before it was Solomon's...and for a king so wise, he was an absolute fool to try to harness its dark power."

"My apologies." The physician continued to burrow in the dirt without looking up.

"None needed. But you're right. Gregory didn't want to reveal too much to William, but he's definitely close." The Djinn walked over to the wooden chair near the physician's table and sat down. "But it sounds as though I'm finally getting under his skin. All is not lost yet."

"Ah-ha!" Tufic exclaimed with a smile as he reached into the pile of dirt and extracted a small oval object. He held it up with an air of satisfaction. A single, multi-colored mushroom. "We're running out. The fungi are becoming much more elusive to find."

"We can worry about that later. Right now, we need to discuss stepping up the timetable," the dark-robed figure said. "I'd assumed we would have much longer to carry out our plans. As you've noted, that might not be the case now. Our strategy will need to change."

The physician gave a stern look at his friend as he moved over to the table, placed the mushroom into a crucible, and began grinding it to dust. "But if we run out of these, you might not be around to enjoy the fruits of all your labor. With the way you've been pushing yourself...the injuries you've sustained...my potions are all that is keeping you alive now and you know it."

The Djinn sighed as he pondered this. His own mortality mattered little to him. He'd already lived much longer than anyone such as him had a right. But his mission...his mission was something that he could not jeopardize. "Very well, Tufic. Just how much of the concoction do we have left? How long will our supplies hold out?"

His friend stopped his grinding for several seconds as he mentally calculated the numbers. "At best, we have a week. Two at the most if I ration it."

"And then?"

Tufic could only shrug. "I'm afraid it has escalated in recent weeks. However..."

The Djinn cocked his head. "Yes?"

"Well, I was thinking...they say that the Seal of Solom... excuse me, Aandaleeb's Ring...had many magnificent properties."

"Strike that notion from your thoughts," the living shadow said, standing unsteadily to his feet. "Have you heard nothing of what I've said about that infernal talisman? It was wrought with the most evil of magic. The ring cannot be used at any cost, do you understand me?"

"But sire...it is said that the Seal not only has the power to bind the spirits and bring life to the inanimate, but also heal grievous injuries. And on at least one occasion, it is said to have even raised someone from the dead."

"And besides being called by its forger, the Babylonian sorcerer Aandaleeb, the ring is known by yet another name...a secret name. Are you aware of what that is, Tufic?"

The physician shook his head.

"Solomon himself is said to have spoken of it on his death bed. He called it Wisdom's Bane." The Djinn looked his friend in the eyes. "No. No good can come from such a thing. The wise king himself understood this in the end. It's why he petitioned his high priest to remove it from his grasp and hide it for all times."

"But you will die."

"Which is something I'm completely prepared for, my old friend. But not quite yet." He took his seat once more and held out his hand. "So, I'll have the potion now...as loath as I am to imbibe it."

Tufic nodded with a wan smile, then poured the ground fungus into a vial filled with a strange amber liquid. Giving the concoction a careful stir, he handed it to the enshrouded man and watched him drink it.

"Ah, Tufic, that has got to be the worst tasting swill in the history of mankind," he said with a weary laugh. "But now on to more pressing matters. The medallion I recovered from Isabella. Have you had time to study it?"

The physician pulled out a key from his tunic and used it to unlock a small chest resting among his scientific equipment. He reached in and extracted a gold chain with an intricately carved gold medallion attached.

"Aye," he said, handing the necklace to over to the Djinn. "It wasn't easy, but with the help of an old man I met in Acre, I was able to translate the script."

"And?"

"Besides a vague recounting of Rakeesha's golems, it tells of how Azariah, the high priest, entrusted Solomon's ring to a band of nomads. My research suggests these were the progenitors of a group of desert monks known a few centuries ago as the Essenes."

The Djinn nodded at this. "I'm familiar with them. They were a group of ascetics that practiced Jewish mysticism for many centuries. They thrived in the land up until around the time of Christ. Then, the Romans drove them into the desert once more. Fortunately, Samir befriended their descendants several years ago."

"The Sheik knew them?" Tufic asked, a little surprised.

The Djinn sat silently for several seconds, staring absently into the golden face of the medallion he now held in his bandaged hand.

"You'd be amazed at who the old man had become friends with over the years, Tufic. And lucky for us, Samir introduced William to their chieftain about a year before his death. He should still be in good standing with them, I'd say."

"So, what do we do now?"

"Simple enough," he said, rising from his chair as he clutched the medallion tight in his hand. "I leave at once to find the Essenes. It won't be easy. They're nomadic and will be difficult to locate. But it's our next step. Just pray I get there before Gregory's forces do."

5

"You will tell the baron what he wants to know!" Gerard DuBois roared as the back of his hand slammed across the battered nomad's jaw. The chains binding the pathetic man's wrists rattled against the impact. "He is losing his patience with you, Jew."

Gregory arose from the wooden chair he'd been occupying since entering the cell to observe the interrogation and sighed. This simply wasn't going nearly as well as he'd first hoped. When he'd first received word that his men had been able to capture one of the Guardians—the group of nomadic warrior-priests, who at one time had been known as the Essenes and had been charged with protecting his prize for nearly a thousand years— he'd been ecstatic. He'd believed it only a matter of time before the emaciated and dehydrated desert-dweller would crack under the brutal hand of his mercenary lieutenant and share the secrets he'd sought for so long now.

Instead, the nomad had been ridiculously stubborn. Even now, at Gerard's latest beating, he merely spat a wad of congealed blood from his mouth and glared at his interrogator.

"Enough!" the baron said, walking casually up to his prisoner.

"Enough," he said a bit more gently, then nodded to Gerard to back away. "Seriously. Must we continue with this charade, Ibrihim? You know, as well as I, that you will invariably tell me what I want to know. One way or another. We have no intention of letting you die…so you will have to endure this…" He waved a hand around the cell. "…for a very long time."

The nomad smiled grimly. "And I am prepared to endure to the very end. There is nothing you can do that will force me to break my vows…or betray the trust placed in me."

This is getting tiresome, Gregory thought as he stared at the man with a smug smile. *A different tack is needed for this one. But what?*

Though he knew he could continue with the torture, he was becoming even more convinced that such tactics simply would not work on someone this zealous. He'd need to be creative, if not even a bit dishonorable. In the end, the method of obtaining the Solomon's Seal was inconsequential. The only thing that mattered to the baron was its possession.

Gregory turned to Gerard and nodded once more. Understanding, the mercenary and three of his men unchained Ibrihim bar Jonas, the Guardian of the Seal, and forced him to the ground. They then re-chained his wrists and ankles in such a way as to force him to lay face up and unable to move. One of Gerard's men handed him a wooden bucket filled with hog swill and the mercenary unceremoniously emptied the contents all over the prisoner.

It was a great insult to a man of Jewish heritage. Swine, after all, were unclean. To have their excrement poured over his entire body would be enough to make him think about his vows. But that, in itself, wasn't what Gregory had in mind. No, he had something far worse in store for the stubborn nomad.

"Our friend is a dedicated man, Gerard," the baron said as he strode casually toward the cell door. "He won't easily loosen his tongue to tell us the location of the Seal. You'll only tire yourself out trying to make him talk." Gregory opened the door and turned to face the nomad. "So, we'll simply allow the rats infesting these dungeons do much of the work for us. We'll talk soon, Ibrihim. I pray you'll be much more cooperative by then."

He strode out of the cell, thankful he wouldn't have to hear the impending screams of his prisoner.

6

Two days later...

G erard DuBois, the captain of Gregory's secret mercenary force, scanned the eastern horizon from the edge of the ridge his soldiers now huddled upon. The orange-red glow of the sun descended behind him, blinding those encamped in the valley below from his presence.

'Twill be a cooler evening than we've experienced in recent months, he thought, taking a deep breath of the humid air. A thunderstorm had rolled into the valley earlier in the afternoon. The moist breeze cooled the white-hot armor against his skin. Western armor wasn't designed for such hostile environs as the *Outremer* and it could make a waiting soldier miserable just from the heat building up inside the chainmail.

He inhaled once more, then looked down at the settlement below.

It had taken some doing (and the loss of an eye by the teeth and claws of hungry rats), but the nomad had finally revealed the location of the Guardians' camp. Now, he and his men waited patiently for the time to strike. Soon, Gregory would have his precious ring and Gerard would be one step closer to gaining the prize he most desired—the baron's lovely daughter.

The thought of her alabaster skin against his raised the temperature even more within his armor and he turned his attention again to the camp below lest he lose himself in his fantasies about Isabella.

The nomads were casually preparing for the evening, unaware of the danger that lurked over the horizon. Cooking fires burned—the succulent smell of stew rose up from the smoke—making Gerard's stomach rumble. Children laughed as they chased a pathetically scrawny dog around the camp's ramshackle huts. A group of women huddled together in hushed chatter as they carried pots filled with water on their heads from the Jordan.

It truly was a beautiful sight to the Western warrior. Not for its pastoral perfection, but for what was soon to come—mayhem, terror, and death for any who stood in the way of his mission.

His purpose here was, of course, two-fold. Primarily, he was to retrieve the fabled ring known as the Seal of Solomon. But there was a secondary reason for this raid as well. The baron was in desperate need of laborers to continue work on the tunnels he'd been excavating for the last seven and a half years. Tunnels deep in the underbelly of the City of David. Tunnels that would lead Baron Gregory to the final piece of the puzzle to his lifelong quest. The nomads who survived the initial raid would be taken prisoner and forced to work. The baron never asked how his workers were procured and of course, what he didn't know wouldn't hurt him. But Gerard savored such moments as this.

He had come a long way from his humble beginning. The illegitimate son of a Saxon nobleman and a Jewish whore, he had been born in Bethany, a tiny village on the outskirts of Jerusalem. His suspect heritage prevented him from any positions of honor among the nobles. But he hadn't let it stop him.

"Sir, Balian's group is now in position," reported Archibald, his second in command. "Durgan's forces are almost in place."

"Thank you, Archibald. We will now bide our time until the infidels are deep in slumber. Be ready for my signal."

"Aye, Captain."

Gerard watched as his closest friend marched toward the rest of his mercenary force. They were feared throughout the *Outremer* and with good reason. They were the best. They had never known defeat and with a few exceptions for Gregory, they rarely took any prisoners. He was most proud of his men.

IT HAD BEEN a perfect victory and took less than fifteen minutes altogether. Not even one of Gerard's men had been injured, though the same could not be said for the Guardians. Six strong men, and one impulsive lad, had died in the attack.

Of course, there was never really any chance the campaign could have turned out differently. The camp, which had been set up on the western shore of the Jordan, had been surrounded. Balian's knights had ridden in from the north, while Durgan's from the south. Gerard's men had marched in from the east, all while the camp slept in the stillness of the night.

They had struck swiftly, silent as a bird of prey. A bird of prey...the unnerving memory of the falcon shot a shiver down his spine. It was the only thing that disquieted him about the entire affair. *An omen if there ever was one*, he thought.

The bird had swooped down upon them in the thick of battle —black as jet with eyes that glowed red from the camp's firelight. It had done nothing but perch itself upon a withered old tree near the tent of the tribe's chieftain and watch the battle unfold.

At first, Gerard had opted to ignore the strange sight as the battle raged on. Things had gone well until the young boy fell. It was such a useless death. The lad would have been a strong worker in Gregory's tunnels. But he'd been too proud for his own good. Taking a sword from a fallen warrior, the whelp charged at Gerard like a moon-vexed lunatic. Instinctively, the larger man had cut the boy down with a single swipe of his blade.

It was at that moment the bird made itself known again. Shrieking like a fell banshee from Irish tales, the falcon flew into the air, diving straight for Gerard's head. Its lance-like talons raked against his face, and it was all the mercenary could do to keep from losing an eye. Then, as quickly as it had appeared, the bird was gone. It simply had disappeared, and no one had been able to see in which direction it had flown.

It was a very bad omen indeed, Gerard thought, pulling a round metal object from his pouch and appraising its workmanship. *But well worth the risk.*

The gold ring in his hand glittered in the pale firelight, its strange and ancient symbols etched onto its band seemed to glow an eerie hue of green and yellow. But it was the gemstone in the ring's cradle that captivated him more than anything. An unusual looking pentacle that seemed to shimmer and move as if its very lines were made of water.

"Gerard," said Archibald, huffing as he made his way up a steep incline to reach his captain. "Both Balian and Durgan have taken their men back to Bethany as you requested. We are left with our regular men, fifteen in all."

"Good." The mercenary captain stuffed the ring back into his pouch and looked at his lieutenant. "That's more than enough to keep these heathens in line."

"Shall we make preparations for our journey to Jerusalem, sir?"

Gerard looked at his men. It had been a short battle, but it had been grueling. It was also never wise to travel the desert at night unless you knew the terrain well. His men didn't. Besides, the added burden of herding a group of twenty-seven prisoners through a nighttime desert just seemed liked suicide. No, it would be better to wait.

"Nay, Archibald," said Gerard. "I think we'll stay here for the rest of the night and break camp at dawn. Give the men some time to rest. But set up a two man watch every hour."

"Aye, sir," said his lieutenant, who continued to stare at Gerard without moving.

"Something on your mind, lad?"

Archibald hesitated. He appeared contemplative…almost anxious. Gerard knew what was coming and he dreaded it. He wasn't sure how he was going to respond, and his indecision vexed him.

"Spit it out, man. I'm tired and would like a bit of sleep myself," growled Gerard.

"Well, sir, it's just that the men have been talking…about the falcon, I mean."

"What about it?"

"Well, it seems that the bird was something a bit unnatural," said his friend. "And, well, with all the talk about the Djinn and all, some of the men were wondering if there might be some connect—"

"The Djinn?" asked Gerard, who was already very tired of the conversation. "That's what this is about? A fairy tale? Archibald, you of all people should know better."

"Of course, sir, but it's not me, remember. It's the men. You know how superstitious they can be," Archibald explained. "A number of them have Arabic roots and say that such creatures were often known as shape shifters…creatures known as the *Al-Ghul*, from what I understand."

"Pah! 'Tis the most ridiculous thing I've ever heard of."

"That may be so, but it doesn't help the men's morale, sir. What shall I tell them?"

Gerard had heard enough. It was bad enough that Gregory's own elite force of knights was suffering from these silly nightmares. It was something altogether different when his own men, professional killers, began fearing little black birds that fluttered in the night.

"Tell them what I told you. Tell them the whole thing is ridiculous and to go to bed."

"Yes sir," said Archibald as he turned to walk away.

"But lieutenant? Don't forget to set the guard…just in case."

His old friend smiled nervously with a nod and walked toward the camp in silence. The whole notion was preposterous, but Gerard had to admit, thoughts of the Djinn had crossed his mind as well. The rumors were everywhere, and news of the heathen creature's antics were growing in both audacity and cunning. The Muslims' imams were praising Allah and Christian clerics were praying for deliverance. And knights and foot soldiers alike were afraid to lay their heads down for fear of being snatched away to some unknown hell.

Something had to be done about it. But for now, it was time that Gerard enjoyed some much-deserved slumber.

7

As far as he could tell, it was nearly three in the morning and Gerard had managed to get an hour or so of sleep. But disturbing thoughts of the falcon had swooped into his slumber and jarred him awake. After nearly twenty minutes of tossing and turning on his horse blanket, he decided to relieve one of his sentries and take watch for a while.

Gerard sat on a wooden stool, his back to the fire, looking out into darkness. To his right, young Geoffrey paced nervously around the camp's perimeter. The sound of ragged snoring ripped through the camp, threatening to lull Gerard into closing his eyes for just a few minutes. He grumbled to himself at his weakness, sitting up straighter on the stool.

It wouldn't be prudent to be discovered by the others napping on guard duty. What would his men say to that? He had disciplined the last sentry that had fallen asleep severely—twenty lashes with a leather strap.

No, it wouldn't be good at all to nod off, so Gerard stood up, stretched with a suppressed yawn, and walked to the edge of campfire's light in hope that the cool desert air would revitalize him. He nodded to Geoffrey as he passed him by and looked out onto the night. Not much to see…nothing but a few angular silhouettes of cacti against a vast canvas of purple and blue.

He glanced up into the sky and spotted a dark shape flying toward him—a small metal ball hurled over his head and landed in the center of the campfire as Gerard watched spellbound. Nothing happened.

That was strange, thought Gerard as he fruitlessly scanned the darkness.

Geoffrey, who had seen the strange apparition too, turned to his captain. "What was that?"

"I've no idea, lad. It seemed to be some sort of…" Gerard's words were cut short with a blinding flash of light erupting from the campfire, followed immediately by a giant plume of smoke and ash that enshrouded the entire camp. The flash-blinded mercenary blinked back tears as the sulfurous smoke wafted into his eyes.

Instinctively, the captain drew his sword from its sheath and floundered sightlessly through the camp.

"To arms! To arms!" cried Gerard. "We're under attack! Make sure the prisoners are secure and prepare for battle!"

The clatter of armor and weapons arose throughout the camp as Gerard's men scrambled to follow his orders. Sleep still clung to their eyes as they filed out of their tents, slinging on their chainmail and helmets in the smoky haze.

"Captain, where are you?" asked Archibald from somewhere to Gerard's right. "What is happening?"

"Over here," the mercenary answered.

The lieutenant blindly made his way to Gerard, and they locked hands tightly to feel where the other was. Both men jumped involuntarily when the metallic clank of another object fell into the campfire, releasing a second eruption of smoke from the pit.

High above them, they heard the shriek of a bird. And though they could not see it, Gerard knew without question that it was the same falcon from earlier that evening. The mercenary felt his heart rise higher into his throat at the realization, effectively knocking the breath out of him.

"The Djinn," Archibald said, his voice quivering. "We have angered the Djinn and now he attacks."

"*Quiet!*" Gerard hissed. "We don't want to panic the men. It's probably something else. Let's just wait and see what happens."

As if on cue, a scream arose from Nicholas, one of Gerard's most seasoned men, from across the chaotic campsite. Another terrified wail erupted from two more men. No one could see anything with the ever-present smoke blanketing their surroundings in shades of gray and black. Gerard could only guess what was happening to his men as he dashed in the direction of shouts.

The captain rushed through the campsite, leaping over the prone bodies of several of his soldiers, and finally skidding to a halt at a sight he would never forget. The smoke had cleared somewhat, and Gerard was able to make out the forms of six of his men surrounding a visage of pure darkness—a manlike creature clothed in a black billowing cloak and turban. Its eyes burned through the haze with a ghostly green glow.

Two of his men charged toward the Djinn, who gripped one man's wrist, twisting it furiously and bringing him down to his knees. A nerve-shattering crack sprang out from his soldier's arm as bone and tissue rent in a single motion. The creature then brought one boot down against the soldier's left ankle—breaking it clean. The man let out a heart-piercing shriek.

The second soldier pounced from behind the creature, which stepped effortlessly to the side, causing Gerard's man to fall forward to the ground. The Djinn's heavy black boots came down hard against the man's neck, shattering the spine in several places.

The mercenary stared impotently at the attack. The creature was a blur of motion and fury that simply would not be tracked. He knew from witnessing the Djinn's fighting prowess that hand-to-hand combat would lead to nothing but defeat and probably death. They would need an organized attack against the monstrosity that threatened them this night.

As the dark spirit continued battling the fearful soldiers, Gerard found three of his men who were most formidable with a bow.

"Shoot it," he said. "Bring it down now!"

Without question, the three archers sheathed their swords, took their bows from around their shoulders, and nocked their arrows. In unison, all three shafts sung through the air, striking their intended target with expert precision. One arrow struck the creature in the left shoulder. Two others imbedded in the square of its back, between the shoulder blades.

Seemingly unfazed by the arrows that pierced its flesh, two more of Gerard's foot soldiers fell as the creature spun around, its cloak gliding through the air as if made of ethereal mist. The creature barely glanced at the arrow imbedded in its shoulder as it reached inside its tunic, retrieved three metal objects, and hurled them through the air simultaneously at Gerard's archers. Three thuds preceded the crash of each archer to the ground, a tiny black dagger protruding from their chests. Mindlessly snapping the arrow's shaft off from his shoulder, the Djinn continued its assault on the mercenary's soldiers.

Gerard stood motionless as he watched the onslaught; Archibald swayed spellbound beside him. The creature danced through the air as if riding the wind itself, whirling and striking its enemies in multiple sweeps of its arms and legs. The Djinn's movements reminded the captain of the dust devils and tornadoes that swept through the desert from time to time. One by one, each of Gerard's soldiers fell, screaming into the night sky.

Out of the original fifteen men left to guard the nomadic captives, only four remained standing. Three had deserted altogether. The rest had fallen—either dead or severely injured. And the strange beast before them still moved with a fury of the heathen gods. It simply wasn't going to let up until every man was down.

Without warning, Gerard rushed toward the specter that assailed his men; his long broadsword extended over his head. With a roar, the mercenary lunged, sweeping the blade in a downward arc—swinging toward the Djinn's head.

In an instant, the head was no longer where it was supposed to be. The creature crouched low to the ground to avoid the blow and spun around in one fluid motion with one foot extended. The sweeping leg struck Gerard from behind his knees, sending him sprawling backwards onto the ground.

A flash of light gleamed in the pale moonlight that had eaten its way through the smoky terrain. Gerard looked up to see the Djinn's broad scimitar pointed directly at his face.

"Enough!" the fell creature bellowed. "If anyone else moves, your captain will lose his head."

Gerard closed his eyes tight. He was ready to die but hoped it would not be this night. He had too many plans and now he added revenge against the Djinn to his list. Surely, he would have his vengeance on the creature if he survived tonight's encounter.

Thankfully, no one moved.

"You!" said the Djinn, pointing to a soldier, blood trailing down his face from a large gash in his forehead. "Release your prisoners."

The soldier, whose name Gerard could not place at that moment, stared wide-eyed at his captain.

"Do it," Gerard said.

Without another word, the young soldier turned and walked toward the tent that held their prisoners. Archibald walked over as well and helped him free the tribe from their chains.

The Djinn turned its attention back to its fallen foe on the ground. Gerard's eyes bore into its veiled turban, trying in vain to distinguish some feature that would give a clue as to who or *what* the Djinn really was. Having watched the demon move and fight, the mercenary was convinced that the being that had plagued Gregory and his men for the last several months could not possibly be a man—it was a monster straight from the pits of Hell. Still, with its turban wrapped so tight around its features, there was no way to discern anything of the Djinn's appearance save the glowing green eyes that stared back at him.

The black clad figure looked up in the sky for a moment and sent out a sharp whistle. Within seconds, the shriek of the falcon signaled its swift descent to its master, where it alighted on the Djinn's left forearm. Gerard's assailant turned its eyes back to the captain who was still sprawled out on the ground.

"I have eyes everywhere, murderer," said the Djinn. "I know what you have done. You have murdered a child, and your treachery will not go unpunished."

"Go hang yourself, demon!" spat Gerard. "I have the blessing of the Pope himself, and by nature, the blessing of Jehovah God."

The creature let out a soft chuckle that sent a wave of ice down Gerard's spine.

"That's funny, little man," said the creature. "It was Jehovah who sent me to stop you from enslaving these innocent people. It was Jehovah who commissioned me to stop your dark mission."

Gerard cringed as the Djinn's blade pressed firm against his throat. The hot, sticky wetness of blood trickled down the mercenary's neck as every muscle in his body tensed for death. He saw no way out. He would be killed by this abomination that spat in the face of all that was holy.

The pressure of the black scimitar continued for several long seconds with nothing happening. Although his eyes were shut tight, Gerard knew the smoke had nearly dissipated from the campsite. He could breathe freely again. He wondered how much longer he'd be able to say that.

Finally, the cold steel was removed, replaced by the eerie cold voice of the monster who had defeated him.

"Now, *murderer*, take your men and leave this place. Don't return here again. These people are under my protection now."

Gerard slowly opened his eyes. He was surprised that the Djinn was no longer hovering over his inert body. Instead, the monstrous creature was bent down over one of his fallen soldiers.

Doing some ungodly thing to him, no doubt, the captain thought.

To his surprise, the Djinn stood, and Gerard saw that the young soldier the creature had crouched over had been bandaged. A splint tied around his right leg. The Djinn had tended to the boy's injuries.

Without a word, the dark apparition moved to each of Gerard's men, treating their injuries with the skill of field surgeon. Some, of course, could not be mended. But those that were salvageable, the Djinn treated with the same tenacity he had used to incapacitate them.

Gerard looked over to his lieutenant, who watched the entire affair in stunned silence. Archibald was just as flummoxed as his commander.

The Djinn, having done all he could for his victims, stood and moved over to the mercenary captain who was still flat on his back. Without hesitation, the creature reached down, snatched the leather pouch containing Solomon's ring from his belt, and tossed a small oval medallion near Gerard's feet.

"A trade," the creature said. "The Seal for that medallion. Give it to Gregory. He'll divine its meaning." It backed away and pointed toward Jerusalem. "Now go."

The Djinn's last two words left no room for argument. Seething over the loss of his prize, Gerard palmed the medallion, placed it in a pocket in his tunic, and stood up shakily. He could not allow the creature to leave with Gregory's ring. To do so would be a devastating blow to the baron's plans and his employer would not take his failure lightly. There would be dire consequences.

But how could he do anything to wrest control of the mystical relic once more? Out of the original fifteen men that stayed behind to guard the prisoners, six were now dead. Five were injured but bandaged up. The remaining four, though relatively healthy, were in no shape to take on the Djinn again.

No. Gerard had no choice. To try and fight would certainly mean their gruesome and unholy deaths. With a sigh of resignation, he ordered his men to obey the Djinn's command. The mercenaries set to taking their wounded by whatever means they could and limped from the campsite into darkness.

As the beaten mercenaries moved toward Jerusalem, Gerard turned to look back at the camp they had taken so easily—the camp that had been so costly to him and his men. The Guardians who had just moments before been his prisoners were busy at breaking camp, preparing to move somewhere probably more isolated and safer.

Nowhere on earth will be safe enough for them, thought Gerard. *Nowhere will be safe for the demon either. One day soon, I will find them both and make them pay for this humiliation."*

Gerard realized as he stared back at the camp that the Djinn was no longer visible. He wasn't sure whether that made him feel better or worse. But with a high-pitched shriek of a spectral falcon from high above the desert plains, the mercenary had his answer. *Worse. Much worse.*

As he turned around to face Jerusalem, and safety, Gerard pulled the medallion out from his tunic. The sun was rising in the east and its subtle rays revealed strange markings engraved on the piece of jewelry. The mercenary was unable to decipher its meaning. The unsettling feeling he had upon hearing the demon's bird flying high above them grew even stronger at the sight of the medallion.

Yes, it was much worse than he had ever thought possible. He was sure of it.

8

The next night...

I sabella De L'Ombre could not sleep. Although the last few weeks had been thoroughly exhausting—both physically and emotionally—slumber refused her pleas at every turn. Of course, she was perfectly aware of the reasons for her insomnia. With the turmoil rapidly escalating around her in the lives of those she loved, her mind refused to remain quiet despite her most adamant of commands.

Her father's situation was weighing heavily upon her. His obsession, which was gradually turning to madness. And then there was the Djinn. Her father was becoming even more haggard with each new account of the dark creature's exploits. No matter where Gregory turned, his enemy was nearby. He was becoming delusional, even paranoid.

It was these things...these thoughts and worries...that drove the sweet bliss of sleep from her this night.

Casting aside her oriental silk sheets, she moved her legs over the edge of the bed and set her feet against the cold stone floor. Putting her face in her hands, Isabella let out an audible sigh. She really was tired. But unfortunately, restlessness outweighed any fatigue she felt.

Standing up, she pulled a cool linen robe around her shoulders and walked to the balcony outside her bedroom. She had no idea of the time, but a beautiful full moon hung in the night's sky like a pearl amid a sea of black. Propping her hands on the railing, she peered out onto the quiet skyline of Jerusalem. Down below, palm fronds swayed in the gentle breeze as a symphony of katydids serenaded her. She inhaled deeply of the fragrant warm air.

She loved this city...enjoyed its culture and history. She cherished its people with their seemingly infinite courage and strength. Isabella could never understand why her father refused to see the beauty here that she did. He constantly lamented about a homeland she had never stepped foot in and the wonders that she was missing by being sequestered in the *Outremer*. But she was happy here and had no desire to be anywhere else.

Taking another deep breath, Isabella said a quick prayer for the chaos this beautiful city was facing in the coming days.

A gentle rap at her door startled her.

"Isabella dear? Are you all right?" asked the sweet, reedy voice of Margaret, the nanny and maidservant who had raised her since Isabella's mother had died.

Whirling around, the young woman walked to the door and opened it. Margaret stood there fidgeting in place, her graying hair disheveled inside a kerchief, worry engraved in her eyes. Her short, squat body cut a comical figure in the wool nightgown she wore. Her hands rung together in circles as she looked at Isabella.

"My dear," the older woman said. "I heard you rustling around in here. You know you need to get your sleep. It's not right..." Her nanny's eyes caught sight of the open doors that led to the veranda. "Oh Isabella, it's much too dangerous for you to have those open. Your father has given express orders that they remain closed and locked."

Isabella had to force herself to keep a level head. Her nanny only meant the best for her, but it was becoming increasingly difficult to deal with Margaret's over-protective nature. She was, after all, no longer a child and despised being treated as such.

Besides, she of all people had nothing at all to fear from the Djinn. But of course, her nanny had no way of knowing that.

"I know Margaret, but it's such a beautiful night. I just wanted to…"

Her nanny pushed right past her without listening to a word she was saying. Without a word of her own, Margaret shut the veranda's large oak doors and lowered the bars down into their slots to prevent the world from intruding on her precious charge.

"There now, my dear," Margaret said as she turned with a bright smile. "You'll be safe now."

Isabella knew better than to argue. "All right, you win," she said. "Now, I really am rather tired. I think I'll try to go to sleep now."

Margaret beamed at the young lady she had raised. Taking and pulling her close, the nanny squeezed Isabella tight.

"All right, love," she said, walking out the bedroom door. "Have a good night and I'll see you in the morning."

Isabella shut the door and leaned back against it, exhaling deeply as she closed her eyes. She loved Margaret dearly, but sometimes she felt so smothered.

"That woman truly adores you."

Her eyes snapped open at the disembodied voice; her heart pounded against her breast. Across the room, the doors to her veranda now stood wide open once more with the bar that had held them secure resting idly against the frame. The linen curtains around the door fluttered back in the light breeze that blew from the Jerusalem streets, revealing the outline of a black-robed figure leaning carelessly against a stone pillar with arms folded. She scolded herself for being so surprised. Now that she saw him, Isabella detected the faint odor of brimstone coming from his direction.

"What are you doing here?" she whispered as she dashed toward her father's most deadly nemesis. "Do you have any idea what would happen if you were discovered?"

The Djinn leaned forward, his warm, gentle eyes—no longer glowing green—betraying the smile she knew so well under his dark hijab. The creature moved quickly, sweeping Isabella off the floor with powerful arms and twirling her around the room...her feet flying behind her. She stifled a girlish giggle.

"Put me down," she commanded in a harsh whisper. "I'm serious. You can't be here."

The Djinn complied without a word, but she could see the hurt look in his eyes.

"I'm sorry," he said. "But it has been so long since I last saw you. I've missed you."

"I've missed you too."

"But..." He paused for effect. "You're worried."

"Of course, I'm worried," she said. "You've turned the whole world upside down. My father is beside himself. He sees demons in his sleep. His obsession with you is almost as great as for those twelve abominations that he discovered in the tunnels below the city."

"Good," he said with a chuckle. "Then our plan is working perfectly."

"Yes, it's working! But to what end?" she asked. "What happens next? Would you...would you kill him? Would you really kill my father?"

The Djinn stood silent for several minutes, his gloved hands wrapped gently around hers. It was a harsh question, she knew, but one that Isabella felt compelled to ask. He needed to consider all the possibilities.

"I don't know," he finally said. "I would rather not. But he simply cannot succeed in his quest. Too much is at stake. I may have no choice, Isabella."

Her heart sank. She understood, but it didn't make things any easier. The baron's daughter wasn't entirely sure what danger twelve old statues could pose for the people of Jerusalem. Nor did she know the extent of her father's plans. But she was convinced it was nothing good. The Djinn had always taken great pains to conceal what he knew of Gregory's aspirations. For both her sake, as well as Gregory's.

He still believes there's a chance for my father to repent, she thought. *He's giving him every opportunity.*

"And what if he kills *you* instead?" she asked. "You may hesitate, but he will not. You have truly rattled him, and he will stop at nothing to see you hanged if he is able."

"Well, if that happens, then so be it," he said in a tone more grim than she had heard in a long while. "Only let me die with the honor befitting a knight of the cross."

Tears welled in Isabella's eyes. She knew he meant it.

The dark figure pulled her to him, his arms wrapping tight around her slim frame. His warmth reassured her.

"It's all right, dear one," he said. "Remember, Christ is on the throne—not Gregory or the Pope. This foolhardy crusade of theirs goes against everything He stands for. He will see them vanquished."

The Djinn gently pulled away from her and looked deep into her eyes.

"I love you, Isabella…very much," he said. She noticed a single tear running from his right eye. "The day I first held you in my arms was truly the happiest of my life."

She smiled at this. "Save one other day," she reminded him.

"Aye. Except *that* day," he said gently. "But that day is past. You are here now. The other is not. And it is you who I will protect and love 'til my dying breath."

"I know you will, and I cherish you for it."

The two stood silently, gazing at each other. They needn't say another word. Both knew how the other felt. True, unconditional, and unfettered love passed between these two souls. It was a thing of beauty in Isabella's eyes.

The sound of shuffling feet from outside Isabella's chamber door broke the spell. Her head turned around, muscles tensed, as three loud bangs exploded against her door.

"M'lady," came the nervous voice of Horatio, one of her father's knights. "M'lady, beggin' your pardon ma'am and sorry to wake you, but your father sent us to check on your welfare."

"Just a moment." She turned to face the Djinn, but he was gone. The curtains still blew in the warm breeze, but he had vanished like the spirit he pretended to be. She never would get used to that—his startling entrances and insufferable exits. But she knew that he would always be there when she needed him most and that was truly something to be thankful for.

Isabella hurried for the door and for the second time that night, opened it to the anxious faces of her father's knight and squire.

"Yes?"

"I'm truly sorry, miss," said the humble knight. "But your father's been worried about you. He just asked us to check on you."

"Thank you, dear Horatio," she said with a smile. Of all the baron's knights, Horatio was by far the kindest and most noble of the lot. He had always treated her with great affection and kindness.

Perhaps it was his friendship with her uncle that made him pay special attention to her. Her Uncle William had always treasured Isabella more than all his amassed wealth and had showered her with love that even her father had never provided. That is, until William was taken prisoner and disinherited by Gregory.

But Horatio had been William's closest friend. When all

others claimed her uncle had rejected Christ for the Muslim prophet, Horatio had bravely defended him time and again—to his own ruin. His loyal devotion to his friend had brought the wrath of the nobles down upon him and now, Horatio had been reduced to guard duty and minor errands for her father.

But if the loyal knight regretted his devotion to William and his present situation, he never voiced it to Isabella. On the contrary, he lavished her with all the fondness he could muster in her uncle's absence.

"You're welcome, m'lady."

"Hello, ma'am," said Samuel with an awkward wave.

Isabella's smile broadened.

"Why, hello Samuel," she said. "It is good to see you."

The young squire blushed. Horatio turned around to face his squire with a scowl.

"Well, m'lady, we should let you get back to bed," the knight said. "We're off to a very important meeting with your father now. We'll tell him you're fine."

"A meeting? At this time of night? What kind of meeting?"

"Oh, well now, I'm not at liberty to say," he said, obvious pride evident in his voice over being invited to such an event. "But it's something big, I'd say. Probably has to do with that nasty ol' hob what's been bothering us of late."

Isabella stifled a smile at the mention of the 'Hob.' She had heard of the poor knight's recent encounter with the Djinn and felt bad that he had to go through such an ordeal. Still, the good knight had handled himself bravely from what she understood.

"Well, then Sir Knight, I bid you a good night."

Bowing low, Horatio beamed back at her.

"You too, sweet Isabella. Sleep well."

With that, the knight and his squire turned and walked down the hallway toward the stone stairs leading outside. Isabella quietly closed the door and skittered once again onto the balcony.

She scanned the city below for any signs of movement. Nothing stirred. After several moments, she saw Horatio and Samuel leaving the palace in which she lived and sauntering down the street toward the Dome of the Rock.

For a while, nothing else stirred. Then, out of the corner of her eye, she saw a strange shadow come to life from the flat rooftop of a home across the street. The shadow dashed away, leaping into the air and landing on another rooftop.

Isabella's heart skipped a beat. He was following them. He had heard. She uttered a silent prayer for the Djinn. *God, please protect him. Please protect them all.*

9

"Hurry up, Samuel, we haven't got all night," Horatio said as knight and squire loped up an uneven stretch of a stone walkway in the east end of the city. "We wasted too much time fawning over Lady Isabella. We were supposed to be there five minutes ago."

Samuel huffed as he scampered up to his cousin. He was nearly five years Horatio's junior and already more unfit than the elder knight. Of course, it could have something to do with Samuel's massive girth around the belly, mused Horatio.

"I'm sorry, sir," the squire wheezed, gripping the right side of his ribs with one hand. "But your legs are much longer than mine and this hill is killing my shins."

"Much longer? You're four inches taller than me, Samuel."

"Am not. Remember when Gram measured us back home? You were a full foot taller than me."

Horatio shook his head in disbelief. "I was ten years old. You were six."

"Oh, that's right," Samuel said as he absently pulled a greasy lock of his chestnut hair away from his eyes.

Turning away from the dull squire, the knight pushed on up

the steep incline. The crier had already announced the midnight hour several minutes ago—the precise time Gregory had instructed the two of them to arrive at the Jehoshaphat Gate. He was not going to be happy about their tardiness and Horatio was growing quite ill of being scolded by the arrogant jackal.

"I'd be better off in William's house," the knight mumbled to himself.

"What did you say, cousin? I didn't quite hear you."

"Nothing, Samuel. Just move it."

The two picked up their pace when the hill gave way to flattened cobblestone. No torches lit the series of alleys and back streets Horatio and Samuel trod and the going would have been much harder if not for the unnaturally large moon that hovered in the sky. Its eerie glow brightened their way as easily as lanterns blazing through the fogs of London.

Horatio's mood lightened as he spied the great gates of Jehoshaphat only yards away.

"Be stout, Samuel. We're almost there," he said, a sudden rush of energy fueling his steps.

There was no answer from behind. Come to think of it, Horatio couldn't recall hearing the constant puffing of his squire for some time now.

"Samuel?"

The knight stopped in mid-stride and turned back to look for his cousin, but there was no sign of him.

Oh no, thought the knight. *Not again. Please not tonight. Not ever again, Lord.*

Horatio retraced his steps, scouring the darkened doorways and deserted alleys they had passed since the knight had last heard the footsteps of his cousin.

"This can't be happening," the knight muttered as his heart drummed against his chest. "Samuel!"

Nothing. Not a sound.

He was alone.

Horatio struggled with indecision. Should he keep searching for Samuel or continue to the meeting with Gregory and his foul mercenary Gerard? He couldn't believe his misfortune. He prayed silently to God for a simple reason for all of this. He prayed he would not have to face the *Demon* tonight and that his squire was safe from harm.

Samuel had not quite recovered from his recent encounter with the Djinn. He had refused to speak freely of his ordeal, but he had been a different person since that night. He was no longer as quick to laughter as he once had been, and his stride appeared to be much heavier now as if burdened by a great weight. Horatio winced at that thought. Despite his overwhelming flaws, his cousin had always been the purest of sorts. He was not meant for such dark things.

He remembered the boy, a mere twelve years old at the time, running around their farm back home…chasing that crazy pig of his and oinking uncontrollably, convinced he could communicate with the dumb beast. Samuel had eventually fallen headfirst into the slop trough after an ill-formed strategy to lure the swine into his arms. The pig trotted around him like a victorious conqueror, but the boy's laughter could not be stifled despite his failure. It had been positively infectious. His entire clan, including Horatio, had joined in the merriment.

That was how he remembered Samuel. But the lad was a different person now.

Several days ago, Horatio's cousin had confessed that he had not been entirely truthful in his account of the Djinn's attack. He told the knight that the creature had spoken to him about grave matters—things that were dark and sinister. Samuel had refused to reveal any more than that. He had given his word to the demon that he would keep silent. And while Horatio doubted such an oath should be kept to a creature so vile, he didn't press his cousin for any further details. He just hoped the lad would tell him when the time was right.

Now he truly feared he might never get the chance. There was
nothing for it. Horatio knew he could not go onto the meeting
without his loyal friend. He turned around and continued his
search.

———————

"SAMUEL!"

Samuel's head jerked up to look around the darkened alley.
His cousin was nearby and searching for him. His pulse
quickened.

"Don't worry, lad," said the living shadow standing in front of
the squire. "We'll be through with our business before he
finds us."

"He'd understand, you know. He's brave and strong—and
above all, good."

"I know he is, Samuel," said the Djinn. "There's no finer man
in all Jerusalem than your master. But he wouldn't give us the
chance. He's too blinded by *duty*."

The squire's eyes dropped once more. The creature was right.
Horatio meant well, but until he opened his eyes to evil the baron
and his ilk were committing, he'd continue blindly serving the
wrong side.

"What would you have me do?" asked Samuel, who had
given up the silly notion that the creature before him was an
evil spirit. In fact, despite the Djinn's own protests, he had
become convinced that he was, in fact, an avenging angel of the
Lord.

It had been in the way the creature had spoken to him—just
days ago now, but seemingly like ages—when he had spirited
Samuel away and tied him up. The Djinn's words had been so
comforting. He had told the boy that he would not so much as
hurt a single hair on his, or Horatio's head. Not a thing easily
believed except for the kind eyes hidden in the dark recesses of

his turban—once he'd seen past the greenish glow, that is. Samuel had believed him instantly.

Everything he had thought of the creature until that moment had skittered away on the desert wind. At that very moment, Samuel had known he was in the presence of one who served the True and Living God. Of course, if Horatio had heard that, he would have been convinced that the "demon," as the knight often referred to the Djinn, had used some wicked enchantment to beguile him. But the only enchantment the squire had seen in the creature was the truth.

And hope.

"Did you hear me, Samuel?" asked the Djinn, who had been instructing the boy of his plans.

"I'm sorry, sir. I was pondering."

A gentle chuckle escaped the linen fabric of the angel's turban. "That's all right, lad. I know all this is a bit much to ask of you. I wouldn't have, but that I gathered you for a man of stout heart and noble courage."

"Aye, sir. All I wish is to serve Him what saved me from my sins."

"Good," said the Djinn. "So, this is what I ask of you."

The man in black explained the task he required from Samuel. Patiently, he answered the squire's questions with warmth and concern until they were both convinced the lad understood his role.

"Samuel!" Horatio's voice was growing nearer.

"Now, hear me boy, your cousin is upon us," the Djinn continued. "There is danger in this. If you are caught, do not resist. Tell them all you know, and they may go light on you."

"But I'd never..."

"Listen to me. Tell them everything. You do not know enough to jeopardize anything that I've worked on. You only know your part. You will betray no one by giving them what they ask. It would pain me to see you come to harm, lad."

"All right," said Samuel, as he knelt at the Djinn's feet, his eyes clenched with pride over his task. "I will do all that you ask of me."

"Stand up, Samuel. I am no god to be worshipped, nor king to be revered. I am but a mere servant—like you. Now be strong and find your cousin. He worries for you."

The squire looked up to find that he was now alone in the alleyway. It seemed to Samuel that the creature had simply stepped into the very shadows like a doorway and disappeared. The thought of it unnerved him. There was just so much about the Djinn that he didn't understand.

Still, he knew there would be time enough to reflect on the creature's nature after tonight. Now, he must get back to his cousin, who was at this point, frantically scouring the streets for him.

Samuel smiled. No matter how much Horatio pretended to dislike him, the lad knew his cousin would go to the ends of the earth to protect him from harm. Muttering a quick prayer, he ran out of the shadows and into the moonlit streets.

———

"SAMUEL!" Horatio cried as he sprinted around the corner, nearly bowling his cousin down. "Thank God you're well. I was worried."

"I'm fine. Everything is all right. I just had a bit of a fall back there and became disoriented." Samuel hated lying to his cousin, but he saw no way to avoid it. "You know me. I've no sense of direction at all."

The knight smiled at his young charge, relief flooding his veins at having finally found him—and none the worse for wear. But something in Samuel's eyes disturbed Horatio. Something was not quite right.

A scuffling noise above broke the knight's gaze at his squire.

Looking up, he caught a fleeting glimpse of something black moving about on the rooftop of a small mercantile.

He turned his eyes back to his cousin, who casually looked down at his feet as if mesmerized by the shape of his shoe. Horatio looked up at the roof one more time but saw nothing. Perhaps it had been his imagination, though there truly was something about Samuel's demeanor that unnerved him. The knight vowed to get to the bottom of it before the night was through, but now they needed to make haste to Gregory's meeting. The baron was no doubt cursing them at that moment for being late.

With a smile, Horatio placed an arm gently around Samuel's shoulder. "Come, cousin. We have a meeting to attend."

The squire returned the smile. Whatever dark shadow loomed inside Samuel's soul seemed to vanish with his contagious grin. For one brief moment, Horatio saw the same light-hearted boy he had remembered from their youth. The knight promised himself that he would do all he could to see it for years to come.

10

G regory's patience was wearing thin. Horatio and his halfwit cousin were nearly thirty minutes late. One of the baron's greatest irritations was the lack of respect by his men and recently, Horatio had been the most disrespectful of all in his employ. He wasn't sure why the knight's absence surprised him.

Granted, Gregory had asked the two simpletons to check on his daughter before coming to the meeting, but they still should have been here by now.

Unless...No! He wouldn't even entertain such notions. The damnable creature that had haunted him in these last few months was beginning to plague his every thought. He was seeing the Djinn in every shadow. In every flicker from the corner of his eye. And this had led to a nagging sense of dread—dread of the Djinn's next attack. An unreasonable fear that the creature would get to him at his weakest point. It's what he would do if roles were reversed. He would go after the one thing his enemy treasured most. In Gregory's case, that would be Isabella.

It was bad enough the demon had absconded with Solomon's Seal...an object of immense importance to his plans. But that simply wasn't enough for the Djinn. No. He'd sent a not-so-subtle threat in his latest attack against Gerard and his men. The baron reached into his tunic and absently pulled out the oval medallion from around his neck.

Gregory traced the medallion's inscription with his finger. It had taken nearly six years and a veritable fortune to translate, but he had finally done it. He'd unlocked the secret location of Solomon's Vault where the baron's life had changed forever. He'd been searching, under the Holy See's instructions, for the fabled *Urim* and *Thummim* stones...but what he'd discovered once opening the tunnels that led to the Vault made those relics insignificant by comparison. The medallion had been the key to the discovery of a lifetime. Perhaps even the greatest discovery in the history of the Crusades.

Of course, after he'd gleaned all he could from the medallion, he'd given it to his daughter on her eighteenth birthday. A prize worthy of a princess. A divine gift to a divine gift.

Then, one day, two months ago, the medallion had disappeared without a trace—from Isabella's very bedchambers, no less. At the time, it had not concerned him too much—after all, he already had the information he needed from it. He'd simply assumed his daughter had misplaced it. An irresponsible oversight, to be sure, but nothing to raise suspicions of sinister dealings afoot.

Now, he knew differently. The Djinn had been in his daughter's bedchambers. He had taken it from her while she slept. Its return was a clear warning: "I could have taken your daughter any time I chose." Gregory shuddered at the thought. It was why he was taking such special precautions with her now—why he'd practically sequestered her in her room and why she was being watched so tenaciously. He would not allow the demon to have her.

But he could not think such thoughts tonight. Not now, when the hour he had worked for was so near. Soon, the Djinn would be a mere trifle and the prize Gregory had sought—had sacrificed so much for—would be his. The baron shrugged off the gloomy thoughts and turned his gaze to the five other men who *did* have the courtesy to arrive on time.

Well, not all who were present had arrived on time. Tufic, his brother's physician, had only just arrived. The insufferable heathen hadn't even apologized for his audacity. It was out of sheer grace that Gregory had invited his brother to the meeting in the first place—William had, after all, been invaluable in his research into Solomon's golems and his guidance and wisdom would be needed before the final stages of the baron's quest were complete. But, of course, his brother couldn't attend due to his illness—or perhaps, the fact that most of the gentry in Jerusalem considered him unclean. Unwelcome. So, instead of attending the meeting himself, William had sent his loyal representative.

The baron shivered under Tufic's cold glare. There was just something unsettling about the physician, though Gregory could not discern what it was. He was typical of most natives of the *Outremer*—dark skin with close cropped black hair and a neatly trimmed mustache and beard. His mustache was curved with wax at the ends to form two tight loops above his upper lip. Thick, bushy eyebrows hung over a narrow, beaklike nose.

No, Tufic's appearance was that of any other Saracen. Gregory's apprehension of the doctor was not from his looks—it was in the way he stared at the baron. It was clear that the heathen held great animosity toward him. Tufic's eyes burned with rancor whenever they met Gregory's own. And the baron had the sense that, if left unchecked, the physician might use one of his surgical instruments on him one day.

Remembering the task at hand, Gregory pushed back all thoughts of mistrust, fear, and irritation. This meeting was just too important. He forced a broad smile as he motioned for his guests to enter the large, stone doorway that led down to his private tunnels.

"Come, gentlemen, the time is at hand."

"But what of your men?" asked Tufic with a sardonic grin. "You have complained of them since my arrival. Are you so quick to give up on them now?"

"Obviously, they have been delayed," Gregory said, taking a deep breath to ease the irritation building within him. "They'll catch up to us, I'm sure. Horatio knows the way."

All six men turned to the heavy oak door that had been pulled open by Gerard's own men just prior to their arrival. Besides the baron, his brother's physician, and Gerard, the group consisted of Monsignor Tertius, a Moroccan nobleman who had renounced his title, wealth, and land to serve the Holy Church. A direct representative of the Pope, Tertius had been sent to the *Outremer* to check on why Gregory's mission had been delayed. The Vatican, it seemed, was getting impatient and they would be most displeased when they learned the truth behind this expedition. This, of course, did not concern Gregory in the slightest.

The fifth man invited to the meeting was the most unusual, if not dangerous, choice for Gregory's endeavor. Unfortunately, the baron had *no* choice—Al-Dula ibn Abdul was a necessary evil in the purest sense of the phrase. Al-Dula was an infamous Moslem warlord from Egypt and one of the top-ranking officials in Sultan Saladin's cabinet. He was also ravenously ambitious. Claiming to be a direct descendent of the Prophet Mohammed, Al-Dula held aspirations to wrest control of the Sultan's realm and establish himself as the new Caliph. He'd also been the one to provide the medallion to Gregory that pinpointed the exact location of Solomon's Vault. An heirloom from when his family held considerable power while Jerusalem was still in Saracen hands. Though the baron had despised forming a partnership with the man, he would never have discovered the Vault without him.

Of course, he'd nearly had to sell his soul to obtain the piece of jewelry. Al-Dula had wanted nothing less than the means to overthrow Sultan Saladin and he was convinced, just as Gregory, that the power to do that lay deep within Solomon's Vault. In the end, the baron decided, the price would actually serve his own purposes quite nicely as well. After all, Saladin had his eyes set on Jerusalem at that very moment. To remove him from power now could only benefit Gregory in the end.

Of course, Al-Dula had not come alone. He brought an uninvited guest—the sixth and final member of their party. Gregory had not been told the man's name and truth be told, he wasn't sure he cared to know. Al-Dula had volunteered some information on the strange and silent guest, dressed in a black and gray tunic, a dark red turban, and a thick black beard that hung down to the man's chest.

Apparently, the sixth guest was a member of a secret Saracen society—a group known and feared throughout the Muslim world as the *Hashshashin* and made up of elite clerics, completely devout in their religion to the point of fanaticism. And, if what Gregory had heard about the sect was true, they had honed the art of murder to the point of almost supernatural perfection.

The baron glanced at the silent killer in their midst, and couldn't help but utter a silent prayer to whatever god would listen that he would find an ally in the man—the cleric would make a ruthless enemy.

"Come, gentlemen," Gregory said. "History awaits us this evening."

The baron led the way down the stone staircase that descended into the bowels of the city. Flickering torches, interspersed several feet apart, lit the long, spiraling steps. Fire-cast shadows danced along the curved walls as the seven men struggled to maintain solid footing on the narrow stairs. After several minutes, the group came to level ground—a long dark tunnel stretching deeper into the earth before them.

"Just a little further," said the baron, turning around to look at his guests. "What I have to show you is just—"

His words hung in his throat. The hashshashin was no longer with them.

"My friend," Gregory addressed Al-Dula, "it seems as though your man may have gotten lost."

"You needn't worry yourself, Baron. Emir is quite capable of taking care of himself."

"Yes, well, be that as it may, it is essential that we all stay together."

Panic began to swell within the baron's chest. He didn't like this at all. It was bad enough that Al-Dula had brought this killer with him to their meeting. He was an unaccounted variable in the entire scheme and Gregory did not like unknown variables.

Al-Dula was a man motivated by greed and ambition. This made him predictable and, thereby, trustworthy to a certain point. But this 'Emir', as the future Caliph had called him, was motivated by something altogether different—fanaticism. To a man like Gregory, whose only commitment was to himself, these were alien and unfathomable concepts. He simply could not be sure how to anticipate the actions of such men.

For a moment, thoughts of William flitted through his mind. *You would know, wouldn't you, brother?* Gregory thought. *You've always acted according to your convictions. You would know exactly what to expect from this hashshashin.*

Taking a torch from a wall sconce, the baron turned toward the darkened tunnel just as a scream from above echoed down the narrow confines of the stairwell, stopping Gregory in his tracks, and chilling the hearts of the entire group. In unison, they spun around as a great commotion descended the steps toward them.

Suddenly, Samuel careened down the stone steps, tumbling end over end. The young squire crashed to the dirt floor at the feet of Tufic, who immediately stooped down to examine the lad for injuries.

Sounds of a fierce battle ensued, the clatter of clanging

swords exploded above them. Horatio jumped into view, his back turned to Gregory and the four other men who watched slack-jawed at the duel. The knight was pushed back, blocking a blow from a curved scimitar—the attacker still unseen around a corner.

Gregory froze with dread. He had heard rumors of the curved black blade wielded by the Djinn—a blade exactly like the one now struggling to hew the outmatched knight to pieces.

Horatio took another step backwards, bringing his assailant finally into view—it was Emir. The brutal hashshashin pushed his advance, nearly knocking Horatio from his feet, but the knight brought up his shield, narrowly escaping a decapitating blow.

"Lord Gregory, get out of here!" cried Horatio as he glimpsed over his shoulder to see the baron and the others. "It's the Djinn!"

Emir crouched down as the knight swung his blade around in a full arc, attempting to slash the cleric in half. The hashshashin swung his right leg up, entwining it between Horatio's own legs and twisted. The knight flew helplessly, tumbling straight for the crowd of onlookers.

The cleric bounded down the steps three at a time until he came to Horatio's inert form. Grabbing him by the neck, a long slender dagger appeared out from a fold in Emir's tunic and flew towards the knight's throat.

"Enough!" commanded Al-Dula.

With skill that Gregory had never known possible, the zealous Emir flipped the blade into his palm in mid-swing, striking Horatio with the butt of the dagger. The knight gasped from the blow as Emir raised himself to his full height and looked down at Horatio, bloodlust in his eyes.

"L-Lord Gregory," said the knight. "It's the Djinn. Don't let him escape."

The baron raised an eyebrow, an amused smile growing across his face.

"Pick yourself up, fool," he said. "This isn't the Djinn."

Tufic, finished examining Samuel's wounds, held out a hand for the knight and pulled him up. A quick examination revealed no serious injuries and Horatio explained what had happened to initiate the fight.

"We were running late because of a disturbance in the eastern sector," Horatio lied. He was in no mood to explain Samuel's brief, inexplicable disappearance. "We realized you must have gone down into the tunnels ahead of us, so we hurried along."

The knight glared at Emir, rubbing his bruised jaw before continuing.

"Anyway, as we made our way down the stairs, I spied a shadow moving below us on the staircase. I've seen the way that foul creature moves with my own eyes, and I'd have sworn it was the same beast...so I attacked."

"That was rather brave of you," said the physician with a warm smile.

"I'm not sure about bravery, sir. It was more out of fear than anything else," the knight continued. "Anyway, it turns out it wasn't the Djinn. It was this bloke here. It's eerie how much he moves like the demon, though."

"Yes," said Gregory, looking the cleric up and down. "Very *eerie*, indeed. Anyway, gentlemen, now that the excitement is over, shall we proceed?"

With everyone's assent, including a bruised Horatio and a bewildered Samuel, the group moved forward into the recently excavated tunnel.

11

T here were no torches in this section of the excavated tunnels, so the only light came from those held by Gregory, Gerard, and Al-Dula. Each flicker of flame cast dark shadows that seemed to dance rhythmically to the light, making it difficult to see sudden drops in the stone floor that could cause one to stumble.

The group moved slowly, stooping low to avoid hitting their heads on the cross beams supporting the ceiling, for about a quarter mile until they came to a rather vast chamber.

"My men unearthed this four months ago," said Gregory, walking into the center of the great hall with arms spread wide in pride. "The chamber has been examined by both a Roman priest and a Jewish rabbi. They both agree on its origin…as well as purpose."

Each man stood awestruck by the sight. Spanning nearly fifty feet in height with a vaulted ceiling, the chamber was ornately decorated and trimmed with gold. Lavish relief carvings and mosaics covered the smooth surface of the walls—scenes depicting great battles and miracles from God intervening in the lives of the Jewish nation.

But the baron's guests gasped in near unison at what he'd brought them all here to see. Along the circular walls of the chamber stood twelve large statues that towered over the guests like dark juggernauts guarding the gates of Hell itself. Each figure was roughly nine feet tall with massive shoulders and arms that gripped the hilts of enormous bronze swords. Their faces, malformed in ancient clay, were depictions of various animals. An eagle. A wolf. A bear. A viper. And so on, with the most striking of all resembling that of a roaring lion.

"What is this place?" asked Al-Dula, his eyes wide as he scanned each of the statues. "What do your clergymen say this was?"

"That, my friend, is the question," the baron said, his sightless, graying eye shining brightly in the torch light. "From what we have determined this was the central hub, of sorts, to a vast repository known only in whispers as *Solomon's Vault*. It was constructed directly underneath what was once Solomon's Temple."

Complete silence reigned throughout the chamber. No one moved as they absorbed this information. The implications were staggering to all save Horatio and his squire, and Gregory could not have been more pleased. It was exactly the reaction he had hoped.

"So that means we are directly beneath the Sacred Dome?" asked Al-Dula.

"Exactly."

"But how has no one ever found this place?" Tufic asked. "The Temple was destroyed over a thousand years ago. Jews, Romans, Saracens, Christians…all these have searched this land high and low for any secret treasure chambers such as this. How could no one know this was here?"

"Because no one knew where to look," said Gregory. "By the time of Christ, the Jews had all but forgotten this place even existed. It was built by Solomon himself, well before Jerusalem was sacked by the Babylonians. It, at one time, was his personal treasure vault."

"Treasure?" asked Gerard.

"Don't become too excited, Captain. This chamber was not for just anything that glittered or shined. It was for objects of a particular variety. For things beyond all the treasures of the earth."

The Saracen warlord walked over to the southern wall and examined an intrinsically detailed painting of a group of men carrying a strange looking gold box. Lightning and fire seemed to surround not only the box, but the men carrying it as well. "You're talking about the Ark of the Testimony, aren't you?" Al-Dula hissed, a look of true understanding washing across his face. "Don't tell me you have found it!"

"No, I haven't. At least not yet. But then, as you are aware, it was not for the Ark that I have been searching all these years," said the baron.

Al-Dula nodded. "The Urim and Thummim. The stones of 'Revelation' and 'Truth.'"

Gregory smiled. "Well, that is what I was originally searching for, yes," he said, glancing slyly toward Monsignor Tertius. "But I long since gave up that search for something...much more tantalizing."

"What? You've given up?" the Vatican priest asked, his eyebrows furrowing. "Lord Gregory, this is most displeasing. His excellency, the Pope himself, specifically commissioned you to find the stones. When he hears of this..."

The baron waved him off. "Please, do shut up," he growled, spinning around, and pointing at one of the statues. "I've no interest in your opinion in this matter. Nor that of the Holy See. What I'm presenting to you is much more powerful than anything the divining stones of David could provide."

The guests stared at the clay figure to which Gregory was pointing. A look of confusion plastered across each man's face.

"What? These statues?" Tertius asked harshly. "You have forsaken your quest for a handful of old clay totems?"

A hiss of understanding erupted from Al-Dula's lips as he moved over to the lion-headed statue and examined it more closely. Its frame was littered with intricately carved pictograms and designs, depicting what looked to be some type of fierce battle scene. Script from some unknown tongue was etched along its arms, legs, and forehead with exacting precision.

The Saracen spun around to face Gregory, a look of awe on his face. "Are these what I think they are?"

The baron nodded with a smile. "They are."

Al-Dula's eyes widened. "But are they active? Have you reactivated them yet?"

The group stared silently at the exchanged until Monsignor Tertius cleared his throat and interjected. "See here," he began. "What are you two going on about? What on earth is so special about these statues?"

"Allow me start from the beginning, Your Excellency," the baron cooed, moving over to a figure whose head was shaped like a boar. "When I first arrived here, I was driven to succeed in the Pope's task in recovering the fabled Urim and Thummim. Through several years of research, I'd discovered that one of the last known locations for those relics was hidden somewhere underground. Some kind of vault created by King Solomon." He nodded over at the Saracen warlord and held up the medallion that hung from his neck. "Thanks to this heirloom provided by our friend Al-Dula here, I was able to determine the precise location and immediately set about excavating. Six months ago, my men finally broke through and discovered this central Hub."

Gregory raised a gloved hand and caressed the broad arm of the statue and smiled.

"That's when I discovered these, and my mission immediately changed."

The monsignor turned around in a full circle, examining the

Hub and the six darkened passageways that lined its rounded wall. "I don't understand. Surely you searched these tunnels further for the stones," Tertius said. "You said so yourself that they were last known to be within these walls. A little more effort on your part and surely you will find them."

The baron whirled around and glared at the priest. "You're missing the point, Monsignor. The stones are useless. Mere baubles for the Church to hide within their own coffers. Completely useless to anyone." He smiled once more, trying to calm himself. "But these statues. Your Grace, these mere 'totems' as you call them represent near limitless power. A force which nothing on earth could even remotely hope to stop."

"I must admit, I'm a bit taken aback by all this. Confused."

"Of course you are," Gregory mumbled, running a hand through his thinning hair. "I would expect nothing less from someone with as little imagination as you."

At this, Tufic cleared his throat and stepped forward. "Monsignor, I believe I begin to understand. These things that line the wall...Lord Gregory does not believe them to be mere statues." The physician looked over at the baron. "You believe these are the twelve golems that are said to have been created by King Solomon's vengeful wives, don't you? The ones that legends say nearly destroyed all of Jerusalem until they were imprisoned by the king himself."

"Indeed," said Gregory. "But I don't just believe that's what these things are. I *know* it.

"But how? How can you know for sure?"

"Never mind that," growled the Monsignor. "Just what exactly is a *golem*? And why would it supersede the importance of the Urim and Thummim?""

"Because, Your Grace, the Seeing Stones are simply powerless relics," the baron said with a sigh. "But golems...golems are something far more useful. You see, they are living, breathing creatures...as Adam, they too were formed from the dust of the ground and were given life by the mystical means of Solomon's very own Seal.

"Tufic is correct. These are the very same that are said to have been created by a woman unwillingly forced into marriage with the king. She despised him and she loathed the kingdom. So, she tricked him. She promised to show him the secret that her own people had been doing for centuries...creating clay automatons that would do the bidding of the one who brought them to life."

"Blasphemy!" the priest said. "Only God can create life. For anyone else to even attempt it would be..."

"Disastrous," the physician said. "Catastrophic. As Solomon himself discovered."

"Only because he had no way to know of his wife's plan," protested the baron. "By the time he realized what was happening, it was too late. She had already given her creations their instructions and there was nothing anyone could do."

Al-Dula stepped in between Gregory and the others.

"You didn't answer my question, Lord Gregory," he said. "Are they active?"

The baron smiled at the Saracen for a few moments without saying a word, then shrugged. "Yes," he finally said. "In a manner of speaking, the golems you see before you are awake even now."

"In a manner of speaking?" Al-Dula asked. "What is that supposed to mean?"

"It means that they've been active since they were first animated. They do not die. They do not sleep. They are, as far as I know, fully aware of us and our presence within their prison."

"Then why aren't they moving? Why not command them to do something so that we might know the truth of the matter?"

Gregory let out frustrated laugh. "Because I do not have the power to command them just yet. Rakeesha, the wife of Solomon who created them, was their last master. They would only respond to her instructions. I am still attempting to discover the means to wrest control of them. I have no doubt that a scroll I'm currently searching for, the *Sefer Yetzhirah*, or Book of Creation, will provide me with an incredible fount of information on this subject. This book is said to have been kept in a secret library within these very walls and contains specific details on how to construct these creatures. Until I find those instructions, I'm afraid, the golems are—"

"Excuse me, sir," came Horatio's grating voice. "I don't mean to interrupt, but has anyone seen Samuel?"

They all turned to face the knight with looks of incredulity on their faces. Gregory glared at Horatio. He wasn't sure how much more of this imbecile and his idiot cousin he could take. What did he care where Samuel had wandered off…

Oh no.

"Where is he?" said Gregory, suddenly anxious over the chilling thought that had just occurred to him. "Find him! We must find him now."

Gerard bolted toward the far-left passage in the opposite end of the chamber from which they'd entered. The rest of the group waved their torches in front of them, peering into any dark recesses they could find within the vast Hub.

"Samuel!" Horatio's voice echoed through miles of tunnel. No response. "Samuel! This isn't funny now."

Still nothing.

Gregory turned on the knight, grabbing him by the arms and pulling him close. His foul breath and spit flew into Horatio's face.

"Tell me now, fool, did you not tell me that your squire was captured for a time by the demon?" the baron hissed, trying to keep the others from hearing. Waiting for the knight to respond, Gregory scanned the chamber to account for each member of their party.

Gerard was nowhere to be seen, but then, he'd gone off in search of the squire. Al-Dula and the Saracen cleric were to his right. The priest from the Vatican was behind him.

Wait. Where was the physician? He was missing as well. This could not be happening. Not now.

"Tell me!" he shouted, drawing the attention of the would-be Caliph.

"Um, yes sir. He was taken by the creature...but only for a bit. I found him soon enough. No harm done."

Pushing the knight away, Gregory spun around, spittle flying from his lips as he yelled. "If that whelp finds it..." the baron's thought was interrupted by the sound of Tufic's voice coming from their original tunnel.

"He didn't go back the way we came," the physician said as he walked up to Gregory and the worried knight.

The baron nodded as relief flooded his body. At least his concerns over William's man could now be laid to rest. His whereabouts was now accounted for.

Al-Dula came to Gregory, leaned in close, and whispered, "I am not sure what is going on here, Baron, but there is too much at stake to allow such incompetence in your ranks."

"Don't you think I know that?"

"I'm not sure you do. You have not done well against this spirit that haunts you. Now, you allow this man's squire to wander off unhindered into your treasure vault."

"I can assure you, Al-Dula, everything is under control."

The Saracen warlord grabbed Gregory by the collar and pulled him to his face. Fire burned in his eyes as he glowered at the baron.

"Listen to me, little man," Al-Dula hissed. "We had a deal. The price for helping you find the Vault was that you would provide me the means to do away with the Sultan once and for all. An army of golems could do just that. There is simply too much at stake to—"

His words were cut off by the sound of scuffling feet and a cry of pain in the passage that Gerard had been searching. Several seconds later, the mercenary walked out from the dark, holding Samuel by the scruff of the neck.

"I found him marking the walls with this," said Gerard, shoving Samuel to the ground and holding up a strange writing instrument. "He was leaving some kind of secret message to someone."

Gregory slapped Al-Dula's hands away from his tunic and stepped toward Samuel's prone form. They had been infiltrated. Somehow, the Djinn had bewitched the whelp...the baron was sure of it. Kicking the squire in the gut, Gregory spun around and walked toward the tunnel that led back to the entrance.

"This meeting is over, gentleman," the baron said. "Gerard, take the traitor to the dungeon and prepare him for questioning. We will continue this tour of the treasure vault when I have the answers I seek."

Horatio hurried over to his injured cousin and lifted him to his feet, but Gerard pushed him away.

"He's mine now," the mercenary said with a malicious smile.

12

" Horatio! Come in, come in," said the familiar voice of William De L'Ombre from behind the beautiful, red velvet curtains.

The knight hesitated, struggling to prepare himself for what awaited him upon entering his old friend's parlor. He had not seen William in years—not since before he was taken prisoner and came to live with Samir ibn Nassad, the sheik who had taken such a liking to him that he made him officially an heir to his title and fortune. He'd not seen him since before he had contracted his horrid disease.

Horatio shuddered at the thought. It was just so difficult to accept. William had always been so strong, so vibrant. And while he was by no means the biggest and strongest of the knights, he had always been the most courageous and...Horatio sighed at the next thought...loyal.

Yes. William had always been loyal to a fault. Something that Horatio knew could not be said about himself. It had been because of him that William had been injured and captured in the first place. It had been because Horatio had been flung from his injured horse...because he had lain helplessly immobile on the battlefield, his fallen horse pinning his legs, that his good and *loyal* friend had turned around to save him. It had been because of him that William was loathed by the other gentry in Jerusalem.

And what had Horatio done to repay him? Nothing at all. Not once had he ever come to William's chateau to check on him. Not one single time had he visited, seeking to discover the truth behind what the others were saying. He hadn't even bothered to come when the sheik and his other sons—William's own adopted brothers—had been massacred by Gregory's mercenary army.

No, Horatio didn't know the meaning of the word loyalty. Only now, when his cousin and squire lay helpless in Gregory's dungeons did he bother to show his face to his old friend. He was so ashamed. But he didn't know what else to do. Only Gregory's brother had any chance of influencing Samuel's release.

Taking a deep breath, Horatio pulled the curtain back and walked into the parlor. His tension eased when he did not walk headfirst into the leprous monster his imagination had concocted over the years. William was covered from head to foot in loose fitting white robes and a semi-opaque veil that covered his entire head. His hands were even gloved with some fabric that the knight had never seen before. Shiny. Smooth. He wasn't sure what the material was, but it looked very expensive.

"My friend!" William's joy over seeing Horatio seemed to reverberate around the room. "It's so good to see you. I have missed—" He paused, cocking his head as he looked at the knight. "Are you all right, brother?"

The knight's head hung low. He wasn't sure what he could say. He knew that William loved him as a brother and would never hold any grudges against him, yet he could not bring himself to look at him. Shame welled up, threatening to rupture inside him like an ulcer

"I'm sorry, William," he said. "This was a mistake. I shouldn't bother you with my troubles." Horatio turned to walk out of the parlor but was stopped by a bandaged hand on his shoulder.

"Don't go. I've missed you, my friend. Please stay. Tell me what troubles you."

"It's wrong of me to be here," said Horatio, turning to face the man he had let down so many times in the past. "I just didn't know where to else to go. I don't deserve your help, but I had nowhere else to turn."

To Horatio's surprise, William let out a soft, warm laugh as he led the knight to a circle of plush pillows on the floor. He motioned Horatio to sit.

"My dear Horatio," William said. "You are one of my oldest and dearest friends. I would do anything for you...you should know that."

"But it's all my fault. It's because of me that this...this..." He gestured at William's leprous form. "...curse fell upon you!"

"What? Are you the one that gave me leprosy? Did *you* turn my brother, gentry, and even Jerusalem's king against me?"

Hearing his friend put it that way, Horatio realized it sounded preposterous. Still, he could not help but feel responsible. No worthy response came to him.

"Listen to me," continued William. "You are no more responsible for the things that have happened to me than you are for the sun rising and setting. You are my friend. You are more of a brother to me than Gregory ever was. I would not turn my back on our friendship for all the treasure in the *Outremer*."

"But I..."

"No 'buts.' There is nothing you could ask that I wouldn't turn the world upside down to accomplish."

Without waiting for the knight to respond, William beckoned to a servant girl, who came over and crouched low to hear him whisper something in her ear. Nodding, she walked out of the room and came back soon after with two goblets of wine. Horatio took one graciously and sipped at the sweet liquid.

"Now, please. Tell me what troubles you," William said.

Horatio knew that his friend truly meant everything he said.

He would do whatever it took to help him—even if it meant storming Gregory's dungeon himself to free Samuel. *There is truly no nobler a man in the world than Sir William.*

Resigning himself to overcome his shame, the knight told his friend everything that had been happening in Jerusalem for the last several months. He detailed his encounter with the Djinn and how the dark spirit had been plaguing Gregory and his men. He told of Samuel's strange behavior and his actions in the tunnels that led to his arrest.

"I just don't know what to do," Horatio said. "They won't even let me in to see him. Gregory will not see me. And that scoundrel of a mercenary—Gerard—there's no more evil man in all Jerusalem than he. He takes pleasure in all of this."

William leaned back against one of the pillows, his veiled eyes looking up toward the ceiling in thought.

"Yes, I have heard most of what you have told me already," the leper said. "Tufic has filled me in, and Gregory came to consult me on this *Djinn* problem."

Both men sat silently for several long moments. Horatio could not remember ever having been in a more uncomfortable position. He loved William as much as anyone could love a brother, yet despite the leper's abounding forgiveness, the knight had difficulty letting go.

"This Djinn is a very serious problem, Horatio," William said, breaking the unsettling quiet in the room. "Samir spent many hours regaling me with tales of the Muslim lore and legend. The djinni stories were some of his favorite myths."

"Myths? But surely, he believed in such things. All Saracens do, don't they?"

William burst out with his all too familiar laughter. Horatio hadn't heard his friend laugh in years, yet for some reason, it felt as if it were only days. Still, he enjoyed seeing his friend in such high spirits—even in such dark times as these. It brought a certain calm to him, as if all was well with the world.

"Aye, my brother, most Muslims do believe in such things. Such creatures are written about in their holy book. Yet Samir was no follower of Allah."

"What? But I thought..."

"You thought what Gregory and the others wanted you to believe, Horatio. Samir was a Christian. Yes, he was born a Muslim and inherited a Saracen's title, but he was more a believer in the Nazarene than any of the so-called Crusaders that invade the City of David."

"He was a Christian? But how is that possible? How did he carry out the sacraments without a priest?" Horatio's eyes grew wide at his next thought. "If he was Christian then why would Gregory's forces ride in and kill...oh, no."

"Yes, dear brother. Exactly. Samir, his sons, and his entire household were killed under false accusations of following Islam. In reality, he was considered a threat to the kingdom," explained William, who had become quite somber. "Of course, truth be known, much of the blame should fall on his eight sons, who conspired with the Christian Noblemen to usurp their father." William sighed. "How unfortunate their treachery didn't prepare them for the betrayal my brother and his ilk would levy against them once Samir was gone."

Horatio took another swig from the wine and William filled his cup to the rim again. Without a word, three servants were ushered into the room and set down large bowls of fruit on the table before the knight.

"Eat up, Horatio. My tale will take some time and it's time you know everything. Don't worry about Samuel. Everything will be taken care of soon enough."

S amuel knew things were bad when he could smell himself. He hadn't bothered to bathe for several days before being arrested and now, being stuck in his cell overnight—it was just too much. Even for him.

His nose wrinkled at the foul stench wafting up from his fetid rags. Unfortunately, something as simple as a nose twitch sent waves of burning pain over his entire face—thanks to Gerard's handiwork. He wasn't sure how long the mercenary had beaten him, but it had felt like forever.

The young squire couldn't believe he was in this mess. It was bad enough that the rats scampering on the stone floor of his cell were gradually gaining the courage to move ever so much closer to him, but the food that was brought for him to eat was little more than liquid slop that swine might find unappetizing. And Samuel knew all about pigs—oh, he missed Master Flatnose so much. He couldn't help smile—despite the pain it elicited—at the thought of his faithful pig from back home.

The smile quickly faded, however, as doubt crept into Samuel's mind. Had he made the right choice in obeying the

Djinn's request? Why had he even listened to the creature? At the time, it had made perfect sense. He had been confident that the spirit had come from God and not, as others were saying, from the fires of Gehenna itself. He wasn't sure why. It had something to do with the creature's voice…it just sounded so soothing and gentle.

Now, as the squire's eyes tried to adjust to the squalid dungeon, he wondered if, perhaps, that voice had not been laced with poisoned honey. An enchantment designed to enthrall him.

"Bloody demon," he muttered to himself as he shifted his weight to the left to ease the pressure on his right leg. He sat uncomfortably, cross-legged, on the stone floor. Chains stretched from both wrists and ankles to the wall. Blood trickled down his hands from gashes made when the irons were bolted around his wrists.

Oh, why did I do it? Why didn't I tell Horatio about the Djinn?

Since that first night, Samuel had been visited by the creature four separate times—always while he slept soundly in the backroom of the barracks. After the first visitation, he had been convinced that he had dreamed the whole thing up. But after the second…well, there was little room for doubt.

The Djinn had told him things. Things that Samuel wished to the Lord Above he could forget. He had told him about Gregory and the evils the man brought with him from France. He had explained the baron's plan and how, if he succeeded, thousands of people would be enslaved—all hope being squeezed from their lives with no recourse at all. It just seemed so gruesome. Samuel couldn't help but want to offer any assistance he could to stave off such tyranny in the land.

And what harm had Samuel really done, anyway? None that he could see. He couldn't figure out why Lord Gregory and that buffoon Gerard had treated him as badly as they had. All he did was walk down one tunnel, attaching funny little pouch-things to each of the torches that lit the way. The pouches had all been connected by a strange thin wire. Then, there was that peculiar marking he'd been asked to make—"...on the eastern wall," the Djinn had told him. "Be sure it's on the eastern wall." But it hardly made any mark at all. It had been some weird yellow-green color that he could barely see.

No, Samuel just couldn't figure out what all the fuss was about. Still, he hadn't told them about the pouches. No matter how rough Gerard got with him, he just felt that they were something he ought not mention. Somehow, he knew they were very important to the Djinn and despite his nagging doubts, in his heart of hearts, he still believed he had done the right thing.

The clank of a key and creak of the great metal doors opening from around the corner of the cell jerked Samuel back to the present. Someone was coming and so far, whenever anyone had come to visit him, it had usually ended with a severe beating. He prayed that it wasn't Gerard.

His hopes, however, were dashed as the large mercenary swaggered around the corner, an ominous grin spread across his face. Samuel's throat constricted at the sight. This couldn't be happening again. *Oh, please Lord, no.* Then, someone behind Gerard appeared that sent a tidal wave of relief washing over him—Tufic strolled casually to the barred door of the squire's cell.

The physician and mercenary glared at each other for several long seconds without a word. Gerard was obviously not happy about Tufic being there, but it was clear that he had no choice.

"All right," said Tufic. "Now, open the door and get out. The agreement is that I have ten minutes alone with the poor lad."

"If you don't watch your tone, Heathen, you'll be spending a much greater time with him than ten minutes."

"The baron wouldn't like that, now would he?"

"It makes no difference to me," growled the mercenary. "He doesn't pay me enough to care what he thinks."

Tufic gave a gentle smile at the larger man. "I'll be sure to let him know that when I present my diagnoses of your captive."

Gerard's face reddened, but he didn't take back what he'd said either. He wheeled around to the door, inserted the oversized metal key, and turned the latch. He had to pull hard on the door to swing it open, breaking off bits of rust that encrusted it.

"You've got ten minutes. No more," he said as he spun around and loped from the dungeon. The door clanged shut around the corner.

Tufic stepped into Samuel's cell and crouched down close to him. A great white smile broke out across the Saracen physician's swarthy face as he inspected the bruises and gashes across the squire's forehead.

"Good," he said. "There doesn't seem to be any serious damage to you. How do you feel?"

Samuel felt oddly comforted by the physician's presence. He couldn't figure out why. He had only met the doctor a handful of times—the last being in Gregory's tunnels. His gentle hands had mended him well after his encounter with the strange hashshashin that accompanied the baron's Moslem friend. Somehow, down deep, he knew that this was a good man, and his warm smile and soothing voice expelled the doubts he had been harboring.

"I'm fine, sir. Just a bit uncomfortable—oh, and a bit hungry too, if you understand my meaning."

Tufic laughed. "Yes, I can imagine the food here isn't very appealing." He rummaged through the folds of his tunic and produced the largest fig Samuel had ever seen. "Here you go, lad. Eat up."

Samuel grabbed the luscious fruit and bit down deep—its juices exploding into the back of his throat. He didn't think he'd ever tasted anything so good in his entire life. As he relished every savory morsel, Tufic stood, crept to the edge of the cell, and peered around the corner. As he turned back to face the squire, who was still gnawing enraptured on the fruit, he placed a finger to his lips and crouched down again at Samuel's side.

"Now listen to me, lad," he said in a hushed tone. "I haven't much time. A mutual friend has sent me to tell you to be prepared to flee this place at a moment's notice."

Samuel stopped chewing. "Mutual friend?" he asked, pieces of fig spewing out of his mouth.

"Yes. You know who I mean. He's coming soon. He will free you. When he does, you must use this map...go immediately to the place that is marked," Tufic said as he produced a small piece of cloth with markings that resembled a map from his robe and handed it to Samuel. "Do not stop for anything or anyone. Just go. Once you are there, all will be made clear."

The squire swallowed the last bit of fruit in his mouth as best he could. He tentatively wiped the juice-covered hands on his tunic and took the cloth map, staring at it without saying a word. The "x" marking was near the Jordan River, about ten miles south of Jerusalem. No one lived out there but nomads and...oh!

Samuel slowly looked up at the physician. "Are...are you him? I won't tell anyone. I didn't tell that Gerard anything. You can trust me," he said, beaming from ear to ear. "You really can, you know."

Tufic returned the smile and clapped his hand on the squire's shoulder. "I know I can trust you, lad. But for now, just do as I say. Be ready to move. And when the time comes, run. And keep the map hidden somehow."

"Don't worry. I know exactly where I can hide it. Gerard will never find it!"

"Good lad. Now, I've got to leave. But don't worry. We'll see one another again very soon."

The physician stood and looked down at the young squire, confined in cold rusted chains.

"I really am proud of you, lad. Our friend is, too," he said with a wink as he turned and walked around the corner to the large metal door that led to the outside world. "Don't worry, Samuel. Soon, all will be well."

As the doctor's footfalls echoed out of the dungeon corridors, Samuel could not help but say a prayer of thanksgiving as a strange calm settled on him like a warm down blanket in the cold of night. He felt completely at peace. He knew without doubt that all, soon, would indeed be well.

14

G regory seethed as he stormed through the dank, narrow hallways of the palace dungeon. Everything— his plans and ambitions—were rapidly spiraling into chaos. Gerard's incompetence had cost him dearly. The loss of Solomon's ring to the Djinn was a major setback. Possibly even an insurmountable one. Without the ring's power, he was now powerless to revive the twelve golem warriors that lay dormant within the subterranean vault underneath the city.

Of course, that wasn't the worst part. The second phase of his plan—the part that would assure his own status of emperor— would be a mere pipe dream. He'd heard rumors that there might still be a way to reanimate the golems without the ring, but it would be impossible to craft an army of new ones.

Fortunately, the baron had not yet disposed of the one person who might provide the key to rectifying his dilemma. If anyone knew a way to attain his goals without Solomon's Seal, it would be the Essene nomad he held prisoner within these dungeon walls. He would force the man to reveal his secrets and his plan would be salvaged from ruin.

Gregory heard the screams before he even rounded the corner to where the prisoner's cell was. The mercenary, eager to rectify his failure before the baron could devise a way to punish him adequately, had already begun the interrogation process. He shuddered to think of what atrocities Gerard had planned for Ibrihim this time. After the last rat-infested interrogation, it was an absolute miracle the nomad was even able to speak coherently.

As the baron approached the cell, a grim-faced guard opened the gate to let him pass. One step through the threshold and Gregory reeled from the horrid stench that greeted him. He glanced around the room to see the prisoner hanging two feet off the floor by chains bound by shackles around his wrists. His shoulders and arms were stretched to an almost implausible length. What was left of the man's face, after the rats' feast a few days earlier, was marred by caked blood, feces, and all manner of ungodly things. His emaciated chest heaved for breath as Gerard slammed a fist into his distended gut.

As soon as the mercenary sensed the baron's presence in the room, he stopped and turned toward his employer.

"I believe he's ready to talk," Gerard said with a growl. "I don't think we'll have as much difficulty with him this time."

The baron stalked over to the suspended prisoner, reached out a hand, and forced the nomad's chin up so that he could look into the one eye the rats had left relatively untouched.

"Is this true, Ibrihim?" Gregory asked with a smile. "Can we dispense with all this unpleasantness? All I need are a few answers. It's as simple as that. You've already betrayed your tribe by revealing their location to me. What is a little more information going to hurt between friends?"

The Essene stared back at Gregory. All hope was gone from them. Through the mercenary's previous torture, Ibrihim had given up his people and their sacred trust. He'd shown Gerard exactly where they would be on a map and had even revealed the secrets of the Seal. The baron knew that this man truly had nothing else to live for.

When the prisoner sighed, Gregory knew his assessment had been correct.

"All right," Ibrihim said, wriggling his wrists to ease the tension in his iron shackles. "What would you like to know?"

The baron weighed his next few words carefully. After all, despair was a powerful motivator. If the Essene discovered that Gregory's assault on his village had been unsuccessful...if he learned that his people were still safe and that he'd been unable to acquire Solomon's ring...well, Gregory could not allow that to happen.

The baron cleared his throat. "Tell me...these golems that I've discovered. They're inert. Inanimate. If someone were to stumble upon them without the Seal, would there be any way to activate them? To bind them to their will?"

The nomad pondered this for several seconds in silence. He shifted his weight to one leg, then back to the other in a futile attempt to make himself more comfortable.

"That would be a very difficult thing to do indeed," Ibrihim finally spoke. Gregory thought he caught the slightest trace of a smile play across his lips and he wondered if he'd revealed too much with his question. "Granted, the ring itself isn't essential to reviving these creatures. After all, the *Breath of God* was sent into them by the power of the ring when they were first created. So, on the one hand, a person wouldn't need it to animate them. They'd simply need to wake them up." The nomad coughed and a gelatinous string of congealed blood spewed from his lips. "I thirst."

Gregory forced the irritation at the interruption away and nodded to Gerard. The mercenary strode across the cell, plunged a wooden cup into a vat of water and brought it over to their prisoner.

"You may quench your *thirst* after."

Ibrihim nodded his understanding and continued with a dry, ragged voice. "Your issue with the existing golems is not bringing them back to life, but rather wresting control from their creator."

"But the wife of Solomon has been dead thousands of years. Surely her influence on them is no more."

The Essene shook his head. "It matters not how long she's lain in the grave. She created them and gave them instructions they never fulfilled. The moment they are raised, they will resume their dark task with dispassionate efficiency." He paused again for another coughing fit, then continued. "It won't matter that you are the one who revive them. They recognize only one voice. Rakeesha's. As far as I know, there is only one way to establish your control over them."

"The ring?"

"The Seal is only needed to create new golems. It cannot establish control over the golems already created." The prisoner shook his head once more. "No, if that was the case, would Solomon himself not have used it to bring their reign of terror to an end?"

"Then how?"

"As I said before, it's no easy matter. The way to revive them into your own mastery is a dark path. One that Solomon himself refused to take, though he no doubt knew he could do it."

Gregory growled with frustration. "Just spit it out, man!"

"Blood." The nomad bowed his head as he said the word, as if resigning himself to a nightmarish fate. "The creatures will awaken to the blood of a sacrifice. A human sacrifice."

The room was silent for several heartbeats until Gerard spoke up.

"Then we have no problem. We can easily sacrifice the prisoner. Kill two birds with one stone, so to speak," he said with a hyena-like grin.

"And you will doom yourselves," the nomad said stoically. "True, my blood would awaken them, but it wouldn't give you power over them. For that, the sacrifice would have to be special. Dangerous."

"What do you mean? Dangerous?" Gregory asked, a lump swelling in his throat.

"The sacrifice would have to be a true gamble. High risk," Ibrihim said, a slight smile returning to his nightmarish face. "If you want to have power over the golems, then you must first sacrifice a person who has power over you."

The baron stared at Ibrihim for a few moments, unsure of what to say or do next. The revelation had nearly knocked the wind from his lungs. There were not many within the *Outremer* who could claim authority over him. Not many to choose for this sacrifice as the Essene described. And no matter who he chose, it would indeed be a most dangerous affair. If the ritual did not work, he would be left impotent...defenseless. If he chose to go down this path, there truly could be no turning back.

Gregory looked over at Gerard and nodded. "Loosen our guest's bindings. See to it that he is fed and comfortable for his service to us this day."

The mercenary gave him a puzzled expression. "Sir? I don't understand."

"It's simple, Captain. Our friend Ibrihim will need his strength if he's going to help us with the rites necessary to awaken the golems. I want him as content as we can possibly make him."

The nomad looked up at his captor, his eyes wide. "Help you? With the ritual? I never said anything about helping you kill another man."

The baron, who had already decided on the perfect candidate for the sacrifice, smiled broadly. "Of course," he said, as turned around and headed toward the cell doors. He had many preparations to make before his dinner meeting with Monsignor Tertius and Al-Dula later that evening. "It is, after all, the means to your own freedom."

15

"Enough of this, Gregory!" The Vatican priest slammed his fist against the baron's oak dining table. Mugs of wine and ale tumbled over, their contents sloshing to the stone floor. If Gregory had been a superstitious man, or even remotely religious, he would have believed Monsignor Tertius capable of bringing down fire from heaven to consume him. As it was, the little priest's outrage was a mere tickle in the back his throat. "His Grace will not stand for it. It's witchcraft of the highest order. You cannot seriously be contemplating this."

"Don't listen to him!" shouted Al-Dula, equally enraged. "We had a deal, Baron De L'Ombre. Do not forget it. Those creatures in that vault would give me the edge I need to overthrow Saladin once and for all...to establish my caliphate as is my birthright. I don't care how much your *Pontiff* will disapprove!"

"Blasphemy!" Tertius roared. "Lord Gregory, do you hear the foul poison your heathen guest is spewing?"

Gregory's smile never faded as he sauntered through his dining hall, hands clasped behind his back, as if in deep thought. The fools. How simple-minded...how short of vision were these men he'd invited into his confidence. Actually, neither would be pleased with what he truly planned for Solomon's golems. He would undoubtedly be betraying both men before this affair was over.

The Holy See had commissioned this entire expedition. The Pope, seeking a means to increase his own floundering influence among the nobles, had nearly tripped on his own robes to provide the finances for Gregory's excavation when he'd heard those silly mythical stones might still be underneath Jerusalem.

Al-Dula, likewise, had been only too eager to lend his own unique resources to the venture.

Neither, of course, would receive what had been promised. Once Gregory came into the possession of the book and reacquired Solomon's elusive ring, he would no longer have need of these contemptuous alliances he'd forged. He'd have little need of anything else from that point on. After all, with an entire army of clay automatons at his beck and call, no one on earth would be able to oppose him—lose one soldier, and he need only sculpt another from the dirt of the ground.

Of course, for now, it was essential he keep at least one of his allies happy. The other would not leave this dining hall a happy man in the slightest, but nothing could be done about it. For his plans to succeed, he would need to sever all ties to one of them. The other would soon join his predecessor and Gregory would finally be able to savor the sweet fragrance of ultimate victory.

Spinning around to face his challengers, his smile broadened. "Gentlemen, gentlemen...I assure you...I have considered every possibility in this matter. It is the only way for his Grace and for you, Al-Dula, to embrace what has been sought for so long. Security here in the *Outremer*."

"His Holiness could not care less about this wretched wasteland or its security, Gregory," said Tertius. "He sent you here for one purpose. To find the holy relics that would establish his *own* security among the gentry. You have failed him miserably and you try to make up for it by bringing me these...these abominations?"

"Abominations? Abominations! Oh, trust me Tertius, these creatures represent the true nature of the gods," Gregory said, his smile suddenly wavering with irritation. "Mankind finally breaking away from the shackles of religion and realizing their own, true potential. The creation of life itself!"

The priest moved around the table and squared up against Gregory. One long, thin finger prodded the baron against his chest.

"You dare to blaspheme against your God? Such words could have you excommunicated from the Church. We've long known about, and consequentially, tolerated your atheism. But make no mistake...we have the power to strip you of your title, land, and influence. Be mindful of your next few words, Baron."

Gregory looked down at the priest's finger, still pressed against his chest, then gently brushed it aside with a smile.

"Very well. Let me try to choose my next few words as carefully as I can, then," he said, his face suddenly turning frigid. "Guards. Arrest him."

Instantly, the six mercenaries hovering in each corner of the room converged on Tertius and threw him to the floor. Iron shackles appeared as if from nowhere and slid over the priest's wrists in a frenzy of motion.

"Wh-what is the meaning of this?" Monsignor Tertius howled, his face planted firmly on the stone floor. "Release me at once!"

The baron's smug grin returned as he crouched down to meet the baffled priest's gaze. "I'm sorry, Tertius. I'm afraid I'm going to have forego our rather tenuous partnership. But have no fear. Your role in this historic endeavor isn't over...and to be honest, it is one of the greatest importance. Trust me. You'll be remembered for years to come for the...sacrifice...you're about to make." He stood up, dusted his robes off, then looked at

Gerard. "You can't take him to the dungeon. No one must know what we've done until the rites are ready to be performed."

"I'll take him to the safehouse near the Jaffa Gate. He should be safe from prying eyes there," the mercenary captain said. Without another word, the mercenary and his guards led the priest from the room.

Al-Dula stared in disbelief at his host. "What is going on?"

The baron waved the question off with the flick of the wrist. "Nothing for you to worry about. A necessary evil, I assure you. And one that benefits you greatly, I might add."

The Saracen glanced over at his hashshashin cleric, who stood motionless against the southern wall of the room, then turned back to Gregory. His thick, dark fingers stroked the course hairs of his beard nervously. "I'm not sure I like that answer very much. You betray the Vatican now. How do I know I can trust you not to do the same with me when it is convenient?"

Gregory was growing weary of the entire discussion. If not for the silent figure of Emir, the baron would have physically removed the obstinate Saracen from his presence. As things were, Lord Gregory forced on the best smile he could muster and walked over to Al-Dula.

"My dear friend, the truth of the matter is…you can't. But the other side of that same truth is that you really have no choice. Soon, a golem army will be mine to command and I *will* use them how I see fit. If you wish to benefit from this, you will simply have to learn to trust me."

The Saracen's scowl was sharper than any sword. He hadn't liked that answer at all. Good. Let him fret. He was right not to trust the baron. After all, Gregory De L'Ombre had no intention of allowing any Caliph to rule once he had his army.

16

Al-Dula's feet crunched on the pebbled walkway that led from Gregory's chateau. He walked with stoic calm despite the rage simmering within after the meeting he'd just had with the baron.

"So, Emir, you know what you must do?" asked the Saracen to his taciturn companion as they strode onto the darkened streets of the northern sector of Jerusalem.

"Of course, my lord."

"The Westerner cannot be allowed to have his army."

The hashshashin, arms folded in front of him, looked up into the night sky. There was no moon. No source of light at all, but Al-Dula could swear that Emir's lithe frame cast a dark shadow along the ground. A shiver rippled down his back.

"As I said...I know what must be done," Emir said.

"Good. Very good."

Gregory was a fool among Western fools. His ambitions ate away at the veneer he worked so tirelessly to project—he was as transparent as Spanish glass. Al-Dula had no intentions of keeping his end of the bargain with the baron. He'd rather die than to allow that pompous jackal to succeed with his schemes.

"And what of this djinn, Emir? What shall we do about this?"

The hashshashin stopped walking and turned to Abdul ibn Al-Dula. His eyes burned with savage intensity.

"Be careful, my lord," Emir hissed, "of speaking of this creature so freely. The djinni are not to be taken lightly. They are spirits—both good and evil—with powers beyond anything we can comprehend."

"Surely, you don't believe such tales? You're a holy man."

"It is because I am a 'holy man,' as you say, that I do take such stories seriously."

The Saracen had to admit the tales of this djinn's exploits had rattled him. Such myths were engrained in the minds of all those who follow the Prophet. Legends said the djinni and their kin had been around for as long as there was life—intervening in the history of mankind for better or ill. As Al-Dula had grown up, such stories were forgotten or discounted as legends. But now even he wasn't entirely sure.

"Still," Al-Dula continued, "if this spirit creature interferes, what can be done?"

The hashshashin continued walking, moving in front of the Saracen. It was his way of showing the warlord that he was by no means Emir's superior.

"There are ways...ways of dealing with such beings."

"Like?"

"The Ring of Aandaleeb is said to have the power to bind a spirit to the wearer's will."

"The same ring that Gregory is even now searching for? The one with Solomon's Seal embossed on it?"

Emir simply nodded in answer.

"Good. Then we know where to begin," the would-be Caliph said with a smile. "We must discover—"

Al-Dula's words were cut short when the hashshashin came to an abrupt halt, his eyes locking on something unseen above them. He sniffed twice, as if tasting the wind. The Saracen followed his gaze up into the sky, but saw nothing that would elicit such a reaction from—

Wait! What was that?

From the corner of his eye, Al-Dula caught movement of something dark flitting from one rooftop to another...heading in the direction of the baron's home.

Had it been his imagination? It had happened so quickly. It had moved with a speed that Al-Dula had never seen before.

"Was...was that it?" he asked Emir quietly.

Without responding, the hashshashin bolted silently into the darkness and was gone. The Saracen nobleman exhaled slowly. Whatever it was, his companion would find it and would deal with it before it became a problem.

The holy man is a fortuitous ally, Al-Dula thought, but could not suppress the shiver at the thought of the man as an enemy.

Yes, he would praise Allah for the man's friendship. But he would continue to keep a watchful eye on him as well.

———

GREGORY DREAMED OF NOTHING. For the first time in nearly two months, he had managed to climb into his bed, pull the covers up to his chin, and drift off to sleep without any problems. Ever since that infernal Djinn creature first began its rampage, the baron had experienced nothing but nightmares whenever he closed his eyes. His physicians had warned him that if his sleep patterns continued their course, he would undoubtedly become too ill from exhaustion to continue in his current office. So, he'd moved his bedchambers to the uppermost floor of the tallest parapet in his chateau—where even the Djinn would be unable to reach him—and had found the added security helped ease the tensions that haunted his nights.

His slumber now brought oblivion to the entire world. All thoughts of his current plague of complications—thanks to the

Djinn—as well as the preparations for the monsignor's upcoming sacrifice were eradicated and now Gregory nestled his head into the plush pillow with a smile on his face. For the moment, all was right with the world and soon, even the Djinn would have no power over his dreams.

A flutter in his room drew Gregory to the brink of semi-consciousness. Movement. An image of feathers fluttering in the wind cascaded through his mind's eye.

What was that? The baron's eyelids remained shut. He didn't want to open them. He was sleeping too well. So what if a stray thrush had flown into his bedroom through the veranda door. It could find its own way out. He rolled over onto his left side, pulling his sheets around his shoulder.

The flapping of wings nudged him even further toward the waking world. Irritation grew. He could not believe his misfortune.

"Shut..." Gregory sat up to throw his pillow at the bird, only to feel his spine nearly liquify at the sight that greeted him. "...up."

An ebon shadow, in human form, sat on the edge of the bed. Arms folded, legs crossed indifferently, the shrouded figure stared at the baron's trembling form. A falcon, dark as midnight and resting on the creature's shoulders, preened its feathers.

Lord Gregory had never seen the Djinn before. Of course, he'd heard the descriptions from the reports. He'd listened to the nonsensical ramblings of cowardly knights, foot soldiers, and mercenaries. But he'd never been prepared for the horrible blackness that sat mere inches away from him in his own bed. It was as if all light was inexplicably sucked into a void shaped like a man—a hollow space carved out of some tangible darkness. Only the otherworldly green glow about the creature's eyes gave any indication that the figure was more than a shadow in his room.

The baron's tongue seemed to swell, blocking the words that

would summon his guards from just behind his chamber doors. Why wouldn't the words come? He heard only a soft whimper escape his quivering lips.

The beast before him laughed softly—a sound like that of a funeral dirge.

"Where, dear baron, is your boasting now?" the shadow rasped. "Perhaps your courage is still asleep?"

Gregory attempted to stumble out of his bed, but with a speed defying all belief, the creature spun around—its falcon alighting from its shoulder at the sudden move. The Djinn then slapped the baron against the chest with the palm of his hand and shoving him back onto the warm comfort of his pillow.

"No. You're going nowhere for the moment, De L'Ombre," said the Djinn. "I have something most important to say and you'll sit quietly and listen."

Summoning at least some control of his faculties, the baron whispered hoarsely, "W-what do you want?"

"Just what I said…I want you to listen."

"All I need to do is call out. My guards will be in here in seconds."

"That's more than enough time to cut your throat."

Gregory contemplated that. It was true. The creature had immeasurable speed. He could kill him and climb out of the balcony before his guards had even unlocked the door.

"Besides," said the Djinn. "The sentries at your door…they're already here."

The creature stood from the bed, unblocking the streams of moonlight pouring in through the open veranda. A gasp escaped unbidden from Gregory's lips as his vision cleared. Four armored and well-armed guards lay in a heap on the floor near the balcony's entrance. They must have heard the creature enter his room, come in and tried to stop it—and had failed miserably. The baron hadn't even heard a sound. A chill shivered down his spine at just how dangerous this creature really was.

"Don't worry. They're still breathing."

"What do you want?" asked Gregory. He couldn't care less about the wellbeing of his incompetent sentries.

"You've already asked that."

"And you never answered."

The Djinn spun around, his cloak swaying behind him as if living shadow clung to his frame. The cold green glow of his eyes bore straight into Gregory's heart, threatening to rip out whatever was left of his defiance.

"I said that I wanted you to listen," the creature hissed as he leapt forward, clamping his clawed right hand around the baron's neck. "And so far, you've done nothing but flap those venomous lips of yours. Now...are you ready to hear what I have to say?"

Gregory attempted to speak, but the Djinn's grip squeezed tighter around his throat, effectively warning him not to say another word. The baron responded by closing his eyes and giving a curt nod.

"Good. This is your last warning, Monsieur De L'Ombre. After this, there will be no others. If you do not do as I say, I will hunt you down, find you, and string you up by your ankles in front of all Jerusalem. You will beg for your life, m'lord...that I can promise you."

The creature moved his hooded face closer to Gregory's. He reeked of brimstone, and it was all the baron could do to keep his dinner down. The black falcon perched itself on the baron's headboard, peering down at the Djinn's prey—ready to attack at any moment.

The baron struggled to swallow. His bedclothes had already been stained with urine the moment he laid eyes on the foul spirit in his room. His heart pummeled against his chest like war drums. He had never felt so helpless. Or so afraid.

"I know what you are up to, Baron. I'm here to tell you to stop now. You still have a choice. If you continue down your path, you will destroy an unimaginable number of lives...including, quite possibly, yours and your lovely daughter's. It is madness to attempt to revive Rakeesha's golems. Even more lunacy to create your own army of them. They cannot be controlled, no matter what you might believe. The forces that bring them to life are corrupt. Their very nature is to destroy. And they do not care who their fell swords cleave."

Gregory stared back defiantly at the Djinn. He didn't care about anyone other than himself—and naturally, his daughter. The lives his golems would snuff from this world mattered little to him. No. Soon, he would establish himself as king of the entire *Outremer* and he would finally have the means to the revenge he had sought his entire life. No one—whether Saracens or Jew—would be safe from his wrath. They would all fall before his might and the world truly would be a better place because of it.

"Doing this will not bring *her* back, Gregory," the creature said, sorrow strangely evident in its voice. Suddenly, it was a voice that sounded oddly familiar to him, though he couldn't place how. Worse still, the creature knew what no other could possibly know…his true motive behind his plan.

Gregory had never been sure who had murdered his beloved Christina. Some said it had been a lone Muslim raider consumed with hatred toward the Crusaders who'd invaded the Holy Land. Others claimed it was a Jewish merchant, who had lusted after his wife for years. It really didn't matter. He hated them all. And they all would pay.

Suddenly, recognition struck him. The voice. He knew it. In another life, in a different world, he would have felt completely betrayed. Yet here and now, it made a certain kind of sense. He should have suspected. He had done so much for the soul that hid behind the shadows and superstition—and this was how he was to be repaid.

Rage welled up from deep inside the baron's soul, squeezing out the fear that had only recently overwhelmed him. Slapping the Djinn's hand away from his throat, Gregory roared with anger.

"Take your filthy hands off me!" He sprang from the bed in a moment of mindless abandon, grabbed his sword, and whirled around to face the dark form enveloped in the shadows of his room. The falcon screeched a warning.

The Djinn's dark blade was already unsheathed, glinting in the pale light of the moon.

"How dare you!" Gregory spat. "How dare you show sympathy to me? Not after what you've done. This is not about Christina. This is about what is right, and you know it. Those people do not deserve to live, and I aim to see an end to them all."

The baron moved slowly forward, his blade at ready, testing the metal of his opponent. He wasn't sure how his opponent would react to an all-out assault. Gregory knew, if push came to shove, that he had no hope to win in an open and fair fight. He'd have to find a way to even the odds.

"You cannot win, old man," hissed the creature. "And I don't want to fight you. At least not yet."

From behind the Djinn, Gregory saw two of his men stirring. They moaned softly as they attempted to untangle themselves from the limbs of their unconscious comrades. Knowing he had to keep his enemy preoccupied to allow his men time to awaken, the baron lunged forward, his sword singing through the air.

His foe spun right, blocking the thrust with the scimitar. In a single motion, the Djinn ducked down, curling into a ball, and rolled backwards toward the recovering guards. Springing into the air, he swung around with one heavy boot slamming into both guards' jaws, causing them to collapse once more into unconsciousness. As the creature glided down to the bedroom floor, a single dart flew from his fingertips, imbedding itself into Gregory's right thigh. He screamed in pain as he collapsed to the floor.

The baron's hands probed for the projectile in his leg and

yanked it out. Blood seeped from the open wound as flesh and tissue tore free. The blade of the dart was serrated, Gregory observed as he tossed the thing to the ground.

The Djinn backed slowly to the balcony doorway.

"I never wanted this, Gregory," he said. "But I will finish what I started if you don't give up this obsession of yours. I can't let you succeed in this."

The baron writhed in pain, clamping down on the gash in his leg to stop the bleeding. Looking up at his enemy, Lord Gregory couldn't help but laugh, but there was no mirth in it.

"You have no choice, *boy*. There is nothing you can do now to stop it. I know who you are...your reign of fear is at an end. Soon, I will awaken Rakeesha's golems. I will recover the *Book of Creation* and I will recover Solomon's Seal from your dead hands. You have lost this night, traitor. And you have been stripped of all your power."

The Djinn had edged his way to the railing of the veranda.

"Perhaps. But I know you will not out me. Not yet anyway. To do so would eat away at any confidence your men still have in you. In the meantime, I will do everything I can to stop you. Next time, I won't be merciful. Next time, if you continue your course, I will have to..." The dark-clad man hesitated. "I will have to kill you."

Without another word, the Djinn vaulted over the railing and into the night. Its wretched bird flew from its perch and followed into the shadows.

Gregory limped toward the edge of the balcony and peered over. No sign of him. He was gone. But he would be found soon enough.

"Guards!" he cried as he hobbled down the stone staircase from his room. "Guards!"

He would send his men to scour this city for the Djinn despite the sudden dread that plagued his thoughts. His enemy was right about one thing: once the Djinn's identity was revealed, the humiliation would be unbearable. His reputation would be ruined. The betrayal would be revealed, and it would be discovered that the Baron Gregory De L'Ombre could not keep his own house in order. If a man couldn't manage his own people, how could he possibly rule an entire land?

No. Despite his misgivings, the creature simply had to be found. Gregory's plans were nearly complete. He could not allow his betrayer to succeed. But, Gregory decided, he would keep the truth a secret until the very end. He would not tell a soul what he knew...at least not yet. If he planned this just right, he might find a way to turn the situation around.

A weak smile crept onto his face as he descended the staircase in search of his guards. Yes, this just might turn out all right after all.

17

Guards scrambled through the streets surrounding Gregory's chateau, searching frantically for the Djinn's trail. As usual, he had disappeared as efficiently as a mist evaporates at dawn. The creature had simply melted into the shadows of the Jerusalem night as if made of the same dark substance, and it infuriated Gerard.

He had heard the clanging of the alarm bells just as he had ascended from the dungeons. He had no need to be told what the commotion was about. The dark spirit's presence had already been felt within the dungeon walls. The idiot squire, Samuel, had vanished from his cell—not only the barred doors, but the iron manacles that had restrained him were still insufferably fastened. To add to the mystifying disappearing act, Samuel's dungeon rags were folded neatly on the dirt floor as if the vile spirit had merely whisked him magically away to his otherworldly abode.

That was the second reason the Djinn would pay. He had still not yet recovered from his encounter with the creature in the nomad camp. Not only had he lost the Ring of Aandaleeb that day, but the damage to his ego and the loss of respect from his men were potentially irreparable. And now, the demon had rescued the simple little squire right from under his nose as well.

Gerard thanked the lord above for having given him the good sense to move the Essene nomad to a different section of the prison when that Saracen physician had visited the whelp earlier that day. Otherwise, the Djinn might have taken him as well, and all truly *would* be lost.

One of Gregory's personal guards rushed past the seething mercenary. Gerard clutched his arm and twirled him around mid-stride.

"What news is there?" he asked the man who was wheezing from his exhausting search.

"None, sir. The foul thing is nowhere to be found."

"Keep looking. He must be here somewhere. As far as we know, he hasn't sprouted wings."

The young guard stared slack-jawed at Gerard.

"What is it? Why are you looking at me like that?" Gerard asked, already annoyed with the buffoon.

"Um, sir, it's just that…it's just that the creature's supposed to be a s-spirit. Can't they pretty much go wherever they want?"

Heat rose up the mercenary's neck. With a growl, he spun the sentry around and placed a good square kick to his rear, pushing him down onto the dimly lit, stone-paved street.

"Keep looking anyway," he spat.

The guard, picking himself up, dashed off around a corner. He didn't even bother to dust himself off.

Gerard sighed. One man. One man had done this—made all his men, as well as Gregory's, look like a gaggle of henpecked geese. Oh, the mercenary was sure it was no ordinary man—those eyes, for one, gave testament to that. He could never forget those strange, glowing green eyes. He had suffered from incurable bouts of night terrors because of them. But the more he thought about it, the more convinced he was that their prey was still just a man—more than likely possessed by some foul spirit, but nonetheless flesh and bone just as anyone else. He could feel it.

And if the Djinn was a man, then he could bleed. And Gerard was betting he could bleed quite well. It was a wager he'd made to himself, and he aimed to collect very soon.

The mercenary strolled around the corner of the baron's stately home deep in thought. Torches in their sconces provided decent enough light, but he wasn't interested in catching the Djinn now. Such a search was futile. Someone *that* good would not be easily tracked. It was a waste of time and energy to run around the city half-crazed looking for an almost ethereal adversary. It hadn't prevented him from stopping the young sentry earlier because it had just been too entertaining to watch him scramble nervously away.

He chuckled at the thought as he stopped and leaned against an ancient cedar that grew in the courtyard of the chateau. He reached into a pouch on his belt, brought out his pipe and tender box, and began puffing on the very expensive blend of *charas* he had purchased in Persia three months ago. He'd discovered the intoxicating substance seven years before in an excursion into Asia and had been indelibly dependent on it ever since.

Exhaling the smoke from his lungs, his watery eyes followed the smoke rings that drifted into the air above his head. Of course, he had no interest at all in the rings. It was past them that now held his utmost interest. Four levels above, just past an opulent veranda, was the bedchamber of Isabella.

The *Lady* Isabella.

He had been utterly enraptured with her since the moment he'd first laid eyes on her, though she'd been a child of a mere thirteen years at the time. On more than one occasion, he'd tried bargaining with the baron for her hand, but had been flatly rejected. The pompous Gregory had even had the audacity to laugh at him in his face at the mere prospect.

In days past, before coming to Jerusalem, he would have

simply taken the lass, had his way with her, and sold her to a Nigerian slaver he'd been acquainted with from years before. But now he simply had too much to lose. He'd already invested more into Gregory's scheme than he'd ever intended. To pull out now would be disastrous.

His eyes scanned the balcony for signs of the lady who made his loins burn with desire. The door stood tantalizingly open, and the dancing glow of candles flitted around her bedroom as if beckoning him to come to her. But she was nowhere in view. There was nothing but empty space.

He pulled another toke from his pipe and savored the sensation. He closed his eyes and thought of the lady's exquisite beauty and the many ways he could force her to be his. He visualized how he would mark her. Scar her so that no other man would ever desire her again. He would make her his and then, when finally sated, he would cast her aside for the mongrels.

He smiled at the images flashing through his mind's eye.

Soon, Gregory would have his indestructible army of clay and his mission would be over. He'd be paid handsomely for his part in the whole affair. Then, after all was complete, he would wrench her from the protective grasp of her peacock of a father and carry her off to Egypt, or better yet, Constantinople.

Yes, Constantinople. He liked the sound of that.

Suddenly, his eyes snapped open; his reflections severed by a sound high above on Isabella's veranda. Crying. She was weeping. But what on earth could cause such anguish—especially at this time of night?

He moved around the tree in which he'd been leaning and peered up at the chateau's façade, being careful to remain out of the torchlight. The beauty glided out of her room onto the balcony, her head in her hands, wracking with sobs.

Gerard's muscles tensed. From out of the bedroom, a shadow slithered toward her. A human shaped shadow. One that the mercenary knew all too well.

With Isabella's back to the creature, she had no idea of her danger. Gerard drew his sword and stepped out from behind the tree to shout a warning at the witless girl.

The Djinn's clawed hand slowly reached out to land a blow that never came. Gerard gasped. Instead of attacking Isabella on the balcony, it had laid its misshapen fingers upon her shoulder, turned her around, and pulled her tight against its stout frame. The baron's daughter dug her head into the creature's chest and let the onslaught of her tears pour out of her.

This couldn't be happening. The baron's very own precious child had not only sided with his fiercest enemy but seemed to have some sort of relationship with it. A relationship of some unholy affection.

Gerard crept closer to the chateau's wall, craning his neck to hear what was being said four stories above.

"Will you kill him?" Isabella asked between choking sobs. "Will you really do it?"

"I don't know. I may have to. You've always known that."

Gerard could no longer see the two from his vantage point. But the unusually crisp night air carried their voices perfectly. His brain churned with this new discovery. What could he do with it? How could it be used to his advantage?

"Isabella, you know I love you more than the world itself," the creature said. "But my calling is higher still. I cannot deny my mission. If your father succeeds with his plans, it will mean the enslavement of thousands of people."

"But surely, they can be stopped. There must be a way to...to turn them off. Like blowing out the flame from a candle."

"No. There's not. At least, there's no way that I've yet discovered. I'm hoping the scroll that Gregory so desperately seeks...the text known as the *Sefer Yetzirah* or Book of Creation... might give a clue as to how to bring about their destruction, but I am doubtful. If Solomon's scrolls had the answer, then he would have used his own knowledge to destroy them. Not bury them in his vault."

The Djinn paused for several seconds. Gerard shifted the weight on his leg in an attempt to look over the railings of the veranda to see what was happening, to no avail.

"But even if I can discover a means to stop them, it would prove futile if your father discovers the means to create more of them," the creature continued. "Destroy one, the baron will create two more in its place. No, I'm afraid that my only hope of sparing your father's life is to locate the book before he does. If he gets his hands on it…if he learns the secret to creating the golems…I'll have no choice, but to…"

A scuffle of feet from above caused Gerard to crouch further down in the shadows cast by a torch to his right. The fair hair of Isabella poked out from behind the rail. She seemed to be looking off into space.

"I understand," she said as she turned and disappeared from view.

"But Isabella, just know that I have given him every opportunity. And I haven't given up on him yet. He's not an evil man—just misdirected and beguiled by hate. He's never let go of the pain of your mother's death and it's eating him up inside."

"And what about you?" asked Isabella in a soft, gentle voice. "You loved her too. Probably more than my father. How did you deal with the pain?"

A weak laugh floated down to Gerard's attentive ears. The mercenary's mind raced. The creature had "loved" the baron's dead wife? The very idea spiraled wildly through Gerard's thoughts. He just couldn't quite grasp the implications.

"I took comfort in the single greatest accomplishment of your mother's life," the creature said. "I took comfort in you."

Nothing was said for several moments. The mercenary felt bile rise as he imagined the two once again in a tight embrace.

"What will you do now?" asked Isabella finally.

"I'll do what needs to be done. They have almost reached the Seventh Chamber in Solomon's Vault. The Library is closer than they even imagine. I must get to it before they do. That's why I'm going tonight."

Gerard's eyes widened. *Tonight? He's going to the Vault tonight to try to steal the scroll out from under us.*

This was something the mercenary could not allow to happen. Besides, he now had an advantage over the creature—two advantages to be exact.

One, Gerard knew the Djinn's plan. He would be there waiting when the creature arrived. Two, he was privy to the strange relationship between the creature and the baron's daughter. Both were pieces of information that he was willing to exploit to his benefit.

Voices from above once again halted his musings. They had been speaking, but the mercenary had missed a portion of what they had said.

"Be ready, Isabella. Things will become worse around here before they get better. Be ready to move when I come for you."

"I will."

"Good girl," said the Djinn. "Now, I must leave. But know that I truly love you more than life itself."

"I know that. And I thank our Father in Heaven every day for that love."

A strange hiss spat out from above and Gerard saw a cord fly out from the balcony, attaching itself to the building across the courtyard. Suddenly, a vast black form sprang from the veranda into the air, catching hold of the cord and skimming over to the building's rooftop. And like that, the Djinn was gone.

And so was Gerard. Springing to his feet, the mercenary dashed through the courtyard and into the street, nearly knocking a sentry off his steed.

"I need your horse," the mercenary growled as he pulled the bewildered guard down from his mount.

In a single motion, Gerard swung his leg over the horse's back and darted off down the stoned streets toward the baron's tunnels. He didn't have much time. He and his men had to be ready for when the creature struck. They would be ready. And the Djinn would most certainly bleed.

CROUCHED DOWN unseen on another rooftop not far from where Gerard commandeered the horse, an altogether different shadow watched with vigilant eyes. Emir, the hashshashin, had left Al-Dula's side the moment he glimpsed the dark spirit traipsing along the rooftops.

He had followed the Djinn back to the baron's home and had watched eagerly from a safe distance the confrontation between Gregory and the creature. He had seen it all. He had even observed the baron's mercenary spying on the creature and the Western female.

This was becoming very interesting. Finally, Emir had an opponent worthy of the hunt. He finally had a foe who would be a true challenge.

The hashshashin rose from his hiding place, allowing his dark robes to blow in the breeze. A dark smile crept up the side of his face. *I am truly going to enjoy this*, he thought as he leapt into open air and into the night.

18

The rain was unusual for this time of year. Steady sheets of water plummeted from the sky, whipping up pockets of steam that rose from the heat-scorched stone pavement of the street. The Djinn savored the wet trickle of relief for several minutes before remembering his objective. He only had two more hours until dawn. After that, he'd be exposed, vulnerable. Slipping out of the city would be impossible.

To make matters worse, the shadowy figure now crouching down on the flat rooftop of the baker's shop knew he was being followed. He had spotted the hashshashin earlier, darting in and out of the shadows like—well, like him. He wasn't sure what to make of this cleric called Emir. He had heard stories of the sect to which the Saracen belonged. They were known as the most lethal of killers and completely zealous for their god.

The Djinn knew he'd have to be extra cautious in dealing with this one…a man of similar training and purpose as himself. But for the moment, there was nothing to be done about his newly acquired shadow. Right now, he had a job to do.

Quietly, he pulled a small, black crossbow from inside his cloak and aimed it at the trellis overhanging the tunnel entrance.

His eyes scanned the surrounding streets. The sentries had just marched off around the corner on their regular rounds. They would be gone for three and a half minutes. More than enough time.

With a pull of the trigger, the quarrel, pulling a sturdy line of rope, hissed from the crossbow. Sailing through the deluge, it struck its target with a twang. The Djinn anchored the other end to the shop's sign over the door and slipped a small pulley onto the line. Without a moment's hesitation, the creature that had struck such fear in the hearts of the Western invaders hurled through space toward the fast-approaching ground.

He let go, tucking his legs into a ball, and dropped into a roll on the mud-caked street. Being careful not to slip on the rain-slick road, the Djinn swung his body up with the momentum and approached the doorway to Gregory's tunnels.

His gauntleted hand turned tentatively on the door's handle.

Strange. It was unlocked. That wasn't good. After the incident with Samuel, Gregory had upped security in this sector and had ordered the door to be locked with irons at all times. They must be expecting him. Of course, it didn't matter. He really had no choice—he *had* to go in.

The creak of the wooden door opening grated against his nerves like the screech of a banshee. His muscles tensed as he peered around it, seeking signs of a possible ambush by unseen guards. Nothing. The quiet ebbed back into place.

So far so good.

He stepped into the gloom of the passageway and closed the door behind him. Then, the Djinn dashed down the spiral staircase, barely touching the steps, making no sound. It was eerie, even to him, how the shadows seemed to enfold around his lithe figure—almost adopting him into its darkened fold. The *old man* had taught him well. A grim smile rose underneath his *tagelmust* as he pressed on toward his goal.

He soon reached the lowest level of Gregory's tunnel system, which carried with it a silence as deafening as the fire powder he'd learned to harness. Stooping down and leaning up against a wooden support beam, the Djinn peered into the darkness of the passage that led to the main Hub, the central chamber from which all the tunnels within the system snaked. His eyes scrambled to adjust to the flickering torch light around him. The tunnel itself was black as pitch, but the antechamber he crouched in had been illuminated with several sconces, practically blinding him. Though his night vision was greatly diminished in the torchlight, he saw no hint of anyone lying in wait in the gloom.

Exhaling, the Djinn crept down the dank corridor that led to the Hub. Soon, he would find out if the suffering of poor Samuel had been worth the price. A twinge of regret crept through his mind at the thought of the good squire. He deserved better. There were few in this bleak world that could measure up to the courage and loyalty of that boy and he had allowed the accursed mercenary to do unimaginable things to Samuel.

Well, the lad is now free, he thought as he vowed silently to make it up to him. It was now a matter of honor. *When this is all over, I'll—*

His thoughts trailed off as he came up short of the opening in the tunnel. More torchlight and even a handful of campfires lit up the chamber before him. There was virtually no cover for him to make his way to the eastern-most passage—which, according to his painstaking research, would lead him to the Library.

Still secreting himself within the safety of shadows, the Djinn squinted into the brightly lit cavern, scouring for potential places to lay an ambush. If *he* could not find a place to hide, then neither could his enemies. Steely muscles tensed, poised to strike at the first sign of attack. His keen eyes scanned back and forth for anything—any movement, any indication of...

There.

The Djinn saw him. A single helmet bobbed nervously behind a rickety wheelbarrow filled with dirt. To the sentry's left, three more figures huddled together behind a canvas tarp. Four guards...at least that he could see. There was no sign of Gerard, but he guessed that the mercenary was lurking somewhere nearby.

His instincts had been correct. They *had* been expecting him and only Gerard possessed the strategic abilities to prepare his men so quickly. He wasn't sure how the mercenary had divined his intentions, but at this point, it was really of little consequence. The Djinn had been brewing up superstition and dread in the hearts of these men for several months now. Their own fear would be their undoing and he was more than willing to use it to his advantage.

They expected a dark spirit of vengeance. That was precisely what they would get. He grinned. This was almost too easy.

19

T he screams echoed through the web of passages that was once known as Solomon's Vault. Gerard stiffened at the sound. The cries had come from the *Hub*. He was here. He had made his first move, and the mercenary was determined to make it the fell creature's last.

Gerard and his men huddled inside the largest chamber of Solomon's treasure repository...its rounded walls lined with twelve lifeless golems standing guard against the wall. Their animal-like faces stared blankly back at him, unsympathetic to Gerard's plight.

The tension was as thick as goat cheese within the confined space. The mercenary captain glanced around the room, looking at each of his men. Their eyes widened with each earsplitting screech of their comrades from the Hub.

After several moments, he craned his head to look at Archibald. Despite the cool subterranean air, his lieutenant's skin glistened with sweat down an ashen face. Without muttering a sound, Gerard motioned for his men to get into positions. Unsteadily, and with great hesitation, they complied. Archibald inched up behind his leader, leaned forward, and whispered.

"Sir, all the other tunnels have been left unguarded. Every able man we have lies in wait with us."

Gerard knew what his friend was trying to say.

"Relax, Archibald."

"But sir, how do you know the thing will head this way? What if we've miscalculated? What if he goes down a different passage?"

"He won't."

His lieutenant shifted on the balls of his feet to maintain his balance, his chainmail clinking haphazardly with each nervous gesture. He was clearly unnerved, and truth be told, Gerard couldn't blame him. Whatever this Djinn was, it would be no easy feat to stop him. He was sure that before this night was done, some of his men would be dead. The creature was just too good.

"But sir…"

"Lieutenant!" Gerard's voice rose involuntarily along with his irritation. Taking a deep breath to calm himself, he continued more quietly, "He'll come down the eastern tunnel. It's where he had that squire scout ahead. He knows where the Library is and it's no doubt in this direction. He'll come this way."

One of his men coughed nervously to the left. The mercenary glared at the offender—a stern warning silently understood.

The screaming from the Hub had ceased. The mercenary wasn't optimistic enough to think his men had succeeded in their mission. The Djinn would be heading this way soon. Gerard and his men had to be ready, prepared for anything.

He willed a determined smile to encourage his men, but the muscles of his face just would not cooperate.

THE DJINN SKULKED AWAY from the last sentry's dormant form and toward the eastern-most tunnel. The entire offensive had taken less than three minutes. Gerard's men had offered very little resistance—a few screams, flashing swords waving erratically, and even a short barrage of crossbow fire whizzing through the air. They'd had very little skill. Even less discipline. In the end, they all lay unconscious—a few broken bones, but breathing—on the passage floor.

His grin broadened underneath his veil. Not bad.

As he approached his target passage, the sound of flesh and fabric tearing filled the tunnel and his right leg buckled. Stumbling, he crashed headfirst to the ground.

Without a sound, he sat up, twisted around to examine the cause for his fall. He winced at the sight of his leg. A single arrow protruded, blood-soaked, just above his kneecap.

He wasn't sure when it had happened. He had seen a number of bolts flying during the fray but had been unaware that any had struck him. *It's getting worse*, he thought. He wasn't sure how much longer he had.

"Well, this isn't good," he mumbled to himself as he grabbed a piece of ember from the nearby campfire and inched himself against the wall of the Hub.

Rummaging through a small pouch hanging from his belt, he quickly plucked out a small silver tube capped with cork. He popped it open carefully and poured its contents, a fine gray powder, around both entrance and exit wounds. Once done, he took his knife and cut a thin groove along the arrow's shaft before pouring the powder along the rut. Cutting the arrow's tip off with the blade, he quickly stuck the ember to the powder. Just as a blinding flare of white light erupted, he yanked the shaft from his leg in a single motion. The searing heat of the flare burned hot around the two openings, fusing the injuries closed.

Bracing himself against the wall, the black-clad figure pushed himself up into a standing position. Standing and crouching several times, he tested the injured leg. It felt fine, though that was no surprise. He knew it would. But he didn't know how much longer it would hold out without proper treatment. Time truly was running out.

As an added precaution, the Djinn tore a strip of cloth from his cloak and wrapped it several times around his leg. That done, he lifted his head toward the eastern passageway once more.

His goal was ahead. There was nothing he could do—he had to proceed as planned and pray that providence would see him through this ordeal.

Crouching down again, the Djinn crept silently into the tunnel. Unlike the torchless passage from the entrance, this tunnel was lined with twenty-four lit sconces. There was no way anyone could possibly make it to the other end without being seen by those in the next chamber.

Thank goodness for Samuel, he thought. *This is where we see if his suffering paid off.*

The Djinn peered down the well-lit tunnel. About midway, it bent, forming a natural barrier to the treasure repository at the end. It was there that most of Gerard's men would be lying in wait.

Reaching again into his pouch, he pulled out a small tinderbox and retrieved a piece of flint. He inched forward to the first sconce and pinched a small thin fuse that connected several small canisters that Samuel had placed along the corridor's wall, just above each torch.

With a clink, the flint struck the wall, sparking the fuse to life. The Djinn stepped back and turned his head, closing his eyes.

One...two...three...four...POP! The canister, a thimble-sized portion of compressed fire powder tightly wrapped inside parchment paper, ignited in a puff of hot air, sucking oxygen from the torch and snuffing its flame. The fuse continued to burn along the tunnel's wall resulting in a series of twenty-three consecutive pops, blanketing Gregory's tunnels in darkness.

Shouts and screams exploded from the other end of the passage as chaos erupted in the pitch-black chamber ahead. The Djinn padded swiftly forward. His grin had spread into a full-blown devilish smile.

Now it's playtime.

THE DAY OF THE UNICORN DISH

20

G erard tensed. His eyes scrambled to adjust to the darkness invading the Vault. His men were panicking. Scurrying around blind, they chattered like monkeys anticipating a fierce lion's attack. This wouldn't do. He had to regain control.

"Quiet!" he said in a hushed but firm tone.

The sounds ceased immediately at the command. He couldn't see a single man but knew they all looked in the direction from which his voice traveled…looking for guidance and courage. He wasn't sure he had either to give.

Durgan, one of his most competent men, sidled up to Gerard.

"This is not going well," the soldier said. "I've never seen them this agitated."

"That's right. You left before we were attacked by the creature the first time."

Durgan stiffened at the rebuke.

"How was I to know he was going to attack? You're the one who sent us on our way."

"Still, you're right. The men are most definitely frightened," said Gerard.

And who could blame them? There seemed to be no end to what this Djinn could do. What witchery had the creature used to extinguish all the torches at once? Gerard realized he was facing not only a cunning warrior in the Djinn, but a sorcerer as well—a prospect that chilled him to the bone. Fighting a man was one thing. They always had a weakness one could exploit if you lived long enough to discover it. But a practitioner of magick was something altogether different.

"They'll deal with it. They are stout men," said Gerard finally.

"Most of them are barely old enough to be called that."

"They're brave."

"How many of your 'brave' young men ran away from the Essene village?"

If there had been any light, Gerard would have glared coldly at Durgan for the reminder. As it stood, he had a different idea. The reedy sound of metal sliding against metal echoed through the chamber as the Gerard slowly inched his sword from its scabbard.

"Any man caught abandoning his post will wish they had been killed by the Djinn," Gerard growled. "Any questions?"

No one spoke. Then, after seconds of complete silence, a symphony of unsheathed blades rang out in the Vault as they all prepared themselves for the Djinn's imminent attack.

"Nicely done," was all Durgan could say.

Gerard spat in disgust in response. The Djinn would be here soon. He could already be in the very chamber in which they now stood. He had to rally his men.

"Archibald," he said into the darkness.

"Aye, sir."

The sudden response—so close behind him—made the mercenary jump.

"Quietly locate everyone. Pull them together, shoulder-to-shoulder, in a circle. Face each man out toward the walls and make the circle big enough to cover the expanse of the chamber but compact enough to allow little room for anyone to squeeze through," Gerard commanded. "And find something to light some of these torches."

"Aye," Archibald said as he stumbled off to collect the men. Suddenly, the lieutenant's movements stopped.

"Sir?"

"Yes, what is it?" Gerard felt the walls and ceilings moving against him in the darkness. He strained to maintain his own calm.

"Look behind you, sir?"

Gerard craned his head to look on the eastern wall. His eyes widened at a strange greenish symbol, shaped like a single letter from some demonic language, glowing dimly in the dark. The mercenary had never seen anything like it in his life—no, that wasn't entirely true. Although the obvious magic employed to create the symbol's ghostly aura filled his mind with dread, he had seen the symbol itself before. It had been engraved on the medallion the Djinn had stolen from...no, been given, he corrected himself, by Isabella. The soft green glow pulsed through the chamber, illuminating the faces of three terrified soldiers who stared at it in stark silence. Gerard shuddered.

"What do you suppose it means?" asked Archibald.

"I've no idea. But we'll worry about that later. For now, just do as I've commanded."

"Aye, Captain."

Quickly, his lieutenant scrambled to position each of the men in his proper place. While Archibald went about his task, Gerard's nose wrinkled at a sudden, familiar odor filling the vault —brimstone.

He's close. Very close.

Soon, all eighteen men stood like statues in the bitter darkness of the chamber. And though they couldn't see them, each of the mercenaries felt the cold, indifferent glare of the twelve golems encircling them in the shadows.

Archibald continued fumbling around the floor until he let out a cry of triumph.

"I've found a torch!"

"Shhhh, you idiot. He's undoubtedly nearby," said Gerard. "Just light it and join the circle."

Gerard's body ached. He hadn't moved an inch since the torches went dark. Sweat beaded down his bearded face and over his lip. He allowed his tongue a swipe and tasted the salt.

Clink! Tiny sparks flew from Archibald's fingertips as he struck flint against stone.

Clink! More sparks, but the torch remained unlit.

Clink! The third try was charm and Gerard's lieutenant triumphantly succeeded in lighting his torch. The warm glow of the flame washed over the mercenary and his men. He could feel his courage and strength returning at the comforting flicker of the light.

Archibald stepped toward the encircled soldiers, ready to take his place among them. He stopped short, just in front of Gerard... his face ashen and mouth agape with terror as he stared dumbly past his commander's right shoulder.

"What is it?" asked Gerard.

Archibald tried to speak, but no words caught on his tongue. Only a gasp of air escaped his lips as he raised one hand and pointed directly behind his captain.

"I've already seen the markings, you fool! Now, get into position."

His lieutenant stood rigid, the torch slipping from his fingers to the floor and casting strange shadows all around them. Feeling bile rise in his throat, Gerard slowly turned around; his men did the same. In the middle of the ring of soldiers, enfolded in a mixture of otherworldly darkness and torch light, a living shadow stood, hunched over, ebony scimitar gripped firmly in hand. Its eyes glimmered with the same eerie green as the marking on the wall and bore straight into the mercenary's very soul. No one moved. Each man remained cemented in place by mind-numbing, irrational horror.

Archibald fainted.

Without warning, the creature kicked high, striking Gerard in the jaw, whirling the mercenary through the air to slam against the hard earth. The blow knocked the wind out of him, and he wheezed from the sudden lack of air.

All around him, his men thrashed in the gloom, striking ineffectually at their assailant. Blades sparked as they clashed against the Djinn's scimitar. Rufus, one of Gerard's more recent recruits, flung himself headfirst at the demon, which swiveled out of the way, allowing its attacker to plummet helplessly into a group of barrels.

The creature spun around, its extended leg sweeping one young soldier off his feet. When it came to a stop, the Djinn found himself surrounded by three more guards. They looked at each other in surprise, a smile forming on their lips. They finally had it at a disadvantage and would use that for all its worth. In unison, they charged. Without hesitation, the Djinn dashed to its left at full speed, jumped toward the dirt wall, spun around in mid-air, and kicked off. It propelled itself over the heads of the attackers, rolled, and incapacitated them with a flurry of kicks.

One by one, Gerard's men fell, moaning from the fury of the Djinn's assault. Archibald, having come to amid the violent struggle, lunged forward, swinging his blade in an upward arc. The creature feigned to the left, ducked, and swung its boot around to strike the lieutenant in the gut. He collapsed with a grunt; blood spewing from his mouth, he went unconscious once more.

Another soldier leapt into the fray, swinging a spiked mace. The Djinn, attempting to pivot out of the way, swung to its left, catching the edge of Durgan's sword on its shoulder. Blood spewed out of the gaping wound, as it smashed its palm to the side of the swordsman's face. Pieces of teeth exploded from Durgan's mouth as he sprawled to the ground.

The demon resumed its attack. Clambering forward, it grabbed the wrists of two more men; twisted upward, resulting in two loud cracks ringing out as bones splintered in both soldiers' arms.

Gerard's men were dwindling. There were only three left, including the mercenary captain. His head throbbed as he pushed himself to his feet, glaring at the spectral apparition in front of him. The thing glided across the chamber, whirling fists and feet with a maelstrom of vengeance. The last two soldiers each lay curled in a ball, holding unseen injuries and moaning.

The Djinn turned silently to face Gerard. Blood gushed unnoticed from the creature's shoulder. It took a step forward and...what was that?

The creature had stumbled, catching his balance before completely falling over. It had instinctively grabbed for its knee. Its right leg. Gerard's memory replayed the fight in every detail. The entire time, it had been favoring that leg, using its uninjured left leg for most of the heavy movement. The thing was injured too. That was its "Achilles' Heel!" The mercenary knew what he had to do.

Gerard readied his sword and hurled himself at the gruesome ghoul. The clash of metal echoed through the web of tunnels as the two blades struck, jarring the mercenary's hands. Pulling back, he twisted round and hurled his sword once more at the creature's head.

The Djinn rolled away, turned, and hurled two darts at Gerard's torso. He managed to dodge one of the projectiles but was struck in the right shoulder by the other. Wincing, the mercenary tore the dart from his flesh and pounced.

The two rolled end over end on the rocky ground of the tunnel, struggling to overcome the other. Risking everything, he pulled a dagger from its sheath and jabbed deep into the creature's leg, twisting it furiously to maximize the damage.

To Gerard's horror, the Djinn made no sound, but leveled a backhand against the mercenary's face with such force that he was thrown from his enemy. The last thing he remembered before everything went dark was the creature's clawed fist barreling down again across his face. Then, there was nothing.

THE BATTLE HAD COST the Djinn precious time, as well as blood. Although the injuries he'd sustained did not cause him physical pain, he felt faint. Too much of his blood had been spilled and a gray haze began to cloud the corners of his vision. The sun would undoubtedly be rising soon, effectively blocking all exits from the city...but unless he found a place to rest and recoup from blood loss, it wouldn't matter.

Following the glowing mark on the eastern wall, he shuffled clumsily down a darkened corridor. One more thing needed doing before he could take refuge among the shadows of the maze of tunnels—he had to find what he had come for. He had to find the Library. Find the *Sefer Yetzirah*...the Book of Creation. Nothing else mattered.

Even though he'd managed to secure the ring that was given to Solomon by, according to the legends, an actual djinn named Aandaleeb, the scroll might contain some secret to creating the golems that would allow Gregory to make his army in another way. He couldn't take the chance. Unless he found the manuscript, the people of the *Outremer* would never be safe.

Stopping, he quickly dressed his wounds and listened for signs of pursuit. Confident that he was truly alone, he reached into the pouch around his waist and pulled out a piece of cloth that shined with the same green glow he'd had Samuel use for the wall marking and wrapped it around a piece of wood he'd taken from the Vault. The illumination was minimal, but it gave off enough light to allow him to proceed.

Taking a deep breath, he pushed on and despite his injuries, moved with amazing speed. He had spent days studying the plans and diagrams of the tunnels that the baron's slaves had made. After careful scrutiny of the maps and examination of Isabella's medallion, the Djinn had discovered the most plausible location where Solomon's prized Library should have been hidden.

It had been a stroke of luck—or perhaps providence—that all the sentries had been drawn into one place at one time. Then, it was only a matter of shrouding them in darkness and taking them out all at once.

It had all worked out fairly well. If he didn't think too much about the blood soaking into the bandages around his leg and shoulder.

He stumbled eastward until he came to a fork. One way supposedly led to an underground river that opened into a small pool on the outside of the city walls. The other led to a secondary Hub, its webbing of passages splaying out in all directions for countless miles. It was the tunnel with the water he wanted. He chose the left one.

As he marched, he reflected on the medallion Isabella had given him. It had been the key, quite literally, and Gregory had missed it. The answer had been in front of the baron all this time, but he had failed to see the importance of a single chip of ruby embedded in the piece. Pushing his thoughts aside, the Djinn trudged on through the darkened labyrinth.

After a quarter of a mile, he stopped abruptly. He'd heard something, something faint, behind him. Footsteps? He couldn't be sure. It sounded nothing like the clanging stomps of the metal greaves and boots of Gerard's soldiers. Still…something was not quite right.

He craned his neck to hear better, peeling back the hood that covered his head. Nothing. There were no sounds, except for the occasional plop of water dripping further down the tunnel. At least he knew he'd chosen the correct passage to follow. Wiping the sweat from his eyes, the Djinn sprinted forward towards the sound of the water.

21

"**A**rgh!" Gerard awoke with a jolt, sword slinging blindly through the air in panicked ferocity. The Djinn was no longer there.

How long had he been out? There was no way to tell. The chamber was still as black as pitch save the small area behind him that flickered from Archibald's torch, still resting uselessly on the ground.

All around him, his men stirred—moaning and writhing from injuries incurred by the filthy demon's attack. The world spun uncontrollably around him as he clambered to his feet. The mercenary limped to the torch, bent down, and picked it up. The room once again was bathed in blessed light.

"Archibald," he said, as he stooped over his injured friend.

His lieutenant lifted his head; bewilderment and no little pain were etched into his face.

"Yes, Captain?"

"Gather the men. See to the wounded and get back to the chateau. I've got to report to Lord Gregory immediately."

"Uh, sir?"

"What is it, Lieutenant?"

"Well, sir, I was just wondering why we weren't going to search the tunnels for the...the...creature," Archibald whispered the last word nervously.

Gerard had already considered it but realized it would be futile. They would never be able to find him in this maze. Even if they did, he lacked men healthy enough to do any good against the demon.

"Because I said so," answered the captain. "Now, do as you're told."

"Aye, sir," Archibald said as he struggled to rise. Gerard helped him to his feet and dusted his chain mail and tunic off.

"Now, I'm off. See to it that the men are cared for and report back to me as soon as you can."

With that, the mercenary bounded off toward the main Hub and the entrance to Gregory's tunnels. The baron was not going to be happy about the news. But then, Gerard was getting weary of caring. Besides, he had worse news for Gregory than the Djinn's victory here tonight. He wondered how the baron would react to his daughter's nocturnal visits as he pressed on through the passages.

IN A CITY that thirsted for water, it was ironic that such a vast reservoir lay undetected deep within its belly. The Djinn doubted, however, that the water was safe to drink. He could smell its salt wafting through the air as he approached its algae-infested edge.

His keen eyes scanned the darkened shore of the underground lake. Schools of tiny, ivory colored fish flitted through the shallows of the water, oblivious to the intruder from the outside world. The Djinn stood transfixed on the otherworldly creatures that swam effortlessly through the currents, changing directions to form a zigzag pattern in tandem.

Breaking himself from his fixation, he stood erect, every muscle tensing. The Library was near. He could feel it. All his research pointed to this very underground lake as the marker for its entrance.

But where was it? The Djinn looked around the vast chamber. Besides the spider web of passages that spread out along the walls, he could make out nothing that would resemble a doorway. Nothing that indicated a room that housed thousands of years' worth of precious tomes.

It has to be here. I know it.

The lake. The answer had to be with the lake. He rifled through the clues he'd pieced together from the medallion and various other sources, reciting them verbatim. Finally, he remembered the one he felt held the solution to his conundrum.

Drink from the water of wisdom, the medallion's strange script had read. *Enter the Hall of the Wise.*

The Djinn looked across the glassy surface of the water. *It most definitely wouldn't be wise to drink from* that *water.* He paused. A smile slowly began creeping up one side of his face. *Unless...*

Crouching down, he pulled at a pack worn around his back, hidden behind his cloak. Ignoring the numbing sensation around his shoulder, he scavenged inside, pulling out a small parcel wrapped in an exquisite piece of Asian silk.

"That should be enough," he said aloud as he tugged at the string and opened the package. Three strange looking mushrooms lay exposed on the rocky floor of the chamber. Pulling a dagger from his boot, he carefully sliced two of the fungi in half. A plume of green spores spewed from the mutilated mushrooms, casting a weird otherworldly glow all around him. Taking a rag, the Djinn smeared the luminescent slime oozing from the mushroom all over the blackened blade of his scimitar, then sheathed it.

His eyes moved to the rocky floor of the cavern, searching for...

There.

He scurried along the floor, pocketing eight fist-sized rocks, and then returned to his pack. Piling the stones in a small circle, he picked up the last mushroom and squeezed. Its haunting green juice bled onto each of them. They glowed satisfyingly at him as he cast each one out into the abysmal pool—each one further away than the last.

Standing up, the Djinn edged his way to the lip of the pool. The stones emitted their greenish incandescence through the darkened water.

That will have to do, he thought as he waded into the lake, inhaled, then dove into the murk. If the incandescent stones weren't radiating their eerie glow, he would have been completely blind. Slowly, his eyes adjusted to both salt and shadow and he gradually began to take in his surroundings.

The water, at its deepest, was about twenty feet deep with a solid, stone bottom. Besides the tiny schools of fish, there was no movement within the pool. The Djinn hovered just above the floor, scanning the almost perfectly circular lake for...he saw something to his right.

Kicking off the bottom, he sped to the southernmost wall of the lake until he could make out the beginnings of an intricately carved archway that reached to just below the waterline. From above, it would have been practically invisible due to the slime and algae that skimmed the surface.

Pulling out his spore-covered scimitar, he used the blade's light to see past the almost imperceptible entryway and beheld a narrow staircase leading up through the tunnel walls.

Of course, he thought as he swam to the steps. *It's brilliant. The perfect security measure. A person could get into the Library from the lake, but they couldn't leave with any of the parchments or scrolls*

housed inside without utterly destroying them with water. A person
would be able to read all they wanted but would never be able to remove
them.

Feeling the slight tug at his lungs signaling that he was
beginning to need air, he swam up the staircase until his head
broke the surface. The stairs continued up for about another
twenty-five steps and opened suddenly into a vast, unlit chamber.
Only the green glow of his sword provided any illumination. He
looked along the wall to his right and then his left, until he found
the wooden stalk of a torch resting within a sconce. There was
no telling how long the torch had lain dormant within the room,
but the Djinn was confident that any pitch that could have been
used to light it had long since evaporated.

Fortunately, the man who'd struck such fear in the hearts of
Gregory's knights, had come prepared. Reaching into his pouch
again, he pulled out a silver container and poured the contents
along the head of the torch. The acrid stench of whale oil wafted
up from the liquid as it soaked into the fabric. Then, striking his
flint against the stone wall, the torch burst into life.

With a much brighter light source, the Djinn took a moment
to soak in his surroundings. The chamber he'd entered was by far
the largest within the complex system of catacombs. Spreading
far beyond the meager circle of illumination, the room was lined
with row after row of shelves, tables, chairs, and stepping stools.
Standing beside each of the reading desks was a single
candelabrum that could be used to read by.

The Djinn moved his gaze up to see a forest of cobwebs
hanging haphazardly from the rafters that supported the vaulted
thirty-foot ceiling. A bronze chandelier hung uselessly above
him, devoid of any candles that would have been used to light the
room at one time.

All right, he thought, suddenly feeling light-headed. The loss
of blood was starting to catch up to him. Additionally, he wasn't

sure about the library's ventilation either. For all he knew, he was quickly running out of air. *Best find the book and be on my way.*

Raising the torch above his head, he walked along the first row of shelves, carefully scanning the wax seals adorning every manuscript in the chamber. Though he wasn't exactly sure what he was searching for, he'd been told that he would know the correct scroll when he saw it. The medallion had said something about it being "within the Warden's mind"...whatever that meant. But he figured that if he found this Warden, he would be able to find the *Sefer Yetzirah*.

Having searched the first three rows, he moved on to the next, moving deeper into the vast Library. He jerked to a stop at the sound of shuffling in the darkness behind him. He spun around and tried to look past the torch's flame, but to no avail. Shrugging his apprehension away, he continued his search. After ten more minutes, he'd scoured every shelf in the entire room and had not found it. He was just about to move back to the beginning and start the search all over when another sound caught his attention...this time, it was the sound of something brushing up against the wall to his left.

He remembered the stealthy form of the hashshashin that had been following him since leaving Isabella's chateau. Had he tracked him down to the Library? Had he managed to find his way into this very room and now lay in wait within the protection of the shadows?

Somehow, he doubted it. If Emir was there, he no doubt had skill enough to remain completely undetectable. No, someone else was in the chamber with him. And that someone was currently stalking him.

Easing his sword from its scabbard again, he slowly placed the torch on the ground and melted into the darkness. Though the luminescent spores of the fungus still clung to the blade, the glow was minimal, allowing the shadows to wrap around his dark frame with ease. He stole through the labyrinth of shelves, his senses heightened as he searched for his hidden stalker.

Sweat beaded across the Djinn's brow. He felt weak, dehydrated. His injuries were catching up to him and he knew that a prolonged confrontation with anyone would be the end of him. If he didn't take care of this swiftly, he'd find himself a permanent resident within the sub-aquatic Library.

He caught a blur of motion to his right and spun around, but whatever he'd seen was gone.

"All right," he said aloud. "Enough of this game. It's time to change the rules."

Digging into his pouch, he pulled another object wrapped in silk and opened it up. In the palm of his hand, he held a strange putty-like substance, peppered with shavings of a metal the old man had discovered on a journey to Asia. Like the fire powder he'd learned to harness, the metal, when applied to heat, would burn with the brightness of the noonday sun. The Djinn had been loath to use it because the metal was extremely rare and very expensive. But he could think of no other way to locate his stalker than by removing the very shadows in which he hid.

Placing a fuse within the putty, he lit it and hurled the object high into the air. Hearing a satisfying thud, he knew the sticky substance now clung to the ceiling. He clenched his eyes closed tight, counted to three and...the sudden burst of light irradiated through his eyelids, burning at his retinas. Slowly, he opened his eyes...blinking back the brightness that threatened to blind him. A white-hot orb adhered to the ceiling sent a blazing wave of light over the entire chamber. Every shelf...every scroll...every particle of dust shined beneath the artificial sun.

He spun around, looking for his stalker and jerked involuntarily at the sight of a hulking mass of clay only six paces away from him. The thing that lumbered more than nine feet tall was shaped, for the most part, like a human. Its massive hammer-fisted hands were clenched tight and raised above its strange, faceless head. A series of strange symbols and intricate alien glyphs were carved into its clay flesh. And although the thing did not have an animal shaped head like those within the treasure chamber of Solomon's Vault, the Djinn knew he was looking face to face at a golem. But unlike those that Gregory desired to reanimate, this one was already alive. Inexplicably breathing. And hunting the Djinn.

The golem charged without warning, its powerful arms swinging toward the Djinn's exposed head. Although the creature's speed belied its massive size, he managed to avoid the hammer-like blow by diving out of the way just in time.

Rolling to his feet, the Djinn spun around and threw his dagger straight at the monster's face. The blade sunk deep, burying itself to the hilt inside its head, but still the golem kept moving.

Moving. How on earth does it even move?

Though the golem's body was made of soft and malleable clay, there were no obvious means to make an otherwise inanimate object ambulate. No skeletal structure to give it form. No discernible joints or musculature to empower movement. No gears, pulleys, or discernible mechanisms of any kind. For all intents and purposes, the golem was merely a chunk of clay with pillar-like arms and legs. It was like watching a marionette whose locomotion was dependent entirely on the muscles and tactile manipulations of another.

But the mystery of the golem didn't end there. As the fire

metal burned itself out and the chamber began casting elongated shadows around them, the Djinn doubted that being doused into darkness once more would offer him any protection at all. The golem was also devoid of eyes, which begged the question of how it was able to 'see' in the first place. Though he was most definitely a man of science who had preyed upon his enemies' superstitions, thus tricking them into believing he was using the forces of the spirit world to do his great deeds, the only possible solution he could fathom to account for the golem's very existence was simply…magic. Nothing else made sense.

Unfortunately, the luxury of contemplating the monster's mysteries would have to wait. He'd simply run out of time.

Almost faster than the eye could see, the golem dashed toward him once more, backhanding him before he had a chance to move, and sending the Djinn sprawling across the stone floor. Before he could pull himself to his feet, the hulking form reached down, grabbed him by the face, and lifted him off the ground. As he hung helplessly within the monster's grip, he could feel moist clay oozing through the porous linen fabric of his hood and into his mouth and nose. Desperately trying to wrest himself free from the thing's gelatinous grip, he pounded against the golem's face as hard he could. Though blinded by the massive hand engulfing his face, brilliant flashes of light shot through the Djinn's retinas as the last bit of oxygen was squeezed from him.

Consciousness ebbed from his immobilized body, and he knew that if that happened, all would be lost. In a last-ditch effort, the Djinn reached into a pocket within his cloak and pulled out a twelve-inch iron tube with a spring-loaded piece of flint attached to a handle. The contraption was of his own design, and although he'd not tested it enough to trust in most circumstances, there was no longer anything to lose.

The golem's grip oozed its way to envelope his entire head, but with it came a skull-crushing squeeze. An untested weapon was now his only option.

The Djinn's thumb fumbled with the spring-loaded flint and pulled it back. Holding it steady, he lifted the tube and pointed it near where he believed the monster's face to be and released. The flint struck a metal bracket housed within the tube, which ignited a pouch of highly compressed fire powder and iron pellets. With a deafening blast, the tube discharged its contents and suddenly, the Djinn found himself released from the golem's grasp. Falling to the floor, he gasped for breath as he looked up to gawk at his handiwork. The right side of the golem's face was decimated, giving the creature's head the appearance of a crescent moon. The iron shrapnel and concussive blast from his firetube had shredded the viscous clay flesh as easily as a shovel to a grave. And although the giant didn't so much as make a sound, its torment was quite evident as it thrashed around the chamber holding its head.

Still trying to catch his breath while simultaneously collecting his thoughts, the Djinn took a closer look at the monster as it writhed. Something shiny...metallic...protruded from the crater to the right side of its head. In the flickering light of the torch still burning on the ground, he could just make out a brass cylinder—like those used to house ancient scrolls before the time of Christ.

Suddenly, the riddle of the *Sefer Yetzirah* made perfect sense. The medallion had said the Book of Creation would be "within the Warden's Mind." Only he'd mistranslated. A better interpretation would have been "within the Warden's skull." The scroll he and Gregory had been searching for had been inserted into this monster...who acted as a guardian to keep it from falling into foolish hands.

The Djinn shook his head with a rebuking chuckle. "And there'd be no one more foolish than me," he said aloud to the writhing golem. "If left alone, the book would have been safeguarded for years to come. But now that I've found you... exposed your scalp...it would be only a matter of time before Gregory's men recovered it." He sighed. "No. There's nothing to it. I'm sorry my friend, but I must relieve you of your burden now."

The golem, as if hearing the Djinn's words—though it had no ears—stopped its anguished gyrations and seemed to tense.

"It's all right, though," he continued, as he prepared to move the second the monster charged. "I plan not to use the book for evil gains, but rather safeguard it much the same as you."

His platitudes did not seem to appease the golem, who raised both fists in the air in a defensive posture. The thing appeared to be awaiting the Djinn's first move, which brought them both to an impasse.

The monster was smart. Realizing that a steady defense would be the greatest offense, it intended to allow the interloper to draw near enough to crush him within its powerful hands. The Djinn, on the other hand, would have to figure a way to get near the creature without that very thing happening...and with the element of darkness not being of any use at all for a foe with no discernible eyes, he was beside himself on just how to do it. The only way to get to the scroll would be to somehow immobilize the golem.

But how?

Inching over to the torch on the ground, the Djinn crouched slowly, picked it up, and glanced around the dimly lit Library. There wasn't much to work with. His firetube had been destroyed when he'd used it to break free of the golem's grip; its barrel shredded apart like a flower blossom. His sword would be no help either. It would have as little effect on the creature as his dagger had. There were no other tools at his disposal, but a few bookshelves, a desk or two, and the candelabrum that stood next to them.

There's something I'm missing. Something....

He stood stock still, emptying himself of the fear and turmoil that cluttered his mind. The golem continued its statue-like vigil, waiting for his enemy to strike. But the Djinn knew it wouldn't wait indefinitely. Soon, it would renew its attack and it would be over.

So, what is it? What am I missing? What can I use to stop this behemoth?

Slowly, he backed away from the golem, moving slowly toward the eastern wall. The clay man stepped forward, following him cautiously. The Djinn edged his way around the library, his back against the wall as he scanned the room more thoroughly. Sidestep. Two. Three. Four. The monster continued to keep the same distance between them. Moving parallel to the intruder.

Splat.

The Djinn looked down from where the sound came. A small puddle of water pooled on the stone floor from a stream of condensation along the wall. He tapped his foot in the water once more in thought.

Splat. Splat.

A smile spread across his veiled face when he realized what it meant. The Library was under the subterranean lake. The puddles were from condensation running down the stone walls.

Slowly, he reached into his pack and, with both eyes firmly fixed on the golem, rummaged for through it until his fingers latched onto a small silk pouch of tightly wrapped fire powder.

"I'm sorry," he said to the hulk before him. "I'm truly very sorry for what I'm about to do. But I really have no choice."

The golem's crescent-moon head cocked slightly to the left as the Djinn lifted the silk pouch to the torch's flame, dropped it to the floor the moment the fuse sparked to life, and dove toward the nearest writing desk to protect him from the impending blast.

He barely made it in time. Just as he pulled the desk up as a makeshift shield, the silk pouch burst in a blinding flash, rending a jagged hole into the stone wall. A stream of water gushed through, spreading the opening wider and wider apart until a tidal wave of pressure punched through the wall and filled the entire chamber. Both the monster and the Djinn were suddenly swept off their feet and carried along the whirlwind currents of the enraged subterranean river.

Struggling to keep himself from crashing into the debris and stone walls, the Djinn kept his eyes trained on the golem as it floundered helplessly in the flooding chamber. He watched patiently for what he hoped would come...and come before he ran out of air. Gradually, the rush of water subsided, and the two foes hovered in the water. They both had finally stabilized and their standoff resumed once more.

And then he saw it. The golem's arm wavered in the water. Its feet began to twist and swirl. Its barrel-like torso began to dissolve before his very eyes. The sheer amount of water within the now ruined library was simply too much for the creature's clay body to absorb and it began to melt away rapidly into oblivion. After no more than a minute, the entire creature was nothing more than a hovering mass of mud floating harmlessly before him.

Without the golem's mass, the brass encased scroll sunk rapidly to the floor. The Djinn dove down, snatched it up, and swam through the hole he'd blasted and into underground lake. Another ten seconds and he was exploding to the surface sucking in deep gulps of delicious air and clutching the Book of Creation in his trembling hand.

He was so weak. So tired. As he dragged himself to the lake's shoreline, all he wanted was to lie down and sleep for days.

At least for a few minutes. Just a few peaceful minutes.

The strain of the evening's activities had been almost too much for him. The injuries and blood loss from his encounter with Gerard and his men. The near suffocation at the hands of the Warden. Almost drowning in the library. It was all just too much for his body to take.

No. I cannot. To stay is to die, he thought as his head rested against the rocky ground at the edge of the lake. *My death means enslavement to those under Gregory's power. I cannot rest.* He pushed himself onto unsteady feet. *Yet.*

He gripped the scroll tighter in his fist and took a deep breath. It was time to go. Time to get back. His mission was almost over. He was finally beginning to see the light through the murky world in which he'd lived for so long. Soon, he would finally be free. He just had one more thing to do. He had to get the scroll out of Jerusalem and he would finally be done.

He allowed a wan smile at the thought.

Almost free.

A sudden noise from behind spun him around, but it was too late. A shadow leapt from the darkness in a spinning kick that slammed against the Djinn's shrouded face. Recovering faster than should be humanly possible, his arms came up to block a whirlwind of blows from the black-garbed assailant. But he was still protectively clutching the scroll in one hand, preventing an adequate defense. His attacker, observing the weakness, landed a series of blows against the shoulder that had been injured in his fight with Gerard's men.

Countering, the Djinn wheeled around, his arm whipping in a brutal backhand against his attacker's face. Pressing the advantage, he dove headfirst, striking his enemy's midsection and causing both to stumble onto the embankment.

The two combatants grappled, each striving to get the upper hand on the other. Suddenly, with blinding speed, a streak of silver swung out from the assailant's tunic and a razor-sharp dagger pierced deep into the Djinn's gut. Hot, crimson liquid poured out of the wound, soaking the Djinn's free hand as he struggled to close the injury.

"You have fought bravely, Dark One," said Emir, the hashshashin, standing over his fallen enemy who still held onto the scroll with one hand. "I know what kind of disadvantage you've had in this battle and yet, you were unwilling to relent. It has been an honor to fight such a worthy opponent, but I could not allow you to leave with the Book."

The Djinn's eyes began to grow dim. He knew that he had been defeated and was even now spiraling into unconsciousness. He had lost. The thought paralyzed him with dread. The *Sefer Yetzirah* in the hands of Gregory was bad enough. To have such a powerful text in possession of the hashshashin's lord was unthinkable. What such a man would do with the power of creation itself...the Djinn could only shudder at the thought.

"Do not worry," Emir said, a grim smile spreading across his dark face. "I will not kill you here. It would not be worthy. For now, I will merely retrieve the scroll for my lord."

The hashshashin stood above him as the Djinn's vision continued to darken. The last thing he remembered before blacking out was the dark image of his attacker reaching down to take his prize.

23

"He did what?" the baron shouted, spinning around to glare at Gerard.

"He managed to get through our defenses," repeated the mercenary. "He disabled my men as if they were mere squires, m'lord. I've never seen anything like it."

Gregory's scowl never faltered, and Gerard tried to remember the last time he'd seen his employer blink. The mercenary had been right...the baron had not liked the news of the Djinn's infiltration into Solomon's Vault at all.

"And pray tell, how did he get past the ever-formidable Gerard D'Bois?"

The mercenary's eyes traced the outline of the stones in the floor. He simply could not meet the baron's gaze. He had been utterly disgraced.

"He...he used some trickery, m'lord. Some form of dark magic I've never seen before."

"Magic, you say?" scoffed Gregory as he moved over to the mercenary. His index finger reached for Gerard's chin, lifting his face to force the mercenary to look him in the eyes. "*Magic*? Really, Gerard, I am very disappointed in you."

"But…"

"Enough excuses!" the back of the baron's hand lashed out across Gerard's cheek. "I will have no more excuses from you."

The mercenary instinctively nursed his stinging face as Gregory paced the floor of his banquet hall. The baron's thin, wiry frame cast a skeletal shadow across the stones; his head bowed deep in thought. Walking over to an open window, the baron silently stared out at the sun crowning over the horizon.

"We can assume your incompetence has cost us the Book."

"We don't know that for sure," said Gerard hopefully. "We're not even sure he knew where it was located. If we couldn't find it, then how could he?"

"Because, you imbecile, he would have never made his presence known in the Vault if he were not positive," the baron said. "No. He knew exactly where he was going. That was why the squire was sent to mark the walls. It was a marker to show him the correct direction in the darkness."

Gerard reluctantly agreed with his master's assessment. The creature no doubt possessed both the Book of Creation and Solomon's Seal.

"Is there nothing we can do to salvage your quest?" Gerard asked. He still possessed information that could very well change everything, but he was reluctant to share it just yet. First, he wanted to know what his employer had in mind.

The baron's one good eye blinked at the question.

"There's only one thing we can do," he said. "I must proceed with the sacrifice. Awaken Rakeesha's golems and bend them to my own will. We will discover a way to take the Book, as well as Solomon's ring, from our enemy's foul hands afterwards."

"Perhaps there is a way to do that sooner than you'd expect, m'lord." The mercenary felt his voice crack as he spoke the words. He fully anticipated that what he was about to suggest would go even worse than the news of the Djinn's victory in the Vault. But it was the only way he could imagine regaining what they had lost. "What if I said there might be a way to recover them with a simple gambit."

The baron turned; his eyes moved slowly up from thought to face his hired soldier.

"What do you have in mind?"

Bringing himself up to his full height, Gerard tensed as he considered his word choice perfectly. Then, he inhaled deeply.

"There is something that I haven't told you yet. It's about your daughter."

"My daughter?"

"Yes. Last night, after the Djinn absconded from your quarters, I wandered out into the eastern courtyard," said Gerard. "Er...in search of the creature, of course."

The baron's icy stare burned at this admission. Gerard and Gregory had had words over this many times before. The baron knew of the mercenary's intentions toward his daughter and hadn't liked it at all. Gerard had been caught on more than a few occasions staring up lasciviously at Isabella's balcony and Gregory had explicitly warned him not to do so ever again. Gerard was not deemed worthy enough even to *look upon the fairness of such an exquisite woman*, the baron had scolded.

"It wasn't like that, m'lord," Gerard said. "As I said, I was looking for the Djinn. I had no intentions of spying on your daughter."

It was a lie, but Gregory had no way of knowing that. And if his plan succeeded, he would have the best of all possible worlds. The demon would be within Gerard's power and he would finally have the thing he treasured most of all. He couldn't believe he'd not thought of it earlier. It would have prevented the embarrassing debacle of Solomon's Vault earlier that morning.

"Proceed, D'Bois, before I lose the rest of my already waning patience," the baron's voice seethed under his breath.

Gerard nodded, then cleared his throat. "As I was saying...

while searching for the Djinn, I was drawn to the sound of voices coming from your daughter's chambers."

The baron's teeth grinded against his jaw, but he said nothing.

"I looked up and saw your daughter...she was in the embrace of the Djinn."

Gregory's eyes closed as a resigned sigh escaped clinched lips. It was not the reaction the mercenary had expected. Not at all. Gerard tensed again, awaiting the explosion of anger that the baron would undoubtedly unleash upon him. But it never came.

"Of course," Gregory said finally, his voice eerily calm. "It makes perfect sense. He would have naturally sought her help. He would have used her love for his own purposes. I'm a fool to have not suspected it all along."

Gerard couldn't believe what he was hearing. The baron seemed almost relieved, as if he had expected something far worse.

"M'lord?" the mercenary said.

"It's quite all right, Gerard. I'm disappointed, but otherwise fine. My daughter, on the other hand, must be...punished...for her betrayal."

The mercenary turned to look his lord square in the face. It was now or never. Gregory seemed open. He might agree to his plan now.

"I *do* have an idea. If it works, you will not only be able to retrieve both ring and scroll, but the head of the Djinn in the process," said Gerard, a wary smile spreading across his face. "But you've got to let me do it *my* way. You cannot interfere."

The baron turned away, walking over to the window again. The song of a sparrow flitted through the early morning air.

"I can fathom what you have in mind," croaked the lean figure of the baron, his head hanging defeated. He let out another sigh and continued. "I will proceed with my plans to resurrect the golems down in the Vault. While I'm taking care of this, I give

you permission to do what must be done. But hear me, D'Bois...
she is *not* to be harmed. Do you understand?"

Elation flooded every pore in Gerard's body. His plan would
work. He was being handed the prize he'd sought since coming
into the baron's employ. And he would finally have revenge on
the one who had caused him such trouble. Things could not have
gone better.

"Aye, m'lord. I understand perfectly," said the mercenary as he
strode out of the baron's great hall.

24

Isabella stifled a yawn. She hadn't slept at all. Her thoughts had been a jumbled knot of fear, doubt, and loathing. Why must he be so stubborn? He had to know how dangerous it was to challenge her father, yet he persisted. The man the people now called the Djinn would die if he continued down this road—if he wasn't dead already.

She should have heard something by now. It was nearly ten in the morning. He usually sent word to her by this time whenever he went out on one of his excursions. She had told him that entering her father's tunnels was madness, but he just wouldn't listen to reason. His quest, believed to be a holy mission from God, spurred him beyond rational thought. He was a man just as obsessed as her own father and she feared that obsession would destroy them both.

She looked into the fine Persian mirror as she gently brushed the tangles from her hair. She stared numbly at the dark circles that enveloped her eyes and let out a mournful sigh.

They were so alike, the two of them. Neither would ever admit it, of course, but it wouldn't change the fact. Both men railed against what they perceived as the injustice of life. Both men raged against the forces beyond their control.

The problem for her, however, was that unlike the Djinn, her father's ambition would destroy thousands of lives. She knew without doubt that left unchecked, Gregory's schemes would soon be unstoppable. The only hope lay upon the shoulders of the one so many now feared.

Her thoughts were suddenly shattered by pounding on her bedchamber door. She felt the throb of her heart with each knock. This interruption could be anything but good.

"M'lady," said the acidic voice of Gerard from the other side of the door. "I need a word with you. It is urgent business for your father."

Nearly panicked, Isabella searched her room for anything she could use...anything that could be used as a weapon. The Djinn had warned her that something like this might happen and since he had not sent word to her, she could only assume the worst. Somehow, her father's hired soldier had connected her to his enemy.

The pounding became louder, jolting her with every blow.

"M'lady, I'm serious. I must see you immediately."

The door, made of solid cedar, was strong, but she doubted it would hold up long against a full-fledged assault by Gerard and his men. She spun around the room and caught the gleam of silver near her night table.

The curved dagger the Djinn had given her several months earlier. She felt faint at the thought of wielding such a weapon, but she was determined to do whatever she could to escape whatever the mercenary had in store for her. Even though she was confident this unexpected visit was officially regarding her father's nemesis, she knew all too well the mercenary's desires for her, and she would die before she ever allowed him to touch her.

She palmed the blade just as the door buckled under a

heavy crash. They were using a battering ram to make entry. Gerard's face peered through the splintered wood of the door.

"Come now, Isabella. It doesn't have to be this difficult. Your father only wants me to ask you a few questions," he said. "You will not be harmed."

"What's all this?" came the sweet, familiar voice of Margaret from the hallway. "You've got no business with my lady."

"Get out of my way, hag! I have orders from the baron himself."

Isabella stiffened. She wasn't sure whether to be elated at the rescue from her maidservant or terrified. She'd never seen Gerard so grave.

"I'll show you how to treat a woman, you clout," Margaret growled. Isabella, peering through the cracks in the door watched as her closest friend and confidant slammed her walking stick against the mercenary's head.

WHACK! WHACK!

"Enough, woman!" said Gerard, protecting his skull with his arms. "Stop this immediately."

Gerard's men stood helplessly awaiting orders from their captain. Every man in the city had a healthy fear and respect for Margaret's formidable size and strength. She was not a woman to manhandle...especially if that man wished to maintain a respectable number of limbs.

Isabella would have giggled at the sight under other circumstances. She sensed that now was not the time for such antics.

"Margaret, please. Stop," said Isabella, her voice cracking under the strain of fear. "Gerard, I'm coming out."

Her maidservant didn't listen. Her stick pounded violently against Gerard's helmet. A scrape of metal rang out in the hallway as Isabella struggled to unbar the door.

Oh Lord, please, no. Isabella's fingers fumbled over the latch.

With the door splintered as it was, the locking mechanism was jammed. She couldn't open it.

"I said...*ENOUGH*!" roared Gerard.

Isabella's eyes widened in terror as the mercenary's blade swung through the air, cleaving Margaret from shoulder to waist. Blood sprayed as her friend's lifeless form crumbled to the floor.

"No!" Isabella screamed. "No! No! No!"

"Now, my dear, stand aside. I'm coming in."

Isabella dropped to her knees. Sorrow burst from her eyes at the sight of her dead maidservant. How could this be happening? The knife hidden in her palm clattered to the floor. It was useless now anyway. There was no escape. All she could do was trust in God to see her through the ordeal she was certain would come.

The door creaked as more wood splintered from the blow of an axe. When a big enough hole was made, Gerard carefully stepped into her room and squatted down beside her. His hands rested on her shoulders as he leered at her heaving form. A yellow toothed grin splayed across his face at her.

She returned his stare, fury building inside her. No matter what, she would not allow the barbarian to have his prize. She would do whatever it took. No matter the cost. And she vowed at that moment...Margaret would be avenged.

BARON GREGORY DE L'OMBRE looked down at the man who lay trembling, bound and gagged upon the stone table that had once been used by King Solomon himself—possibly as a writing desk for one of his books of Scripture—and smiled.

"My dear Tertius," he said to the Vatican priest. "You should be rejoicing. You are assisting us in ushering a brand-new age into our world. How many people can possibly say that?"

The monsignor's eyes widened, pleading silently for mercy behind his gag. His arms shook against the iron chains that held him fast to the soon-to-be altar. His legs kicked pitifully. Tears streamed uncontrollably down his cheeks.

"Come now. There is no need for fear," Gregory cooed, stroking a single strand of gray hair back from the priest's face. "If your God is as powerful as you men of the cloth believe, then you should really have nothing to worry about, right?"

Someone cleared a throat from behind the baron and he turned to see a nearly emaciated Ibrihim—his surname escaped the baron at the moment—shaking his head with caution. The nomad was dressed in the rich robes of a Jewish priest, complete with chest plate and headdress.

"M'lord," the Essene spoke softly with trembling voice. "I'd caution against blasphemy in this unholy place. At least until our dark deed is complete. It would be unwise on many levels to anger Yahweh when your quest is so close to completion."

Gregory sneered, then waved his hand in dismissal.

"Fine," he said, gesturing toward the twelve golems that lined the chamber. "Then let's just get this over. Proceed with the sacrifice."

Ibrihim gawked at the baron.

"M'lord," he said with a slight bow. "We've been over the specifics of this ritual before. In order for this to work…in order for control of Rakeesha's golems to be transferred to you, it must be you who performs the sacrifice. Your priest is your superior. Your killing him will essentially rob him of his power over you. The blood from his wound, applied to the clay of the creatures, will establish your own power over them. For me to do it would mean nothing." He stripped from the ceremonial robes and handed them to Gregory. "I told your seamstress as much when she dressed me in these robes. They are yours to be worn, not mine."

The baron took the raiment and slipped them over his tunic with a snarl. In all his years, he had killed many men without so much as a quiver. But all of those deaths had been honorable for the most part. Deeds of battle or politics. What he was about to do now was something entirely alien. Different. Unsettling. He was about to take a man's life in cold blood. He was about to slit the throat of a man who was powerless to resist...chained to a stone altar like a lamb of atonement.

Seriously though, what did it matter? The man—even a priest of the Vatican—was insignificant compared to him. He was on the verge of something beyond outdated concepts of morality. He was about to create life itself. About to embark upon a journey that transcended humanity and reached for the vaunted throne of God itself! Compared to that, what value was there in this one pathetic man's life?

Very little indeed, he thought as he placed the priestly headdress upon his brow and smiled. He'd come too far, and he was so close to attaining everything he'd always dreamed. Proper respect from his peers. Fear from his enemies. The ultimate means of revenge for the death of his beloved. And ultimately, true power to conquer this god-forsaken land and beyond. And all he need do was recite the proper incantation, apply the dagger to Tertius' neck, and pull across.

As he began to carry out the ritual as instructed by the Essene, the Vatican priest began to scream behind the cloth gag that covered his mouth. Even as the blood began to pool into the silver goblet he held under the priest's wounds, Gregory began to smile wider as the cries intensified. He decided that he rather enjoyed the sound after all and felt disappointed when it began to fade from Tertius' dying body.

So, when the last drop of blood plopped into the goblet and the priest lay lifeless on the stone slab, he turned toward Ibrihim with his blade and made the screaming start again.

25

For the first time in years, spasms of actual pain shot through the Djinn's battle-damaged body, jolting him into semi-consciousness. His mind raced, straining to recall where he was and how he had gotten there. His eyelids remained closed, no matter how hard he willed them open.

"He's awake," came an oddly familiar voice to his right.

The Djinn struggled to rise, but gentle hands pressed down on his shoulders, keeping him place.

"Nay," said another voice. "Don't try to move. You've been seriously injured and need time to heal."

"W-water," the Djinn's dry lips cracked as they parted to form the word. He realized that he also had no idea how long he'd been unconscious, but he had never felt so parched.

"Of course, m'lord," said the first voice, followed by movement to his right. Where had he heard that voice before? It sounded so familiar...and so calming. It was the voice of a friend, he was sure.

"Now, I'm going to pour a little water into your mouth. Drink slowly." The voice paused. "And not too much, mind you."

Instant relief washed over him as cool liquid poured down dry throat.

My throat! My face!

Instinctively, he reached up and felt for his hood, but it was gone.

"It's all right. There's no need to fret. You're among friends now," said the second voice.

The Djinn's eyes slowly opened. The world was dark and hazy. Two tiny flames flickered in front of him...small oil lamps resting on a pedestal. As far as he could tell, they were the only light source in the room.

He scanned his surroundings. Not much to see, he realized. He was lying deep in a hollowed-out patch of earth...obviously to keep him cool in the arid desert heat. The shelter was sparse, made of camel skin and pieces of driftwood. It was small too, only big enough for three or four men.

He looked to his right and a weakened smile spread across his face.

"Horatio. Samuel. I should have known you would find me."

The knight and his squire beamed down at him.

"It's good to see you too, my friend," said Horatio. "Only, we didn't. Find you, that is. An old shepherd happened upon this hut two days past. He walked in and saw you resting here and immediately went to get help. Since Lord William's chateau is the closest settlement around these parts, he came to us."

The room began to spin around, forcing the Djinn to close his eyes again. He had lost so much blood. It would be a while before he recuperated enough to continue his search for the...

His eyes snapped open. The Book. Gone? It couldn't be. The hashshashin had beaten him. After all he'd gone through to get it —Gerard and his mercenaries, finding the hidden library, and facing the Warden—he'd failed in the end.

The last thing he could remember was passing out on the edge of the underground reservoir.

Then how did he get here?

"When we found you, you had already been bandaged up nicely," said Samuel, his eyes wide and that wonderfully warm smile glued to his face. "Do you remember who helped you?"

He wracked his brain, searching for any memory that would answer that question. By all rights, he should be dead by now...or at least lying in his own blood on the cold stone floors of Gregory's tunnels. But someone had helped him out of the labyrinth under the city. They'd carried him out into the desert, built this shelter, and tended his wounds.

But who? The hashshashin? It didn't seem likely, yet no matter how he turned the most plausible scenarios over in his head, Emir was the most likely answer. The next question could only be why?

"No, Samuel, I don't remember."

"Well, no matter, sir," Samuel said. "You're at least safe and sound now. That's what matters."

Horatio, kneeling down by the Djinn next to Samuel, stared silently at the ground. His arms nervously crossing and uncrossing. It seemed he couldn't help his fidgeting.

"And you, Horatio?" asked the Djinn. "I'm glad you decided to join my merry band. What changed your mind?"

His friend smiled coyly back at him, then nodded. "Aye," he said. "'Tis true. After learning the truth about you...after finally being told the whole story...I wasn't quite sure where I belonged. I wasn't sure I believed the tale that was told me. It all sounded so far-fetched, and I must admit to wondering whether Sir William had not been bewitched by you, as everyone else seemed to be." He nodded toward Samuel. "But it was he that finally convinced me. Or rather, what you did for him that told me William's story had been true all along.

"You see, after doing everything I could to free Samuel from Gregory's prison, I had waited nearby...watching...waiting... biding my time. I knew that whether you were good or evil, you still had plans for the boy, so I let him sit in his cell until you made your move." He paused at this and glanced apologetically over at his squire. The shame over allowing his cousin to suffer under Gerard's stern fists evident on his face. "Soon, my patience paid off and you did what I could not. You freed my squire from his chains and sent him on his way. You asked nothing from him in return for his freedom and it was then that I knew the story was all true. After that, there was no longer a question. I returned to William's chateau along with Samuel and have awaited news of you since."

The knight went silent. His eyes downcast.

"Ah, but I see you're a little upset with me," the Djinn said. "Perhaps a little annoyed that I hadn't taken you into my confidence sooner?"

Horatio nodded. "You know I would have joined you. All you had to do was ask."

"I know, my friend. But I didn't want to put you in that situation unless absolutely necessary. Besides, I needed you close to Gregory. Close to…Isabella. You couldn't have done that if you had joined me on my quest."

The knight stiffened at the mention of Gregory's daughter; a dour look etched across his brow.

"What is it, my friend?" asked the Djinn. "I can tell there is something else on your mind besides my duality."

The knight looked over at him. Doubt and fear echoed loudly through his grim features. Something was definitely not good. Horatio seemed crippled with indecision.

"Just tell me."

"All right," said Horatio, looking at his cousin for support. "As you mentioned, we've been keeping an eye on Lady Isabella's quarters for some time now…just like we'd been asked. Everything was fine until three days ago—the morning after you disappeared into Gregory's tunnels."

"What's happened?" The Djinn willed himself to sit up. For

anyone else, he was certain the pain of that simple act would have been excruciating. Fortunately, he was nowhere close to being just *anyone else*.

"M'lord, you really mustn't sit up," said Samuel, once again placing a hand on his shoulder in attempt to guide him down.

The Djinn slapped the hand away.

"I said, what's happened?"

"She's been taken. It was Gerard," said Horatio. "Killed sweet Margaret and just took off with Isabella. There was nothing that could be done. Our spies were outnumbered and outmanned. They would have been killed if..."

The Djinn stared blankly into Horatio's eyes. He couldn't concentrate on what the knight was saying. All he could hear was the roar of blood rushing through his head.

He had to think this through. He knew that Isabella would be safe...at least for now. Gregory would not allow his daughter to be harmed. Yet once they had what they sought, he was sure the mercenary would leave the city, carrying Isabella away with him to God only knew where.

"Do we have any leads on where she was taken?" he asked while examining the bandages that secured the injuries he'd sustained during his battles in the tunnels. He didn't have time for this. He had to get moving.

"Not yet, sir."

"Where is...?"

"He's already gone into the city to look for her, m'lord," reported Samuel, anticipating his question, while he lifted the bandage around his master's shoulder to check on the wound. "We've heard no word from him. But before he left, he made us swear, sir...he made us swear we'd keep you here safe and sound and that we'd tend to your wounds and make sure you got better. And that's just what we've been doing."

Samuel's grin truly was infectious. There was no sweeter nor noble a man on earth, the Djinn thought as he smiled back at the younger man. And very loyal. He'd take his vow seriously. A twinge of guilt rippled through him at the thought of making them both break their solemn promise. But there was no other choice.

"Get my gear," he said to them, a look of cold determination burning in his stare. He wanted them to understand he was serious. He would not argue about this.

"But you're too weak…" Horatio protested.

"I'll be fine."

"No, sir, I don't think you will." Horatio's glare was equally as determined. "If you leave now, I've been assured that you will die. I, for one, am not willing to let that happen."

"Horatio, I said…"

"I don't care what you said. Your ghost and ghoulie theatrics may have worked on me once, but no longer. You're just a man, my friend…nothing more. You cannot keep going like you are. You could…die."

The Djinn looked at his two friends who had been tending lovingly to his needs. No one could possibly deserve such companions on this earth. God was definitely a God of infinite goodness for blessing him with these two. He let out a sigh as he dipped his head.

"Horatio, my friend, you don't understand," he said in a softer tone than he had planned. "There's no question of that now. I'm dying. No medicine on earth can stop it from happening. My wounds are too deep…my injuries too severe. There's good reason I lay here, Horatio, half buried in the sand. It was to be my grave."

"Don't talk like that, m'lord," said Samuel, trying bravely to sound positive. A single tear streaming from his eye betrayed his confidence. "You'll get better. I just know you will."

"I feel the pain," said the Djinn, looking deliberately at

Horatio. "You understand what that means, don't you? I am actually *feeling* the pain of my injuries."

The knight stared at him silently. His mouth struggled to form words that refused to come. Horatio understood. There was no point in pretending otherwise. It was useless to deny the inevitable.

"Please. Bring my gear to me. Now. She's in trouble. She's my life…my legacy."

His friend knelt silently beside him for several moments, then let out a breath.

Resignation.

Standing up, he walked outside the hut into the darkness. Samuel sat cross-legged, mindlessly rubbing the rosaries that draped across his neck. His eyes closed, his mouth mumbling an unspoken prayer.

The Djinn closed his eyes and joined him.

IT HAD TAKEN LONGER than he would have liked, but Horatio and Samuel had finally redressed his injuries, applied a layer of chain mail, and clothed him in the robes of the Djinn. He stood outside the makeshift shelter in which he had rested for the last two and a half days.

The sun was setting. The air grew cool, and the Djinn felt a small amount of his old strength returning as the moon began to rise high into the desert night.

"What will you do now?" asked Horatio, who led Al-Ghul, the Djinn's black horse, to his master.

"I'll go to the palace first. Look in her chambers and see what I can find," he said as he mounted his steed. "Then, I'll tear the city apart if I have to, until I find her."

Al-Ghul shifted under his weight. The faithful animal could always tell when his master was suffering. A screech from above shattered the air. The Djinn looked up and whistled a shrill cry. The great falcon descended, alighting on his outstretched arm.

"She's been encircling your camp since we found you," said Horatio, indicating the bird. "She's not let you out of her sight."

The Djinn's gloved finger stroked the crest on the raptor's head. Then he looked down at his two friends.

"Go back to Lord William's camp," he said. "Gather the knights and meet me in in twenty-four hours."

"Where?" asked Horatio.

"She knows where," said the Djinn, handing the bird to Horatio's outstretched arm. "She'll guide you."

Then, clicking his spurs into the side of Al-Ghul, he took off into the night. Toward Jerusalem. Toward Isabella.

THE CAVERN in which the underground lake lay was silent as a grave. Nothing but the occasional *kerplunk* of water dripping from a stalagmite made any sound at all. The bizarre, albino minnows streaked just under the lake's surface, feeding on the algae.

It was a scene of quiet tranquility now, several hours after Gregory's men had finally given up their search for the hidden library. Hours after they had traipsed to and fro along the stone floor like a herd of elephants. Hours since the baron's curses had echoed throughout the miles of tunnels.

It had been complete chaos then, but now, it was the picture of pristine serenity.

Until a single bubble blossomed from the center of the lake. Then, another. And a third. Soon, the entire surface of the water seemed to boil with a violent fury. Something within the bubbling caldron moved slowly, deliberately, toward the rocky shoreline.

If Gregory's soldiers had remained a few hours longer, they

would have witnessed this. They would have been enthralled by
the spectacle of it all. And then, they would have run in stark
terror as a single muddy hand stretched out from the water,
clutched onto the stones, and pulled a great hulking mass of
gelatinous clay onto dry ground.

26

The mercenary could not get comfortable. It had been a little over thirty-six hours since he'd taken Isabella prisoner, and the Djinn was still nowhere to be found. He was sure that the creature would learn of his love's disappearance and come to her aid. And the most likely place to start the search would be in the very place from which she was taken. Yet now, as he crouched low in the shadows of Isabella's armoire, doubt crawled its way into his mind.

Twisting on his heel to relieve circulation to his feet, he peered through the crack in the door. Archibald and three of his men lay hidden throughout the bedchamber. Six more men lay in wait just outside the newly repaired doorway. The moment the Djinn stepped foot into the room, he would be theirs.

Gerard's heart thudded rapidly against his chest. Where was he? They were running out of time. Gregory was becoming increasingly unstable with every passing minute. Ever since the ritual and the revival of Rakeesha's golems, he had locked himself down in Solomon's Vault. He'd screamed through the door that he was concocting a plan to retrieve both the Book and the ring —whether the Djinn was captured or not. Gerard was beginning to believe that either his employer had gone completely mad, or he knew more about this Djinn than he'd been letting on. But the baron was convinced that he knew where the scroll and Solomon's Seal would be and was even now preparing his new weapons for an all-out assault on God-knows-where.

But the mercenary wasn't nearly as optimistic. He still believed the best chance they had was in capturing the foul creature that had made a fool of him just a few days ago in the tunnels.

Gerard, however, was beginning to wonder if he'd miscalculated. He wondered what was taking the Djinn so long to pursue his ladylove. Unless the demon had been using the girl all along. Perhaps he didn't care for her at all. Perhaps he was only using her for the information she could provide. It didn't seem likely. He'd seen the two of them on the balcony. He'd heard them talking.

No, there was something very real between the two of them, though Gerard was unable to understand what it could possibly be.

His thoughts raced as the shadows grew longer with the fading sun. It would soon be dark. Surely the Djinn would be here soon.

THE DARK SHAPE struggled up the sheer wall of Baron Gregory's palace, each movement a study in patience and strength. Slowly, one stone at a time, his gauntleted hands pulled him further toward Isabella's balcony. Frankly, as far as he was concerned, he couldn't reach it soon enough. He was neither as young nor as agile as he'd once been. But the rigors he'd faced within the last few days—the sleepless nights and the injuries that needed tending—made this particular climb even more tenuous than he would have believed possible.

He breathed an exhausted sigh as his right hand clutched the rail of the balcony and he hauled himself over the ledge. Once on solid footing, he leaned back against the rail and marveled at how his mentor, in his debilitated health, had always accomplished such physical feats with ease. The scientist in him found such acts to be beyond humanly possible—even augmented with the medications and elixirs that he, himself, had concocted.

Taking a deep breath, he pushed off from his perch, wrapped the black robe tightly around his lithe frame and crept toward the double doors leading into Lady Isabella's bedroom. He reached out, turned the handle, and was mildly surprised to find the doors unlocked.

His hand firmly clutching the handle, he kept the door closed, and tensed.

Remember the plan, he thought. *They took Isabella, which means they know about...*

But even as he thought these things, he realized how absurd he was being. He was expecting this. Yes, it might be a trap. It might not.

Of course, it mattered little. No matter what lay in wait within those chambers, he would have to go in. Search the place for any clues as to where they would have taken her. Short of capturing and torturing one of Gerard's men, it was the only logical starting point. Though, he had to admit...after what they'd done to poor Samuel, he was not opposed to a little torture.

Smiling slyly at the thought, he pushed the door open and stepped into the cool confines of the bedchamber. Two steps in, he stopped to listen for anything untoward. All remained still. He looked around, walking over to Isabella's vanity where she kept her toiletries, and laid a hand gently on the tabletop. Everything in the room appeared exactly as it had been the last time he'd been here. Not so much as a hair in Isabella's brush was out of place. Everything was exactly...wait a minute. The door!

He turned to face the entrance and saw it barred by a thick cedar doorway. Exactly the same as the one he'd seen on the few occasions he'd entered her chambers. But that made no sense. Reports indicated that the door was hacked to pieces. With Isabella gone, there would be no need to hurry to repair the door. After all, there were more pressing matters for Gerard or Gregory to worry about. So why a door?

Zounds, he thought as he slowly crept backwards toward the balcony once again. His eyes locked on the ominous closed doors ahead. *The only reason would be to conceal something on the other side.*

Just as he reached the veranda's doors, something burst from the armoire to his right. A blur of steel and muscle leapt at him, and he was brought down hard to the stone floor. The air rushed from his lungs as the full weight of his attacker crashed down on him. Then, the room was filled with nearly a dozen well-armed guards, their sword blades pointed menacingly in his direction. Yet despite his capture, the man on top of him pounded his fists continuously against his face and jaw. Raw animal rage unleashed upon the shrouded figure's helpless frame.

"I'll kill you," roared Gerard, as his clenched fists thrashed at him. "For the humiliation you've put me through, you will die this night, demon!"

The fierce assault continued for several minutes. Already, he could tell that at least three of his ribs were broken, and he'd lost at least that many teeth. Besides that, his head throbbed with each powerful blow, threatening to throw him into unconsciousness. And he knew that to black out now would certainly be his doom.

"Captain, sir," said one of Gerard's men. "The baron said he didn't want the Djinn harmed. He said that if we caught him, he wanted to question him before—"

The mercenary ignored his man's protest, pulled his robed victim to his feet, and sent his knee into his groin. The captive buckled from the blow, wheezing for breath as he rolled into a ball on the ground.

"Ah, you felt *that* did you?" Gerard growled. "Good. So, you're human after all. Let's see how much pain you can take." The mercenary kicked him, then turned to his men. "Slap him in chains. We'll take him back to the safehouse and have some fun with him before Gregory even knows we've taken him."

The robed man was ruthlessly pulled to his feet and clapped in irons, and it was all he could do to just keep erect as Gerard's men pulled him toward the exit. The pain was nearly unbearable. Almost every limb, as well as his jaw and neck, throbbed. Blood oozed from his nose and mouth as he was dragged across the room.

"Wait!" Gerard shouted from behind. His captors complied and the big mercenary walked around to face his nemesis with a cold, dark glare. "Boys, I think it's time we see who it is that's been plaguing us all this time, don't you?"

Most shouted their assent at the mercenary's suggestion. Their ire and frustration over their numerous defeats at the Djinn's hands now shone through without pity or fear. On the contrary, it seemed that now, while looking at their prisoner, it was as if all the fear they'd once felt for the shadow-shrouded demon was the thing of nightmares evaporating in the light of day. They were reborn. Newly invigorated by his capture. The myth of the creature would be finally exposed. No longer would his magic hold sway over them.

"Gerard, sir," said one of his men. He'd been the only one that didn't seem enthused by the entire affair and the same one who tried to stop the mercenary from beating their enemy to death. "I hate to bring this up, but the baron..."

Gerard spun around furiously, spittle slinging from the corners of his lips. "And I couldn't care less what Gregory said!" he growled. "As a matter of fact, after tonight, I suspect I'll not be taking orders from the likes of Baron De L'Ombre ever again."

And with that, he turned back to his prize, reached out, and jerked the jet-black hood covering his captive's head. Then let out a sharp gasp.

"Well, I'll be…" the mercenary grinned. "I should have known. Makes perfect sense that it would be you now that I think of it."

One of Gerard's men looked at him then back at his captain, shaking his head. "I don't understand," the soldier said. "I've never seen 'im before. Who on earth is it?"

"Oh, you've seen him, all right," Gerard said with a chuckle. "About a week ago now. At Solomon's Vault when Gregory was giving his little tour." He turned to face his men with an exaggerated bravado. "Gentlemen, allow me to introduce you to the Djinn. This is none other than Tufic, the physician of Gregory's brother William."

27

"I said talk!" The back of Gerard's hand slapped Tufic's battered face. "Where are they? What have you done with them?"

The physician's head sank low against his chest, blood gushed from open wounds around his eyes and nose. They had been at it for nearly twenty-two hours. Upon catching the 'demon', the mercenary had immediately taken him to the safehouse in the eastern sector of the city, where they bound him to a chair and began the long—and hopefully, excruciating—interrogation.

"Tell me!" Gerard roared.

Tufic lifted defiant eyes to meet his captor. He had very little strength left and simply would be unable to survive his ordeal much longer. The mercenary knew that he had only a short amount of time to obtain the location of the Book and Solomon's ring, which meant more drastic measures were becoming necessary.

"Archibald," Gerard said, nodding over to the kiln.

His lieutenant strode silently to the blaze, pulling out the fire poker, glowing white from the heat. He handed the instrument to Gerard and walked away to the door.

"What are you going to do?" asked a dazed feminine voice from the shadowy corner of the room.

"M'lady," said Gerard. "You are tired and weak. You need your rest. There's no need to worry about this *filth*. Soon, the spell he cast on you will be over, and you'll finally be free of his influence."

He walked up to Tufic's slouching form, now wheezing for breath. The blistering point of the poker hovered inches from his left eye.

"I'm not going to lie to you," the mercenary said with a malicious grin. "This is going to hurt. It will hurt a great deal."

The physician raised his head again. Slowly, he opened his mouth to speak, but no words came, before slumping back down again.

"Leave him alone!" shouted Isabella, the chains that bound her legs and wrists clinking as she struggled to stand. "You have the wrong man! That's not the Djinn!"

Gerard stifled a laugh. Of course, it was the Djinn. He had caught him in the act, clothed in the black turban and robes of the creature that had haunted him from within his dreams for the past six months. The wench would say anything to save her love.

He looked down at Tufic again, fists clutching the heated poker. Still, something did not seem right about this. He'd seen the creature in battle. He'd witnessed dozens of arrows perforating him with little effect. He had seemed invincible—impervious to pain. Yet now, the dark power of superstition stripped away, he appeared so small. So weak.

Clutching the long strands of Tufic's jet black hair, Gerard yanked his head up once more to appraise his enemy's face. His eyes—what Gerard could see of them beyond the swelling and bruises—were now glazed over. His breathing strained and shallow. How could he and his men have been beaten by such a cur? In hindsight, it seemed utterly preposterous.

The poker had cooled to a dull red hue. He would now get the answers he sought. And soon, the Djinn would be dead.

"You can't do this," cried Isabella. "Please. I'll do whatever you ask. Just don't hurt him anymore."

The mercenary jerked around to look at Isabella. Was she serious? Would she so easily give in to his desire for her? Would she give herself to him for the life of this man?

"I'm serious. I'll be yours," she said as if reading his thoughts. "Completely. Just don't hurt him."

Gerard stepped toward the baron's daughter, the brand forgotten. His rough, calloused hand moved to the gentle lines of her face as he peered deep into her eyes.

"Completely?" he repeated.

She let out a resigned sigh. "Yes. As long as you hurt him no more."

"Captain," interrupted Archibald. "Need I remind you that we are in the baron's employ? We need the information the Djinn can provide."

"Gerard, listen to me," said Isabella. "That is *not* the Djinn. You have it all wrong. You are killing an innocent man."

The mercenary stared into the eyes of the woman he'd longed for since coming to this accursed *Outremer*. He turned to look at his lieutenant and then back to his captive. No matter what he did to the wretch, Isabella would be his. She had no choice in the matter. But to have her freely…that was far better.

However, my hatred for the Djinn possibly equals my obsession with the woman, he thought, turning again toward his helpless foe. *What to do?*

There were other ways of recovering the artifacts. He needn't kill the physician. Besides, how much better to ensure the lady's cooperation than to keep her love under lock and key?

He faced Isabella. Her gentle blue-gray eyes burned deep into his being. They washed over him like a tidal wave of beauty.

"N-n-no," croaked a strangled voice from behind, followed by a horrible fit of coughing.

"So, there's still life in you yet," Gerard laughed as he walked over to his captive. "And it seems as though your tongue has been finally loosened."

"Y-you will not lay a hand on her again," said Tufic, as a clump of blood spewed past his lips.

"I don't think you have much say in the matter, knave."

"You are right, but I'm not the one you have to worry about," said the physician. "She's right. I'm not the creature you seek. The dark spirit of the Djinn is even now on his way here to save me. And her. I promise you, you will not escape his coming wrath."

The mercenary's fist plowed into Tufic's jaw, splintering bone and teeth. He had had enough of this. He no longer cared about "winning" the affections of his love willingly. He would take her against his will. But for the audacity of this upstart, he would suffer greatly. And Gerard would take great pleasure in that suffering.

"Take her away," he said to no one in particular. "She will not use her charms to sway me again."

The rustle of chains, accompanied by screams of protests erupted in the guardhouse, as three of Gerard's men tried to gain control of the woman's squirming form.

"No! Let me go! I said, let me go!"

Laughter exploded from the seven other guards in the house at the sight of their comrades struggling against such a small woman. Isabella kicked and scratched at anything within reach. One guard howled in pain as her nails dug deep into one eye.

KNOCK!

Silence shuddered throughout the room at the sound of a single rap at the oak door of the house. Only a few knew they were there, and those that knew had been instructed that the captain was not to be disturbed.

Gerard glanced at Archibald and nodded slightly. The

lieutenant, understanding the silent command, approached the door and opened it.

Nothing.

"Captain, there's no one there," said Archibald as he turned to his superior.

"Your point?"

"My point is that there's *no one* there…at all. Sir, you expressly placed Jonathan and the miller's son at the door as sentries. They're not there."

The hired soldiers huddled nervously together, looking uneasily at one another…their boisterous confidence suddenly draining from their faces. Isabella, forgotten by Gerard's men, crept to Tufic's side. She tore strips of cloth from her gown and tended to the physician's wounds in silence.

KNOCK!

"Y-your time is up," said Tufic, a knowing grin spreading painfully across his face. "He's here."

"Shut…" The mercenary released another backhand to the physician's face. "…up!" Grabbing Isabella by the shoulder, he threw her across the room onto the makeshift bed they'd prepared for her stay. "Get away from him, wench!"

The distant rumble of thunder rippled through the sky, a harbinger of a great storm moving toward them from the nearby sea.

"You can strike me all you want," croaked the doctor, wincing at the effort of moving his jaw. "It won't stop what is outside these walls. The Djinn, spirit of vengeance, is stalking you even now. Get out while you can."

Gerard turned from his captive to peer at the door once more. What was going on? This made absolutely no sense. He and his men were merely being irrational. They had the *Djinn* in custody. His men had probably wandered off to find wine or to relieve their bladders. There was no need to fret. But if that were so, why could he feel the icy pin pricks of dread oozing down his spine?

"Captain," said Durgan. "The Saracen doctor has the men spooked. What if he's telling the truth?"

"Nonsense. He's only playing to our fears."

"But sir, you've seen the way the Djinn fought. You saw how invincible he seemed. No human could endure what we did to him in the tunnels. What if...what if the Djinn really *is* a spirit?"

"Don't be absurd, Durgan," growled Gerard. "We have the Djinn now. Behold," he said as he lifted Tufic's face up by the chin. "He's flesh and blood. Just like you and me."

"But sir, all I'm saying is..."

KNOCK!

This time, the knocking was louder...more insistent. One could say, angry even.

No one moved. Every muscle in Gerard's body cramped in a rictus of fear. This wasn't right. It wasn't the way things were supposed to be. He had the Djinn! He had Isabella. His victory was assured. Yet now, the smug confidence that had carved its way into the mercenary's heart began to erode.

"Would someone open that door?" growled the mercenary, a marching cadence drumming against his ribcage.

A young soldier moved warily to the door. He stretched out his hand toward the latch, but before he even touched the frame a great crash boomed from above. In unison, every head turned skyward just as the limp form of the miller's son plummeted from the thatched roof above. A deafening thud echoed through the room. Fifteen pairs of eyes fixed themselves on the lifeless form of the guard that lay sprawled on the floor.

"That is enough!" said Gerard, grim determination forcing itself through the mercenary's heart. "Soldier, open that door... now. Men, prepare for battle."

The trembling soldier turned his attention again to the ominous door before him. Every eye stood transfixed as his trembling hand reached for the latch. Suddenly, an explosion ripped through the door, sending shards of wood and smoke throughout the safehouse. The guard crashed to the ground, his face disfigured from the blast, as he breathed his last breath.

Smoke and brimstone filled the room, as puffs of strange green glowing debris flitted through the air. The room was pitch black, the candles and torches being extinguished with the blast. Gerard's eyes strained against the inky blackness and smoke-filled haze, trying to make out whatever was going to come through the door.

For several long moments, nothing happened. The smoke filled the room, burning Gerard's eyes and lungs. It reeked of the fires from hell. He'd smelled the stench before. But that was impossible! He *had* the Djinn. He had captured his enemy. He was sure of it. Yet now, as his throat squeezed tight, squeezing the air from his lungs, doubt spiraled out of control in his mind.

A shadow glided through the doorway—a human shaped silhouette against the night. Two burning green eyes glared hatefully at the mercenary. The creature's cloak appeared ethereal as it flapped soundlessly in a hot breeze that seemed to come from all directions at one time, engulfing it deeper into the shadows. The scrape of steel against a scabbard rang out in the air as the creature drew its sword.

"DuBois," hissed the demon, its voice like none Gerard had heard before. "It is time, DuBois. Time to meet the Creator."

A great crack of thunder erupted, just as white-hot streaks of lightning lit the doorway and the surrounding room in a single flash. The image of the dark spirit blazing brightly in the flash of the lightning bolt would be permanently burned into Gerard's memory for the rest of his life—depending on how much longer he actually had to live.

A great deluge poured down upon the damaged roof and onto the broad, heaving shoulders of the creature that hunched menacingly at Gerard.

"Dear Lord! Protect me," the mercenary muttered at the terror that stood before him.

He'd been wrong. *This* was the Djinn, not the physician. He truly *was* a demon—straight from the pits of hell—and no *man* at all. No power on earth could hurt such a creature. The mercenary had no hope of surviving another encounter with such a thing that now stood before him. Panicked, Gerard plowed forward, past the Djinn and into the downpour from the heavens that would wash away the river of blood that would surely flow from within the guardhouse.

The blood of Gerard's own men. The same men he knew were now doomed, but then, that was their problem.

28

Isabella stared silently at the Djinn as he tore through the remainder of Gerard's men. Archibald now lay dead on the ground, his head severed from the razor-sharp blade of the scimitar. Three others wailed in terror and pain, as they curled up trembling in defeat. Four fled from the house, bleeding with mortal wounds.

Out of the original thirteen of Gerard's men, only three now remained to fight. The odds were decidedly unfair. She felt a sudden surge of sorrow for the mercenaries. The Djinn's wrath could no longer be sated. His rage at the sight of Tufic and her own kidnapping had undoubtedly stripped him of any compassion he might have once had.

The Djinn stood in the center of the room, his blade clutched tightly in both hands. Two soldiers attacked as one, swinging their swords in unison in a frontal assault. Crouching low, the Djinn rolled to the right just as their weapons came down. Before they had time to recover, he came up, whirled around with a blinding sweep of his scimitar striking the nearest soldier across the back of the head.

The second soldier ran out the door screaming in terror.

Sensing the final combatant behind him, the Djinn spun, unleashing three of his throwing knives into the man's chest. He crashed to the ground in a pool of blood.

It was over. The Djinn turned to Isabella and then to Tufic.

"Take care of him," he commanded, his usual soothing voice replaced with cold fury. "I'm going after Gerard."

"Don't," she said. "He's beaten. There's no need for more death."

"He must pay for what he has done."

"And he will. Trust God. Let Him bring about His own justice."

The Djinn stood silently, staring at her. He clutched his abdomen tightly as he heaved for breath. Isabella noticed a tiny stream of crimson flowing between his fingers.

"You're injured," she said.

"It is nothing for you to worry about. Tufic's wounds are more serious than mine."

He was lying. He had always been a poor liar—especially when it came to her. She could now see by his gait that he was in severe pain.

"You're dying."

His head sunk low in response, and he turned toward the door.

"I have work to do," he finally said, turning to glance at her one more time. "I haven't much time left. Get Tufic to the chateau. I'll meet you both there soon."

He bolted through the door before she could protest. It all made sense now. The ferocity of his attack...the guttural snarls during battle. He had been doing all he could to continue the fight.

Fear wormed its way into her mind—fear that she may never see him again. May never be held in his arms again or feel the pure love he had for her. It threatened to overwhelm her as she moved swiftly to free her uncle's physician.

"Dear Lord," she prayed. "Watch over him and keep him. Bring him back to me, please."

29

He had to keep running. No matter what, Gerard knew that if he stopped for even a second, he would die. Every muscle screamed and his lungs cried out in protest, but he pushed on. The demon would not be far behind.

As he fled the safehouse, he'd heard the cries of his men as the Djinn tore through them like a malevolent cyclone. He had encountered the creature on several occasions, but now, it was different. He'd never seen so much fury emanating from any living creature before. Despite his feelings about it, the Djinn had never attacked with hatred before, as he had this evening. On the contrary, he usually had shown a great deal of mercy by treating the wounds of his injured foes. But now…now the mercenary ran from something completely devoid of humanity. Or compassion. Gerard now ran from vengeance incarnate.

His feet pounded the stone walkway while his brain raced to find its bearings. This infernal city was nothing more than a giant maze and at night, in the downpour that gushed from the heavens, the mercenary realized he was hopelessly lost. As a matter of fact, he couldn't remember ever being in the section of the quarter in which he currently found himself.

Gusts of wind bombarded him with a torrential wall of rain, blinding him. It was as if the weather itself sought to drive the running man back toward the demon. How could he have been so wrong? The Djinn could not possibly be a man. No human he'd ever seen moved the way the creature did; as if he were made of nothing more than some dark, baleful vapor.

He had to stop. The world spun uncontrollably around him as his blood pumped feverishly through his veins. He heaved for breath, gulping in as much oxygen as he could during this short reprieve. He couldn't remember how long he'd been running and in the maze of short, squat, identical buildings he found himself in, there was no way to tell how far he'd run, either.

Bending over, he clutched his knees as a sharp pain pierced his sides. He couldn't rest long. It would be suicide. But to not give himself a short respite, he would be dead soon anyway.

A scuffled sound above brought his attention to the roof of a nearby shop. A dark shape slithered out of view just as his eyes drifted upward. He had to press on. The creature was obviously nearby—toying with him—and Gerard was no one's plaything.

Sucking in one last gulp of air, the mercenary burst forward in a full sprint. He rounded the corner to his right into a darkened alley, slid to a stop. His mouth dropped as if a team of oxen were tugging at his jaws.

The Djinn hunched over in the alley, its shadowy form fading in and out with every flicker of lightning that streaked across the sky. A guttural chuckle escaped the demon's covered lips as Gerard wheeled around and bolted in the opposite direction.

He ran faster than he ever believed possible. The creature had caught up to him so easily. How it had managed to navigate the city maze was beyond him, but somehow it had. The only thing Gerard knew was that he had to put as much space between it and himself as he could.

As his boots pounded against the stones, his keen ears strained against the roar of the deluge for sounds of pursuit. He could hear none. It appeared that the creature was not following him. Though he couldn't quite believe the demon would give up that easily.

Gerard bounded past two more alleyways, pausing only briefly to glance back. Nothing but darkness and rain. A streak of lightning hurled across the sky, blasting its way to the ground, striking something nearby. Thunder boomed overhead, causing the mercenary to jerk involuntarily. That was too close and the metal armor he wore did nothing for his confidence. He had to find shelter. A place to hide—a place to regain his bearings and come up with a plan. But where? He had no idea where he was. With the maelstrom lashing down at him from all sides, there was no way to discern even the east from the west. He was utterly blind.

A scraping noise in front of him pulled him from his musings. A figure materialized from the shadows before him. It had come from nowhere. The Djinn had once again found him! What was more, it had somehow made its way in front of him and now, the demon glared silently at its prey. A low hiss exuded from the dark confines of the creature's hood. Its scimitar inched slowly from its scabbard.

This is impossible, Gerard thought, wheeling around and darting toward the last alley he had passed. He careened around the corner, stumbling on a loose stone, and crashed to the ground. Blood and rainwater streamed down his face, burning his eyes as he lifted himself from the street. He had to get moving again, he knew, but his body rebelled against him. It wouldn't move. Several seconds passed before he could figure out why. It had taken that long for his brain to register what his eyes had already seen—the Djinn once again hovering before him, its black robes whipping at the howling wind cascading over the city skyline.

The mercenary fought desperately to remain upright, as dark splotches swirled in front of his eyes, a warning sign of an imminent blackout. He could take no more of this. The demon was everywhere at once. Gerard's body swayed in the wind, as the Djinn glided silently toward him.

As his mind teetered on the brink of madness, the mercenary felt a gentle brush of fabric against his right shoulder. His head slowly turned and looked up; a silent scream filling his paralyzed vocal cords. The Djinn now crouched low upon the wooden beam on the roof of a shop just above him, leaning forward to peer at the mercenary from under his darkened hood.

The mercenary's eyes snapped straight ahead once again. The apparition of the demon that had only moments before stood in front of him was not there. He had seemed to just to have disappeared, only to rematerialize on the roof above.

Spinning around, Gerard's eyes scanned the haze behind him. The rain had tapered off and now, only a light drizzle obscured his vision. A hiss from above reminded him of his current predicament and he bolted again into the labyrinth of alleyways.

He ran several more blocks before coming to a little leather shop that he had visited the day before to fix the strap to his iron greaves. He now knew where he was. The walled fortifications of the city lay to his left, only yards away. There, he would find soldiers, help, to battle the creature that now doggedly pursued him. To his right, only four buildings away, sat the church—a place he loathed more than the heathen Saracens.

Gerard veered to the left, never letting up his pace. The drizzle had now stopped, and steam arose from the city streets like wisps of a spectral net rising from the ground. The mercenary's heart was nearly exploding in his chest with each pump, but he was elated. He was nearly free. He only needed to run a few more yards and...oh no. He skidded to a halt, as the vision of the creature emerged from around the corner of the next building.

The Djinn strode silently, unhurried, toward him. It said nothing as it moved to a nearby lamppost and stopped. Gerard found himself unable to move, unable to scream for the help that was only a block away. The creature leaned casually against the lamppost, arms folding across its chest and a hideous, low chuckle streamed from under the cloak. The mercenary's pulse pounded violently at his temples as his eyes grew dimmer with each mind-rattling thump.

He had no choice now. The church was his only sanctuary. Surely a creature of hell could not enter so sacred a place. Finding strength to power his unsteady legs, Gerard turned and dashed toward the safety of the church. Once again, no sounds of pursuit followed him as he closed the gap, leapt into the church, and slammed the heavy oaken doors shut behind him. Gerard pressed his back against the door as added security and heaved in the air that had eluded him since running from the guardhouse.

He was safe now. His heart, however, struggled to slow its rapid pounding as if unable to believe the news. Gerard breathed again, silently telling his heart everything was fine. It was safe. It could slow down. It could finally rest.

A pathetic whimper wheezed from Gerard's contorted lips from a pair of footsteps plodding down the staircase to his right. He turned to face his own nightmare, only to be greeted by the inviting sight of a monk hurrying over to him.

"My son," said the monk, "What is the matter? You've been injured?"

"I'll be fine, Father. I just need to rest a bit...at least until sunrise."

The monk smiled from under his cowl and bowed his head slightly.

"Certainly, my son. If you'd like, I can show you to a room and then provide a hot meal and drink for you."

"That won't be necessary, Father. If it's all the same, I'll rest here—in the sanctuary—for the night. But some food and ale would be nice."

The monk's smile faded. The mercenary knew he wouldn't like the idea of a soldier sleeping in so sacred a place, but there was no other choice. He had to keep his eyes on the door—he had to be prepared for anything and sleeping soundly in a monastic bed would be a sure way to be caught off guard by the demon.

"Tell me, my son, what troubles you this night?" asked the monk after careful consideration of Gerard's request.

There was no point in lying. If you couldn't trust a priest, who could you trust?

"It's a demon, Father. I'm being chased by a heathen demon."

"Ah, the Djinn. It is the Djinn who pursues you," the monk said calmly as he backed slowly away into the shadows of the sanctuary. "And you thought coming to this church would protect you, did you?"

Gerard looked down at his shaking legs, willing them steady. When he looked up again, the monk was nowhere to be seen.

"Father?"

Silence.

The mercenary stiffened, drawing his sword and inching forward into the dimness of the church. He absently made his way into the center of the sanctuary, turning three hundred and sixty degrees while his eyes scanned every nook he could find.

Nothing.

"Father? Are you there?"

"He's here, *my son*," hissed a horrid whisper from the darkness of the rafters. "And he's safe. He has nothing to fear from me. But *you* do."

A hideous cackle arose, reverberating off the arched ceiling and cascading over the trembling mercenary with a symphonic ferocity. Gerard backed away, inching his way back to the church door.

"You should have never taken the girl, Captain," said the

Djinn, still hidden from sight. "Nor the physician. They were innocent. They are good, decent folk and you will suffer for your sins against them."

The mercenary turned toward the door but stopped himself when he saw the Djinn standing behind him. In desperation, he swung his sword wildly, lashing out with all his might. The creature easily parried with his own blade, knocking his grip loose. Gerard's sword flew harmlessly away and out of reach. The demon's backhand smashed against his jaw, sending him sprawling headfirst to the floor.

The mercenary quickly recovered, turning himself over and sitting up to see his tormenter looming above him. His head craned to the right, as a noise in that direction caught his attention. Two shadowy figures emerged from behind the giant pillars that supported the church's ceiling—they were also Djinn! Three of them? How was that possible? His eyes returned to the creature crouching down in front of him, then back to his right. Yes. They were both still there, standing as still as statues. Neither saying a word.

Movement from the rafters above caught his attention. He looked up to see two more djinni materializing from nowhere, glaring down at him like dark sentries from hell.

Suddenly, Gerard found himself surrounded by an army of the demonic creatures. The djinni crowded in around him. They leered at him, perching from the rafters above. To his right and left, more of demons sauntered in from the shadows to envelope the mercenary with their icy, green stares. There had to be at least fifty of them.

Gerard backpedaled, crabwalking across the cold stones of the church's floor to the northern wall. He had to get away, but there was no place to run. He needed to scream for help but knew that none would come in time. He was doomed.

One of the djinni, the one that had backhanded him at the church's entrance, walked toward him in slow, deliberate steps, then stopped and looked down at its prey. For several long moments, nothing happened. The terrified mercenary's brain searched feverishly for any prayers he had long ago forgotten, but none came to him. The creature's blade inched its way to Gerard's constricted throat, teasing the air as a serpent's tongue flickers.

"No," came a hoarse voice from the midst of the demons. A second djinn stepped from the crowd, glowing green eyes illuminating the darkness of its hood. Gerard knew from the creature's posture and voice that this was the same that had wiped out his men in the safe house. This was the same beast that slaughtered his soldiers in the baron's tunnels. This was the leader.

The lesser djinn moved to the side as its captain made its way to stand over their captive.

"You need not die here this night," the Djinn whispered. "You could walk away from here, your head in its proper place. All you need do is perform a small service for me."

What was he hearing? Did the creature believe he would help it? His soul was lost already, but he would not bring further condemnation upon it by allying himself with the enemies of Jehovah. But what choice did he really have? He was hopelessly outnumbered. He had no weapon. Perhaps a ploy.

"Wh-what kind of service?" he asked, absently pressing himself further against the wall. The stench of brimstone burned his nostrils as the creature crouched down to look him in the eye.

"That, mercenary, will be revealed in time," said the Djinn coldly. "Right now, I need your word. You have the same choice that each of these others had. You can join us. Besides, I really have no desire to kill in the House of the Lord."

"House of the Lord?" Gerard asked. "Surely you jest. The only lord you worship is the Prince of Darkness, vile creature."

The Djinn's head slumped down slightly, as if in thought. Then silently, it arose to its full height and sighed.

"Nay, my friend. I worship not the creatures of hell, but Jesus Christ Himself," it said aloud, no longer the rasping voice of a spirit—but that of a man. It was a voice familiar to him, but he could not place it. "I am not a servant of the devil, as you have believed, but one of the Most High…and it is His hand alone that stays my blade against you. I would gladly relieve your neck of the burden of its head for what you did to Isabella and Tufic, but His mercy is now upon me, and I can't bring myself to do what my heart commands me to do. So, I say again, join us." It paused. "Please."

Without waiting for an answer, the Djinn reached up to his hood and pulled it from his head. Black gloved fingers worked quickly, unwrapping the shroud wrapping that covered his face. Slowly, imperceptibly, the grotesque features of the man beneath the Djinn's hood were revealed and Gerard could do nothing but gawk in silence at the sight.

William De L'ombre's leprous and scarred face stood in the place where only moments before the Djinn had basked in his victory over his foe. The brother of the baron himself had been Gregory's demonic spirit of vengeance.

One by one, the army of Djinn removed their hoods, revealing knights that had gone missing over the last few months after encounters with the creature in battle. Gerard recognized many of them. The one that had wanted to filet him with his sword moved forward and unmasked himself—it was the imbecile knight Horatio. A second later, the half-witted face of Samuel stood by his side.

"I should have cut you down for what you did to my cousin, knave," the knight growled. "But it would be a dishonor to him to do so."

Gerard's mind screamed silently from within his skull. This was lunacy. The very idea was beyond preposterous. William was an invalid. He was dying of leprosy. How was it possible that such a man could do the things that the Djinn had done?

The baron's brother bent down again to look Gerard in the face. The mercenary's eyes caught a glimmer of red trickling down William's side. He was injured. By the way he moved, Gerard could tell it was serious.

"My condition," said William to the mercenary's unspoken questions, "has an interesting side effect. Contrary to popular belief, a leper doesn't randomly lose body parts. He loses them because he can feel no pain. When the leper injures himself, the wound goes unnoticed. Growing infected. It often rots to the point where amputation is necessary."

"So that's why you could take such a beating and never seem to be affected by it," said Gerard, finally understanding.

The man who had been the Djinn looked over to the approaching form of Tufic, leaning on the shoulders of Isabella, as they entered into the sanctuary of the church.

"Exactly. Tufic is a brilliant physician and man of science. He has seen to it that my wounds are always properly maintained," William continued. "His experiments with the fungi known as foxfire have provided me with extended periods of strength and spryness that I would not ordinarily have. In addition, the mushroom provides a natural phosphorous illumination that I've used on occasion to give myself the otherworldly appearance that you know all too well."

To his own surprise, a burst of laughter exploded from the mercenary's belly. Gerard knew that he should be terrified, but seeing his great enemy before him now, he couldn't believe how stupid he'd been.

"This is just too much," Gerard said, stifling the laughter that welled up inside him. "I can't believe we fell for such a charade."

Of course, it all made perfect sense. The creature's knowledge of the baron's comings and goings. His ability to always be one step ahead of Gerard's men. His relationship with the baron's daughter.

The mercenary had completely misinterpreted the secret

liaison with Isabella for that of a lover. In reality, it had been a doting uncle that was simply visiting his niece. It was no secret to anyone that William and Isabella's mother had been hopelessly in love with each other. It must have been utter torment when his parents announced the engagement of Gregory to the woman William desperately desired.

Then, after her mother's death, William had naturally fawned over Isabella—that is, until he was captured in battle by Saracen raiders and sold to a sheik as a slave. It had been shortly after that, William had become infected with leprosy...a punishment from God, the baron had said, for his betrayal at being adopted by the Sheik Samir.

And now, after all this time, William had mounted this great offensive against his brother's plans for an *Outremer* conquest. It was sibling rivalry taken to an extreme level.

"Will you join our cause, mercenary?" asked the leper, ignoring Gerard's outburst.

Gerard pushed himself off the floor and stood squarely before his captor. Suddenly, the "demon" no longer seemed so horrifying. The leper's shoulders hunched as the injury to his gut bled out. William was no longer the formidable beast that had threatened him at every turn. He was now only a dying man, determined to see his brother's plans fail.

His army, on the other hand, was another thing entirely. He had seen many of these men fight on a number of occasions. They were good. Very good. Gerard knew that there was only one means of escape from his present scenario—join the baron's brother.

But it was the one thing that he could not agree to. Not that he had any loyalty to Gregory. Nor was he afraid of losing his soul, as he only moments ago feared. No. The reason he could not agree to the Djinn's demands was simple pride. He had been bested by a foul cripple. He had been defeated by an unclean cretin who could hardly even hold onto his sword, but for the medications the Saracen doctor had given him. And it was for that reason that his own humiliation refused to agree to the Djinn's terms.

"And if I don't join you?" he asked.

"The truth is I'm not sure. I'm not a murderer," said William. "But you would not be allowed to leave here freely. Not until we've ended Gregory's campaign and retrieved the *Sefer Yetzirah*."

The Book of Creation? Then, the Djinn had not secured the Book. All was not yet lost for the baron's plans. And, by William's own admission, he was reluctant to kill him. He had a chance. There was a chance he could escape his fate after all.

Gerard paced forward, dipping his head as if considering the leper's proposition. The djinni spread apart, allowing him room to move freely. The mercenary stopped beside the small frame of a young knight named Adam that Gerard knew to be inexperienced.

"You see my dilemma, don't you?" asked Gerard, turning to face his nemesis. "I've been paid to do a job. Unless you offer more than your brother...well, I don't see how I could help you."

"Gerard, please reconsider. We could use..."

William was unable to finish the sentence, as the mercenary sprung toward Adam with all his strength. Wrenching the youngster's sword from his hand, Gerard spun the knight around and pulled him tight against his body as a shield. The sword's blade rested lightly against the boy's neck.

"Now, I'm walking out of here," Gerard spat.

"We can't allow that, DuBois."

The mercenary backed up, guiding his hostage toward the church's door. The djinni army spread apart, making room for him at a nod from William.

"Now, leper, I will take my leave...grrk."

Gerard released his hostage just as something sharp slipped mercilessly into his back. It was the oddest sensation, but a familiar one, as hot and cold mingled around the blade that now pierced him. Blood streamed from his lips as he slowly turned to see the beautiful face of Isabella standing behind him, bloody knife in hand.

"He might not be willing to kill you, monster," she whispered coldly in his ear as he collapsed to the ground. "But I have no such qualms."

The mercenary's eyes grew dim. A great sound of rushing water filled his ears as his lungs struggled to take in breath. And then, he felt no more.

30

"Isabella!" William's cloudy necrotic eyes widened with horror. "What have you done?"

His niece's lithe frame moved slowly around the cooling body that lay crumpled on the sanctuary floor and spat at the beast that had murdered Margaret. Silently, she looked up at William, not offering a word of explanation.

It was no surprise, actually. Isabella had always been a defiant child. When she believed herself to be right, nothing would stay her course. Her will and determination were indomitable. That was why William had spent years secretly training her how to fight…how to be a warrior. If she was going to run out and fight against every sign of injustice, he had been determined to prepare her for any eventuality.

He had not, however, prepared her for murder. He glanced down at the mercenary, whose blood now pooled around his body, then shut his eyes from the sight. Gerard was not a good man. He should not be lamented. Still, the idea of his precious Isabella bloodying her hands—it was something he had never foreseen.

"I'm sorry, Uncle," his niece finally said, a single tear streaking the porcelain contour of her left cheek. "I could not allow him to leave here. You know that."

"He would not have left, child. I had three men in hiding outside. They would have stopped his escape."

Isabella stared helplessly at William. The men who followed the Djinn shifted uncomfortably in the silence. William knew they believed he was being too hard on her. Perhaps he was. But he could not bear the idea of her being guilty of cold-blooded murder. He had fought so hard to avoid killing anyone through his own campaign against Gregory. Yes, there had been unfortunate casualties—the inescapable result of war—but he had intentionally avoided outright murder.

He looked up at Isabella, who seemed unable to tear her eyes away from him—the dead mercenary under her feet completely forgotten. Her lips trembled as she valiantly struggled to hold back an onslaught of tears.

Oh Lord, how much she resembles her mother, William thought. His heart constricted within his chest at the sight. He missed Catherine so much. His niece was all he had left of her, and he had loved her with every ounce of his being from the day she was born. His every breath and thought had been guided by this love...his desire to keep sweet Isabella safe and to see her happy. Now, here she was standing before him, covered in the blood of their enemy as the full terror of her actions threatened to consume her.

Pulling his hood over his face again to protect her from making contact with his diseased skin, he stepped forward and took Isabella into his arms, pulling her tight against him.

"It's all right," he said soothingly into her ear. His gloved hand caressed her back as she heaved in anguish and a flood of tears against him. "Everything will be all right."

"I'm not...It's not him...it's...."

"Shhhhh. No need to talk now. Just let it out."

She pulled away and looked at him from under his hood, shaking her head in defiance.

"You don't understand," she continued. "I'm not concerned about Gerard. I'm glad he's dead. That's not the problem."

William looked around the sanctuary. His men stood transfixed, staring silently at him. Their mouths agape. Streams of tears streaked across many of their own faces. What was going on?

"Uncle, it's not Gerard...it's you," Isabella said.

William's eyes continued staring at his niece. What was wrong with her? Why was she suddenly fading from his sight? She was only inches away, but she seemed so far. He tried to focus his vision, but her image grew dimmer in front of him. His knees buckled underneath him, and he plopped to the stone floor of the church. Although he could no longer see her, he felt Isabella's warm embrace and heard her sweet whisper in his ear.

"Please, Uncle. Please hold on. I can't do this without you."

He felt a single droplet fall to his cheek. His niece's tear. Then, consciousness deserted him entirely.

———

His dreams were dark and scattered. Fantasy and horror mixed with segments of his past. Images of djinni and all sorts of evil spirits plagued his fevered sleep. Darkness whirled around him as nightmarish phantoms slithered fiendishly through the shadows.

I'm dying, William thought to himself as he scanned the dreamscape surrounding him. This is what dying feels like.

He'd nearly died once before—many years ago. The memory flooded his mind's eye, a whirlwind of sorrow and admiration. If he hadn't already been comatose, the impact of the memory would have floored him.

Samir. The man who would eventually adopt him as an adult son—a custom common in the eastern nations—tended his wounds. The battle had been fierce and by all accounts, he had fought valiantly. But it hadn't been good enough. An arrow to his chest would have killed him for sure if not for the tender care and medical expertise of the Saracen sheik that found him alive on the battlefield.

"Be still, boy," Samir had spoken harshly, but William had known the gruffness had been for his own good. "The shaft must be pulled out. One jerk by you and you might as well get ready to meet your ancestors."

William had been so young...three months away from his seventeenth birthday. Much too young to see the atrocities he'd been part of. Even younger to now lay victim to those very same atrocities.

Thankfully, Samir was no slouch when it came to medicine. He'd been trained by the best. From an early age, the sheik's father had sent him on a journey around the world—his brilliant mind absorbing anything it could. And it had soaked up a great deal.

William later learned that medicine had not been the only subject his adopted father had picked up on his journeys. Philosophy, science, and a variety of special fighting skills had been added to his repertoire as well. As had religion...a simple little detail that would change young William's life forever.

"Steady now," Samir gritted his teeth and his two strong hands wrapped themselves around the wooden shaft of the Saracen arrow. With a great heave, William's rescuer yanked the projectile from his chest and brought down a white-hot branding iron on top of the open wound in a single motion.

William couldn't remember screaming, but he knew he had. Even now, forever marred by his horrible illness, unable to feel pain of any kind...even now, William remembered the horrible agony of that single moment. It was as if he were completely reliving it.

"It's all right," said the soothing voice. "Everything is going to be all right."

This time, William heard himself scream. His eyes bolted open to see Tufic's bruised but concerned face bent over him—a red hot poker clenched in his hand.

"William, listen to me," his long-time friend continued. "You're bleeding out. You've got at least three new injuries. And two older ones have reopened. We've got to stop it."

The smell of Tufic's insufferable medicinal fungi weighed heavy in the air. The stuff smelled worse than his own decaying flesh, but William ignored the putrid odor as his eyes looked past Tufic and locked on their target. Isabella. He looked up into her moistened face and smiled as much as he could muster. He wanted to assure her. He still had work to do. He still had purpose. God would surely not call him home until Gregory's plans were finally stopped.

The fire brand seared his flesh with a hiss. He couldn't feel it, but the smell of burned hair and skin flooded his nostrils and he drifted back into the dreamscape once more.

"You're finally awake, eh, lad?"

The younger William sat slowly up in the feather bed of the sheik's palatial tent. The wizened face of his benefactor beamed back at him. Instinctively, William reached for his chest, which he found covered in linen cloths.

"Don't worry, boy," Samir beamed. "You're going to be just fine. Not a thing to worry about."

Obviously, the older man didn't seem to think a Western Christian, immobilized and powerless in a Moslem's home in occupied territory was something to worry about. Every ounce of his soul screamed at him to jump out of bed and run for freedom. All it took was an attempt to sit up to realize how foolish that notion was.

"I'm serious," the sheik said gently. "You've truly nothing to fear from me."

For some strange reason, William believed him. From that moment on, the two formed a deep friendship that would have lasted forever...if not for the jealousy and greed of Samir's eight sons. It was a friendship that meant almost as much to him as...

"Isabella, no!"

"I must see him immediately," William's niece demanded. When she set her mind to something, there was no stopping her. "Tufic, get out of my way."

"He needs his rest," said the physician. "He's stabilized for now, but I'm not sure for how long. He needs time for the foxfire to work. Needs time to recuperate."

Consciousness was slinking its way into William's mind. He knew it was impossible, but it felt as if pain wracked every inch of his body. Phantom pain. Memories. Nothing more.

You silly oaf, thought William. *Lepers, after all, can't feel anything except shame...humiliation.* As much as he tried, William couldn't muster strength enough to open his eyes. He wanted to see Isabella. He wanted to see her mother again. But he couldn't get his lids to cooperate.

"I don't mean to disturb him," Isabella said. "I just want to be near him. He needs me."

"I can assure you, he doesn't even know you're here. He's completely delirious."

Tufic, you fool, let the poor girl in. William wanted to scream. He couldn't even do that right. What had he done to his body to cause it to rebel so completely?

"Isa...Isa..." it was all the once mighty Djinn could choke out.

Silence.

"See, he's awake. He's calling to me!"

A shuffle of feet and fabric rustled to his left as he felt the presence of his niece drawing near.

"Uncle," her sweet breath tossed the words into his ear. He felt pressure on his bandaged hand. She'd taken it into hers and now sat silently at his bedside. "Don't worry, Uncle. I won't leave you again."

William could hold on no longer. Now in the comfort and care of Isabella, he let himself succumb to his exhaustion and slept peacefully.

31

He wasn't quite sure how long he'd been asleep. When he finally came to, William found himself refreshed. Whatever one could say about the putrid stench of Tufic's mushrooms, they were miraculous in their healing powers. They had certainly been useful enough during his campaign against his brother.

"What are we going to do?" William heard someone ask in the next room. He was in a stone bedchamber with no windows. He must still be in the church. And something was going on... something big from the sound of the commotion.

"The only thing we can do," came Horatio's familiar voice. "We've got to defend his homestead."

"Defend it? Gregory's got nearly one hundred men. At best, we might be able to muster forty. How can we defend against such odds?" asked someone William could not quite place.

Yes, something was definitely going on and he needed to be in the midst of it. He should be part of whatever discussion was causing such concern. He struggled to lift himself from the bed, careful not to crash to the floor. Snatching a walking stick from the corner of the room, William made his way toward the round oak door.

"Horatio's correct," said Tufic in hushed tones. He had been struggling to keep the men's voices down for some time now. Good old Tufic. Loyal to the end. "We've really no choice. Gregory's forces are advancing and it's worse than you all realize." He paused to let that sink in. "Our scouts told me that there are twelve giants leading the soldiers now. Twelve massive, clay giants."

Gregory had managed to resurrect Rakeesha's golems? His forces were moving...the lives of his loyal staff and friends were in danger. Another flash of memories flooded his thoughts as he shuffled slowly toward the door...

"SAMIR!" William had screamed as he rounded the hill, looking down on the sheik's ruined settlement. Fires still raged against the landscape as the sun descended over the horizon. His feet had pounded down the sand swept dune towards the sheik's home.

Bodies lay strewn over the land, burned beyond recognition. Livestock dead. Servants dismembered. Samir's elegant palace was now nothing more than embers flitting carefree through the air.

As he walked through the field of blood and death, he found his adoptive father's mutilated body beside that of a Western knight. Both obviously slain in combat. An axe head was lodged at the sheik's shoulders. One leg was nowhere to be found. Darkening blood dried over his leprous face and clothes. A noble and decent man...and he was no more.

"I should have been there," young William said quietly to himself.

His own words snapped him out of the memory. He found his hand on the door handle of the bedchamber. "I should be there." And he opened the door to the surprised faces of his men, Tufic, and Isabella. William realized then that he had failed to wrap his face in linen. The very sight must have been repugnant to those unaccustomed to his true visage.

"What is it?" he said, a bit more confidently than he felt. "What is going on?"

One of his knights ran to him, Tufic trying to stop him. The knight's face looked haggard and scared.

"Sir, its Gregory. Scouts report that he's amassed a group of knights and they're heading to your homestead even as we speak. Our spies tell us he knows who you are and is going there to take some mystical artifacts he believes you to have."

Tufic stepped up, concern plainly visible on his face.

"Don't worry, William," the physician said. "We'll handle it. You need your rest."

William knew better. He also knew Tufic knew better. He may be temporarily mobile, but it wouldn't last long. William knew that he'd simply lost too much blood. No amount of rest would save him now. He was living on borrowed time. Besides, Tufic was certainly in no shape to lead the men against Gregory. He was still nursing his own injuries.

"I have to be there," William said, memories of the massacre of his adopted family still fresh in his mind. "You and I both know it's true, Tufic. I cannot allow my brother to get his hands on the Ring of Aandaleeb. The lives of everyone in the Outremer are in peril, my friend. I have fought one of those golems. I know its power. An entire army of them would be indestructible." Then, seeing that his friend was about to protest, he raised up placating hands. "No arguments on this. My mind is made up. This is *my* battle. This is my quest. I must see it to the end."

"No!" Isabella protested. "You can't, Uncle. You're too weak. If you go, you'll die."

"Dear niece, nothing will stop that now," he said, his heart feeling heavy in his chest. He wasn't afraid to die, but he hated the thought of leaving her. "I must do this. Your father must be stopped...at all costs. No one person's life is worth the lives of thousands. If Gregory gains possession of his clay army, people will die. It's as simple as that."

She looked at him silently for several long seconds. Fear and indecision were painted on her face. Suddenly, she took a sword leaning against the wall and slid it into the leather scabbard tied to her belt.

"Well, then," she said. "Let's go."

32

S ean Ellis and Richard Nichols had only been in the *Outremer* for six months. They'd both come from a small village in southern England when the Pope called for more soldiers of the cross to defend the Church's interests in the Holy Land. How could they have refused? Their own salvation, according to the Holy See, was at stake. And so, the two, who had been friends from childhood, had joined the first group of soldiers that had passed through their town, sailed *beyond the sea*, and had been assigned to sentry duty the moment they arrived in Jerusalem.

It had not been as dull an occupation as one might expect. After all, they had arrived at the ancient city about the same time that tales of that supernatural creature—the one the Saracens called a djinn—had begun to haunt the streets and carry unsuspecting soldiers away to the gates of hell.

No, neither Sean nor Richard had ever been bored, though they had confided in each other on a number of occasions that they wished they had. Ordinarily, guard duty would have been the sort of thing that would be perfect for them. It wasn't physically demanding. Very rarely did sentries ever see any action—and therefore, the danger should have been at a minimum. And it allowed them a great deal of time to concentrate on the thing they loved more than anything else... weaving stories into songs to be sung back in their local pub.

But they'd had very little opportunity to develop their skill as bards. This spirit...this Djinn...had kept the entire city on edge the entire time they'd been there. Sentries were expected to pay extra close attention to anything strange or unusual and if it was discovered the creature was able to get past any of the guards, severe punishment would be levied for incompetence.

So it was because of this hyper-vigilance that the two, as they patrolled near the Ephraim Gate of Jerusalem as the sun began to rise on the eastern horizon, stopped in their tracks when they heard the heavy footstep from somewhere in the shadows to their right. Simultaneously, they looked at one another with wide eyes and turned to face the darkness of what they hoped was an unoccupied alley.

"Hullo?" asked Richard, waving his lit torch in the direction of the shadows.

"Anyone there?" asked Sean.

Thud.

Another footstep echoed from the alley. Loud.

"I don't quite like this," Richard said to his friend as he withdrew his sword from the leather scabbard at his belt.

"You think it's that Djinn-thing?" asked Sean, extracting his own blade and holding it out in front of him.

"I dunno." Richard took a single step forward, trying to peer into the early dawn gloom. "Way I hears it, the Djinn-thing is a spirit. Don't make no sense he'd be makin' all sorts of noise, cloddin' on around here. I always imagined 'im to be a bit more... I dunno, subtle or something."

Suddenly, a shadow filled the alleyway in front of them. A massive shadow. Richard and Sean stumbled backwards at the sight, falling to the ground as a pillar-like leg stepped into view.

Then another. And as the two guards looked helplessly up, a gargantuan monster stepped out into the light. Its size was immense—nearly twelve feet tall and three feet wide. The thing was roughly the shape of a man with a great head upon its shoulders and no face. It looked as if it was made of mud or slime, and it continued to lumber toward them.

"Sweet Mary, mother of our Lord," Sean muttered as he crab walked backwards to get away from the beast.

Richard was unable to form any words at all, nor move, as he sat paralyzed on the stone walkway. His eyes took in every detail of the monstrosity before him. Every rounded edge of its body. Every carved muscle. Each of the intricately drawn pictograms that decorated its muddy hide—pictograms that almost seemed to glow in the dim light.

It continued to walk toward them with giant, menacing strides and neither of the guards' brains worked well enough to instruct them to lift their swords to defend themselves. Though, in hindsight, it was probably a very good thing they hadn't. The golem known to only a few as the Warden strode past, leaving them both mercifully unmolested as it approached the city gate.

Though the two guards were totally unaware that the creature had been created by King Solomon himself or what its dark purpose had been, they would later swear to their comrades over several pints of ale that as it moved on, they could have sworn the beast uttered a single word...

BOOK.

33

William's homestead was in chaos. Smoke billowed from the servants' domiciles that now burned in the late morning sunlight. Most of Gregory's forces busied themselves tearing the place apart, searching for the ring their master desperately sought. There were a few, however, that focused their attention on more entertaining pursuits, as they, with mocking jeers, impaled the few brave souls who stood up to protect their loved ones from the carnage.

The women they were trying to protect were shoved brutally to the ground, bound with ropes, and forced to watch as their fathers, husbands, and sons were slaughtered before their eyes. Even William's prized hunting dogs were targeted by the baron's horde, clubbed to death to keep the mongrel blood from staining their swords.

A handful of servants almost managed to escape but were targeted by the baron's expert archers as they ran in terror from the bloodbath.

Intoxicated by the rivers of blood that pooled around their feet, the soldiers laughed and jeered, thoroughly enjoying the debauched massacre they had perpetrated. All the while, being mindful to steer clear of the eight living statues that surrounded the encampment...Gregory's golem warriors, who even now kept vigil over the horizon, awaiting the one their master had instructed they should seize on sight.

For the living, breathing, armor-wearing variety of Gregory's soldiers, the golems were something to avoid at all costs. They were happy to continue with their desecration of the property owned by the baron's traitorous brother, so long as they would not have to get within fifty feet of the eight clay horrors that surrounded them.

"It's just the way they stand there," said one of Gregory's knights, as he wiped blood from his blade. "Not moving. Staring into nothing."

"Aye," replied his comrade. "And their faces...why give them animal heads? They frighten me far more than the Djinn ever did, I tell you. There's something just plain evil about them."

The two knights shuddered as they stared unapologetically at the creatures, each with the body of a man and the head of a different type of animal: jackal, magpie, monkey, horse and crocodile were the most recognizable. There was also one that resembled an elephant. Another might have been a hippopotamus, but the final creature was completely unrecognizable from the ravages of time. And these didn't even include the other four—the biggest and meanest looking of them all—that accompanied Baron Gregory into William's tent.

"What do you suppose they're doing in there?" said the first knight, nodding toward the elaborate domicile.

"No idea. Probably the same as we are...looking for m'lord's silly little ring and having fun along the way." The two soldiers laughed as they turned their gaze to the bountiful selection of exotic beauties that now lay bound and helpless on the desert floor. "And speaking of fun..."

SCREEEEEEEE!

The sudden shriek erupted from high above. Every man

looked up for the source of the cry, almost as one. The sun was almost completely overhead, blinding each man as he gazed into the sky.

SCREEEEEEEEEEEEEEEEEE!

Another cry, more piercing than the first. Each soldier knew what the sound was, though no one wanted to admit it. They had heard the stories. Heard about the spectral falcon—black as pitch —that was the harbinger of the creature known as the Djinn. Some said it was no bird at all, but rather all the souls of the men the demon had killed, wrapped up in the form of a raptor, and forced to do the Djinn's bidding.

SCREEEEEEEEEEEEEEEEEEEEEEEEE!

The third screech was loudest of all and demanded even the stoic attention of Gregory's golems. The knights watched as all eight of the clay behemoths turned their animalistic heads toward the heavens and watched silently as a tiny black dot above the clouds drew closer.

"It's the Djinn!" shouted one of the knights from the periphery of the homestead. "The Djinn is coming!"

"We know that, you oaf," yelled another soldier. "We can see his demonic bird. No need to announce it."

"No...no...no!" cried the first, pointing to the eastern horizon. "I mean, the Djinn is coming from over there!"

They each turned to where their comrade was pointing. Sure enough, there, no more than a half mile away, sitting smugly on his black steed atop the closest ridge, was the black-clad form of the Djinn. Even from this distance, they could see his ebon blade gleaming in the sunlight.

Somehow, from this distance and in the light of day, he just did not seem like much of a threat. A few of the knights even laughed, though a bit nervously.

"'Tis but one man," a few chanted. "No matter how supernatural he may be, we are one hundred strong. And we have the Clay Men to watch our backs."

"Let him come!" shouted a few more, as they raised their own swords into the air.

For several long moments, they waited. No one moved. Even the steady breeze that had been wafting up from the Jordan seemed to have stopped. A few nervous coughs erupted here and there, but other than that, every man remained perfectly still. Though, if anyone had been paying the slightest attention, they would have seen each of the eight golems turn slightly to face the Djinn's direction.

SCREEEEEEEEEEEEEEEE! The falcon cried again, this time much closer. A single brave archer nocked an arrow with trembling hand and fired. The shaft flew wide, and the bird veered to the west...toward its master. The archer cringed beneath the icy glares of his compatriots.

Then, the Djinn spurred his horse and took off at a gallop toward William's encampment.

"It's attacking!" cried the knight who first spotted their foe on the ridge. "It's...bloody attacking! Alone. Us."

The sheer audacity of the move sent a shockwave of fear through the troops, their confidence waning. After all, what manner of man—or creature—would dare pursue a full-frontal assault on an entire army by himself? But as the dust kicked up by the Djinn's steed began to settle, a sight greeted them that melted the resolve of all but the bravest of Gregory's men. Close on the Djinn's heels rode a company of well-armed, black-robed figures, their swords outstretched and at a full charge toward camp. An entire army of djinni was descending on the besieged homestead and the invaders could only stare at the wave of death that now bore down on them.

34

T he Djinn and his army drew down on the camp at full gallop. As they approached, eight sets of two men paired together and rode hard toward each of the golem sentries. The rest headed straight toward the cowering soldiers and their hapless victims.

The Djinn watched the scene unfold as if hovering outside his body. As close to death as he already was, that might not have been a figment of his imagination. Still, he watched as his friends and loved ones attacked Gregory's forces as one cohesive unit. His *Knightshades*.

On the ride to his homestead, it had been Horatio who'd suggested the title. He'd pointed out that William's last name—*De L'Ombre*—meant "of the shadows" in the tongue of his homeland, so it only made sense that his knights take on the name as well. It was a good name. An honorable name, though he prayed to God above that these men—and Isabella, whom he loved so dearly—would never have to use it after this day.

Horatio. William watched from his steed as he and Tufic approached the jackal-headed golem. With practiced ease, his friend tossed the Saracen physician one end of a rope and pulled it taut just as they passed the monstrous creature. The line snagged against the golem's legs, sending it to the ground with a vicious crash. Its moist body landed hard, its momentum crushing the golem's backside with the impact.

One by one, each of the golems fell this way, eliciting shouts of victory from the Knightshades. But the Djinn knew their victory would be short-lived. Such a minor setback would not keep the supernatural creatures down for long and then his friends would be lost.

Sagging on Al-Ghul's saddle, he caught the attention of those who had toppled the golems and pointed toward the host of Gregory's men, now in fierce combat with the others. "Go! Help them! I'll take care of our muddy friends."

All but three obeyed the command without question. Tufic, Horatio, and Isabella, however, remained.

"And how, pray tell, do you plan to do that?" the physician said, looking down at the Djinn, who had already dismounted. "I'm not fool enough to think that these monstrosities are defeated."

He pointed down at the fallen golems, who even now struggled to reshape themselves.

The Djinn shrugged the question away. "Never mind that. I'll think of something."

Horatio shook his head. "Even if you could, have you noticed something? There are only eight of these things. There are supposed to be twelve. That's four more you'll have to deal with, even if you do manage to dispatch these fallen ones." The knight jumped down from his horse to face his friend, who slouched over in obvious pain. "Where do you suppose they are, I wonder?"

"Most probably with Gregory, in my tent—his personal bodyguards," He remained silent for several seconds as if in thought, then suddenly spoke. "Which is exactly where I need to draw these." He nodded to the eight that were now, slowly, staggering to their feet.

"What?" Tufic asked. "Why draw them in there?"

"Because there is only one way we can possibly defeat all of them at once. I'll need to lead them down into the laboratory."

The physician grimaced.

"Forgive me, old friend, but don't be daft," he said. "I know what you intend and it's madness."

"What?" Isabella finally spoke up. "What is he planning? Uncle, what are you planning?"

The Djinn stared at her from behind his shroud, then glanced over at the monsters who were fully righted and now lumbering toward them. "We haven't the time to argue!"

The monkey-faced golem lunged forward, its mighty arms swinging wildly toward William's head. Feigning left, he tucked his legs in and rolled to the right, then leapt into the air and brought his sword crashing down into its left shoulder. The blade sunk into its clay flesh and the Djinn hung onto the hilt, swinging up and onto the monster's back. He jerked the scimitar free and began hacking away at the golem's exposed neck.

The other golems converged, moving swiftly to assist their besieged brother. Before they got within ten feet, however, Horatio and Tufic unleashed their own flurry of jabs and parries. Their own swords sung through the air, biting into the moistened clay-like flesh.

"Stop!" the Djinn shouted from his perch on the monkey-golem's shoulder. "They're too powerful!"

But it was too late. The jackal-golem grabbed Horatio around the waist and slung him through the air. The brave knight crashed into the remains of a servant's tent, still smoldering with flames.

"No!" William yelled, diving to the ground and rushing to his fallen friend. Tufic and Isabella joined him as they kicked away the smoking debris. They found Horatio, lying on his back, his right leg bent at an impossible angle. Blood oozed from his nose and mouth.

"How we doing?" the battered knight asked. His words were slurred. "Did I get him?"

William looked over at the physician, his question unspoken.

"I think it looks worse than it is," Tufic replied. "Some broken bones. Possibly some internal damage. If we can get him off the battlefield, I should be able to save him." The physician paused. "But that would leave you defenseless."

William shook his head as he glanced over his shoulder to see the golems now advancing on their position. "Never mind about me. Get him out of here," he said, then nodded to his niece. "Tufic will need your help too, Isabella. He can't carry Horatio by himself."

"I won't leave you," she said, tears streaking her battle-weary face. "You can't take those things on by yourself. I can help."

He turned once more to look at the advancing behemoths. They were slowly gaining ground and there simply was no more time to argue.

"Horatio needs you more," he said sternly. Then, his face softened behind his veil. "Look, I've already told you…I have faced one of these things before. They cannot be defeated with sword or arrow. They cannot be stopped once set upon their mission. The only way we are going to be able to defeat them is to follow in the footsteps of Solomon himself."

"You mean entombing them," she said. Her voice raised a single octave higher. "But how?"

The Djinn's only response was to stand and face the twelve giants that were now only five feet away. He withdrew his scimitar again and gave it a single, fierce swing. "I *am* their current mission. They're fixated on me, not you. If I run, they will follow me. You will be safe. You all will be safe."

"Tufic? What's he planning?"

The physician ignored the question as he cast his gaze back to Horatio. Then he looked over to his master. "How will you get them to the lab?"

"Don't ignore me!" Isabella yelled. "Don't you dare ignore me. I deserve to know."

"Goodbye, sweet Isabella," William said, without turning to look at her. "No one could possibly be prouder than I am of you. I love you."

"Wait, Uncle!"

But he was already gone.

———————

ISABELLA SPUN around looking for William but could only see the golems pursuing him in the direction he'd run. For such large, cumbersome creatures, they were fiercely fast, and she knew her uncle could not maintain his pace for long. Eventually, they would catch up to him and she could only pray he'd survive the encounter.

She knew she should do something to help him, but understood that in the end, she could not offer the assistance he truly needed. As much as she hated to admit it, he was right. The important thing was to remove Horatio and the other wounded from the battlefield and tend to their wounds.

For the first time since arriving at William's homestead, she wondered how the others were fairing and took in her surroundings. To the south, the battle raged on. Though Gregory's forces outnumbered the Knightshades more than two to one, the tide was already turning in their favor. Many of the invaders had fled at the sight of a tidal wave of dark-clad djinni charging toward them for a battle. Those that remained simply lacked the skill, or even more importantly, the heart to defend their position adequately. Even now, the throng of the baron's knights were being pushed back.

"Isabella?" She heard Tufic saying her name, but the fierce battle enthralled her, holding her gaze as if lulled into a waking dream by a siren's song. Steel clashed against steel as the warriors on both sides fought fiercely. Screams and battle cries erupted around her like the baying of great beasts during a full moon. She smelled the iron tang of blood now pooling near her feet and...

"Isabella! I need your help!"

Dazed, she looked down at the physician who was trying desperately to lift the fallen Horatio. Finally, breaking free of the spell of battle, she bent down to lend Tufic a hand.

"I'm sorry," she said, taking the injured knight's legs and lifting. "Where should we take him?"

Struggling to keep Horatio's stocky frame aloft, he nodded to the east, just past the wooden fence that once held William's livestock. It was far enough away from the battle to shield them while Tufic took care of the wounds.

As they stumbled toward their destination, something glinted in the horizon, nearly blinding Isabella. Her eyes, adjusting quickly to the glare, peered into the distance where they made out the source of the light. A man stood alone on the ridge from which only a few short minutes ago they had ridden.

Only something was off. Strange about the man. He seemed too straight. Too tall. Too rigid as it watched the battle below. She tried to focus...tried to get a better look as she continued carrying Horatio to the animal pen...but the distance was too great.

But the odd light that had originally caught her attention seemed to grow brighter with each second. Soon, she realized that it was not coming from a reflection in the sunlight as she had originally believed, but rather, it came from the man himself...sharp lines of pale blue illumination shown from strange patterns carved into its flesh. It was then that Isabella realized what she was looking at.

On the western ridge, casually taking in the scene of the fierce battle, stood the golem created by King Solomon himself. The golem known simply as the Warden. And though she had no idea what its intentions were, its very presence sent a wave of dread down her spine.

35

"Where are they?" Gregory screamed, bringing both fists down on a gold-encrusted chest resting precariously on an intricately carved writing table within William's bedchamber. He'd searched every nook within the antiquated palatial tent but had yet to find either the Book of Creation or Solomon's ring. He had just about given up the search when he'd stumbled upon the strange, bejeweled box hidden in a secret compartment behind his brother's bed. Though the box was much too small to house the scroll, it had been the perfect size for a piece of jewelry. Yet when he'd finally managed figured out the puzzle box's secret, it had been empty.

With a frustrated snarl, he threw the chest across the table. He was running out of time. He'd heard the battle raging outside for the better part of five minutes now. He had hoped to have bested his brother's efforts at hiding the artifacts from him long before his enemies made their appearance known. Soon, he would be forced to admit to William that he'd been unable to find them. He would have force William to show him where the ring and book were, which would merely heap more humiliation on the baron than he'd already had to endure.

With a sigh, he glanced over at the four golems keeping their protective vigil at the chamber door—the lion and boar-headed ones to his left and the eagle and viper-headed ones to his right. They, along with their brethren, had been programmed for one thing and one thing only: to bring the Djinn to him alive. It was yet another cruel injustice he'd had to deal with once reanimating his indestructible minions. They could only be instructed with a single task at a time. A sheet of parchment with only one line of instructions, inserted into the base of the creature's head was the only way they could receive commands. More than one command and the clay automatons would shut down entirely, as if multiple orders overwhelmed them to the point of inaction. It was a flaw that he hoped the *Sefer Yetzirah* would remedy.

So, upon the golems' reanimation, the baron had carefully considered his next move. He knew he would be unable to proceed with his plans without either the book or the ring, so the obvious course of action would be to reacquire them from his irksome brother. But he also knew that William's cunning was formidable. He would not make the search for the artifacts an easy one. Therefore, the only real recourse was to focus his golems entirely on William's capture.

Gregory again turned his attention to the room and with another sigh, began going through the debris from his previous ransacking. They were here somewhere. He knew it. But he was becoming even more convinced that his brother would have chosen a place to hide such prizes where no one could possibly find them. He was just too smart to do anything less. It was maddening to know that the prizes he'd sought for so long were forever outside his reach because of his little brother's craftiness.

The baron suddenly stiffened. His head arched upward. His nostrils flared twice, taking in the putrid aroma that had become so familiar to him since William developed leprosy. It was the stench of decaying flesh. So distinctive. Yet, it had been a great asset to William as he had struggled to create the legend of the Djinn. The stench of brimstone. The essence of hellfire.

But it was the heavy thud of pillar-like feet clomping into the foyer of William's home, that truly told him that he had run out of time. His brother was finally here.

The baron turned to face the bedroom's door just as the black-robed visage of the Djinn entered, held tight by the powerful grip of two golems on either side. The remaining six huddled close behind, blocking his path should he manage to slip free. Despite his predicament, William appeared perfectly at ease. Almost content... as if he'd planned to be apprehended by the baron's automatons.

Gregory's eyes narrowed at his brother. The golems, as if sensing their master's ire, shifted their stances. Their backs arched. Their animal-like heads followed the baron's gaze.

"Where are they?" he asked. "I know they're here. Solomon's ring. The Book of Creation. You have them. Tell me where they are."

Their task complete, the golems released their grip on William, who pulled himself away from his captors and paced casually toward the baron. Though Gregory could tell he was trying hard not to show it, his brother was injured. Severely. As a matter of fact, the slump of his shoulder...the limp in his gait... his nemesis looked to be on his very last leg.

Despite himself, Gregory felt a twinge of regret. They were brothers, after all. So much time wasted. So much pain between them. But he stifled the feelings and gritted his teeth as William approached. He still had a destiny to fulfill and going soft now would result in too many squandered sacrifices.

The *Djinn*—Gregory really had to stop thinking of him as his brother—stepped within three paces of him and stopped.

Silence.

The wretch knew how much refusing to answer his question would infuriate him. William also knew that he needed every advantage he could get if he hoped to win against the baron's superior sword fighting skills. He was good, yes...but Gregory had always been better...except when his emotions betrayed his natural skill at sword play. Driven by anger or frustration, Gregory had a nasty habit of becoming sloppy. It was a fact that had allowed the Djinn to best him a few days before while in the baron's very own bedchambers. Gregory was certain it was exactly what his foe was gambling on now.

"Answer me!" Gregory drew his sword and edged the point directly against the Djinn's throat.

WILLIAM GLANCED SERENELY DOWN at the blade, his hands clasped loosely behind his back. He looked back to meet his brother's enraged gaze. For added effect, the leper reached up and pulled the shrouded hood from his head, revealing the monstrosity that had become of his face. Gregory could never stomach the sight, not that William blamed him. The disease had all but eaten his entire face away. Only his eyes and a portion of lips remained of his once-handsome features.

"I said, where are they?" Gregory's voice now croaked out as menacing whisper. The blade pressed harder against William's chest. "Better yet, show me."

"The book isn't here," he said, his voice soft. Soothing.

"You're lying!" The baron's face twisted with rage. "Show me. Now."

"I do have the ring, yes," William said. His eyes never left his brother's own gaze. "But your friend, the hashshashin, took the *Sefer Yetzirah* from me. I've no idea where it is now."

Gregory's blade eased away slightly. A look of bewilderment etched across his face as he obviously contemplated whether to believe him or not. With a sudden growl, he whipped the sword away and spun, slashing a row of candles resting upon a candelabra.

"That traitor!" he yelled. "That Saracen piece of filth. Al-Dula has betrayed me."

"Did you expect any different, brother? Was he not already betraying his master, Saladin?"

Gregory glared at him, his eyes leaden with molten fury. Then, after taking several deep breaths, he nodded.

"Fine. I'll deal with him later," he said, placing his sword's tip once more against William's throat. His voice was much calmer now, which made his next command all the more daunting. "For now, you will show me where you have hidden the ring."

"And you know I can't do that," he finally responded, gently pushing the blade aside with his gloved hand. He could not give into Gregory's demands too easily. It would draw suspicion. For his plan to work, the baron would have to believe he was doing all of this against his will. "It's too dangerous, Gregory. Solomon's Seal...all it represents...all it can do...it's too dangerous to be possessed by anyone."

But the baron's blade pressed deeper into his neck.

"I'm serious, brother," William said, looking cautiously at the twelve immobile golems that surrounded them in the room. "I will not give you the ring. I cannot."

Suddenly, the baron roared, bringing his sword over his head and back down towards his brother's ghastly visage. "Then you will die!"

William rolled easily out of the way before the blade struck, drawing his own sword from his scabbard as he came to his feet. He'd have to be more careful in the future. The swing had nearly taken his left arm off.

"You don't understand," Gregory seethed. "They are the key, brother, the key to ending this insane quest. The means to destroy the Saracen hordes once and for all. The means of establishing a true divine kingdom right here on earth!"

He swung the sword again, though it wasn't even close. But then, it wasn't intended to be. Despite Gregory's hatred for his brother, William doubted that he really wanted him dead. They were brothers, after all, despite their differences of opinion and common love shared for the baron's dead wife. When all was said and done, the leper believed that bond of brotherhood had never truly been broken.

Gregory heaved the sword a third time, only to have it strike against the Djinn's scimitar in a blur of motion. Sparks blazed from the impact of both weapons. William's grip on his sword's hilt had been too loose and his arms jarred violently from the blow. He stumbled backward and tripped on the debris left over from Gregory's search. Landing on his back, he flipped himself over just seconds before the baron's blade dug deep into the earth where William had been.

"Gregory, listen to me," he said, raising his scimitar in defensive position. "It is madness. The Ring of Aandaleeb will be your destruction."

Another swipe blocked by the Djinn's blade.

"You're wrong!"

William was beginning to think that he'd made a mistake in pursuing Gregory on his own. He'd lost so much blood already. His strength was quickly fading. He had no idea how long he could continue his charade before he succumbed to the inevitable. He also knew that if he couldn't win, the baron would kill every one of his servants until he discovered where he'd hidden the accursed ring. He would have to give into the baron's demands before that happened.

"I'm not. King Solomon himself knew of the ring's danger," he said, side-stepping another thrust. But before he could turn to fend off the next attack, his weakened knees buckled, sending him crashing to the floor.

Taking advantage of the fortuitous turn of events, the baron lunged, bringing his sword down onto the Djinn's chest. Though he held off on plunging it in and finishing him off.

"You're beaten, brother," Gregory said with a sneer. "Show me where the ring is or die now. I will have no more mercy on you."

William lay on his back, the tip of the sword close enough to shave his face if the baron was so inclined. His eyes darted around the room, landing on the exit. Though the golems filled a major portion of the chamber, they had left the doorway wide open.

The baron caught his glance at the door and smiled.

"Oh, I wouldn't try it if I were you," he said. "I could only instruct them for one task, but that happens to be your capture. Even if you made it through the doorway, they would be upon you in seconds. It is the one thing they will do to the end of time or until I give them a new command. So, as you see, there really is no choice. If you want to live—or more importantly, if you want your friends to live—you will give me the Seal."

With a sigh, William closed his eyes and nodded. "Very well," he said. "But know this, I will show you only to save the lives of those I hold dear. If it was only my life on the line, you would have lost this day."

Gregory returned the nod, his smile even broader. "I can live with that," he said, backing away to allow his brother to stand up. "Now, show me."

As William slowly moved toward the door, the twelve golems moved in step, surrounding him as he marched. Silently, the motley group negotiated the voluminous tent that that had been the leper's home for so long. Finally, they made their way to the library, where he pointed to the trap door, carefully concealed in the wooden boards of the floor.

"It's down there," he said, bending down to uncover the opening. "My laboratory."

Gregory peered down into the darkness hesitantly. "How do I know this isn't some sort of trap?"

William shrugged. "You don't. But you asked me to show you where I kept the ring…and if you want it, we've got to go down to get it."

After a moment of quiet contemplation, the baron nodded, then gestured toward the trap door. "You first but remember… my golems are faster than they look. If you try to escape, they will be on you in seconds." He paused, looking at his brother's sagging form. "And I daresay you aren't in any shape to handle much more abuse from them."

Without replying, William moved onto the narrow stone staircase that led to the caverns underneath his estate. Though the fit was tight, and they were forced to crouch, the clay sentries followed next, in single file. The baron brought up the rear. Once they were all safely in the underground labyrinth, the leper reached for a torch resting in a sconce and lit it. He handed the torch to his brother and then took one for himself.

"Be careful," he said as he started walking into a dark tunnel. "It is treacherous down here. Follow closely or you'll get lost."

Within five minutes, the group stalked into the vast underground chamber the Djinn had used for his laboratory. Without a word, William traversed the circular room, lighting each of the nine torches that lined the walls. For the first time in years, the entire chamber was illuminated by pale, yellow flames. The chamber was supported by four sturdy wooden beams made from cedar. A pair of barrels with Asian pictograms scrawled across them rested against each of the beams. Tufic's mushroom patch, along with the laboratory table beside it, were near the center. To their left, several strange-looking stuffed dummies hung from cords attached to the ceiling—telltale signs of combat practice evident on their canvas bodies.

"All right," the baron said, impatiently. "Where is it?"

With a defeated nod, William walked to the lab table, its glass vials and crucible shining in the torchlight. He crouched down beneath the table and pulled out a small golden box. Turning to face Gregory, he opened the box to reveal the arcane ring with which he'd been so obsessed all these years.

"Give it to me!" Gregory shouted, stretching out his hand. "Now!"

Reluctantly, he closed the chest's lid and placed it in his brother's open palm. He was risking a great deal now. The timing would have to be perfect. The last thing he wanted was for Gregory to catch onto his plan before he left the laboratory. Despite the enmity between them, William wanted his brother to survive—for Isabella's sake, if nothing else. He would need to keep him distracted so he wouldn't look into the chest until after he left.

"Tell me something," William said as his brother turned to leave. "Now that you have the ring, what will you do? With the Book of Creation in Al-Dula's possession, what can you possibly hope to accomplish?"

"Have no fear about that, brother," Gregory said. "I'll deal with that traitorous…"

A streak of silver flew suddenly through the chamber, cutting the baron's sentence short and sending William crashing to the floor. Recovering quickly, the leper rolled over and pulled himself into a sitting position. A silver dagger was lodged in his chest, just inches away from his heart.

Though his golems, as usual, remained perfectly still, Gregory crouched down, panic painted on his face. His hands trembled as he reached for the handle of the blade sunk deep in his brother's chest, obviously wrestling with indecision on whether to pull it out.

"Traitorous what?" a voice asked from behind them.

William and the baron looked simultaneously to the chamber's entrance. One of the Knightshades stood in the door, eyes glazed, mouth stricken in an unnatural grimace. The warrior didn't move. He merely stared into the space behind the two brothers, oblivious to their presence. Then, he toppled to the ground, a similar silver dagger shoved through his spine.

A figure of a man, shrouded in shadow, slithered into view from behind the fallen knight. Stepping into the torchlight, the hashshashin sneered victoriously at Gregory.

"Traitorous what?" he repeated.

The baron glanced at William, whose teeth now clenched as he yanked the dagger out of his own chest. Taking his shroud, he pressed it against the wound, hoping to stave off the bleeding. Gregory stood up from his brother's side, his chin lifted defiantly at this new threat.

"Traitorous *swine*," he said, glaring at Emir. To a Moslem, calling them something as unclean as a pig was the most blasphemous of insults. "Both you and your gluttonous master. You had planned on betraying me all along, hadn't you?"

"That had been the plan, yes."

William, watching the exchange, struggled to raise himself to his feet. This was going to get ugly very fast. Gregory was good, but no match for the hashshashin that now threatened them both.

Whether he liked it or not, William would have to help his brother if there was any hope for his plan to succeed.

G regory caught William's attempt to stand from the corner of his eye. *Stay down, you idiot*, he thought as he glanced back at Emir.

William continued struggling, pushing his back against one of the cavern's support beams. He inched his way up, face grim, until he was finally at his feet. *Father would be proud*, Gregory mused. Despite the baron's position as first-born, it had always been William who had demonstrated the qualities and determination of true nobility. Gregory had always envied him for it. Now, he realized, he was proud of him too.

"Now, if you do not mind," Emir said, stretching out his hand. "The chest...please."

Gregory absently backed himself up against the wall as Emir slunk toward him. The hashshashin's eyes gleamed in the torchlight—eyes of Death himself. Undeterred, the baron leveled his blade chest level with the Saracen cleric. His other hand pawed the chest and placed it gently in a satchel around his neck.

"I'm afraid I can't allow that," he said, wishing he sounded more convincing than he felt. Gregory knew that he was no match for a man born and bred to kill people in the name of Allah. "Your master will never lay a finger on the Seal."

Emir's face darkened, eyes narrowing to slits.

"Then my orders are to see to it that you never leave this place alive," he said. "And the seal will be mine anyway."

Gregory looked around, pleading silently for his golem guardians to take up arms against this killer. But he knew it was futile. The only thing they would do now was keep his own brother within arm's reach.

Speaking of...where did he go?

William was nowhere in sight. As the baron and the assassin had kept each other occupied in their current discourse, William had disappeared. He'd obviously fled to save his own skin.

So much for pride, he thought. *Though how he managed to slip past my golems is beyond me.*

Gregory knew that he was in this alone. His golems would be of no help. His knights were busy above fighting their own battle with the Djinn's own army. And his brother had left him to his fate. No, he would have to defend the ring by himself. It was all that mattered now. He could not allow the Saracen to use its power...especially in conjunction with the *Sefer Yetzirah*. He had long ago given up faith in the God of the Pope, but he was a Crusader to the hilt. He would never allow the heathen warlord access to the limitless power those two artifacts wielded. He would see to their destruction first.

Emir struck without warning. Spinning around, the assassin's hand whipped Gregory's blade from his grip. His right leg, following close behind slammed against the baron's jaw. Teeth and blood exploded from Gregory's mouth as he fell backwards, shattering the worktable into splinters.

The baron had never seen such speed. There had been no time to react and now, much like he had done with William only moment ago, the assassin loomed over him, white teeth splayed beneath a thick black mustache and beard.

"I have longed for this day from the moment we first met, infidel," Emir said, staring down at his fallen adversary. "Lord Al-Dula believed we had use for you, but it has always been a dishonor to Allah. I will take great pleasure in bleeding the life from you."

Emir drew his sword from the brown leather scabbard behind his back and raised it above his head. Gregory was stricken with indecision, unable to move...he could only stare up at his killer helplessly.

A strange whistle erupted suddenly, catching both their attention just before a silver object flew into the assassin's back. Wheeling in pain, desperately grappling with the six-inch dagger now imbedded deep, Emir whirled around to see the Djinn's dark form crouching precariously on a wooden cross beam several feet off the ground.

"I believe you dropped something," he said, his gravelly voice betraying his weakened state.

It was all the distraction Gregory needed. Lifting his legs, he kicked the assassin's flailing figure across the room to crash headfirst to the ground.

"Get out of here," William called down from the rafter, just before flipping backwards to land catlike on both feet. He looked at his brother again, eyes now hidden behind the dark turban of the Djinn. "Now."

The baron looked toward the door. Freedom and absolute power were only yards away. Once he crossed the threshold and found his way to the stairs, he'd be safe. Dashing to the entrance, he struggled with the desire to look back. *Not now*, he thought as the doorway loomed closer. *If you do, you'll regret it.*

He halted, just shy of freedom, and turned around. Emir had risen from the floor and was pummeling William with blow after blow to his mid-section. The once formidable Djinn now lay crumpled on the ground, curled up in a ball to protect himself against the kicks of the assassin's pointed boots.

In desperation, William swung his left leg around, knocking Emir off his feet and onto his back. But Gregory saw the move had cost his brother dearly. Several previous injuries secured by Tufic's bandaging had now re-opened with the sudden twist of his lower body. A flood of crimson ebbed out from the wounds and onto the ground.

He's going to die.

The hashshashin raised himself to his feet, dusted his pants off, and looked down at William's battered and bleeding body.

"You have been a most worthy adversary," Emir admitted. "I am honored to be the one to end your life and I pray that Allah will have mercy on your soul."

He's really going to die.

The Saracen stooped down, picked up the Djinn's bloodied scimitar, and twirled it several times in the air, testing its balance. William said nothing but stared back at his opponent. There wasn't a shred of fear on his face.

"This is a fine blade," the hashshashin continued, raising it above his head.

I can't let him die. I can't let him die.

I won't.

The whooshing sound of the sword barreling down toward his brother filled the room. Gregory flashed to action, faster than his next thought. He plowed into the Saracen just as the sword was about to reach its mark. Both men smashed to the ground to William's left, wrestling for control of the Djinn's blade.

In a single motion, both combatants rolled to their feet. Gregory chanced a glance back at William. Still alive, it seemed, but barely. *How much blood has he lost?*

His thoughts were cut short just as the scimitar, having finally been wrested from his grasp by Emir, whirred only inches by his head. Gregory knew he had to end this soon. He was losing this fight fast. One more full-on attack and he'd find himself missing his head.

He waited for another swipe of the sword. Just as it reached its vertex, Gregory ducked into a crouch, sweeping one foot in a circle against Emir's ankles—a trick he'd learned from William. The assassin fell to the ground with a thud, the Djinn's scimitar flying from his grip. The baron quickly snatched the sword up from the ground and swung it to meet the edge of the assassin's jaw line.

Gregory smiled. The cut would leave an impressionable scar.

For the first time, Emir stared helplessly up him. Fire burned in his eyes. Defiance. He would not give up. Gregory's throat squeezed tight. He'd won. He wasn't sure how, but he had won. He decided to press his advantage. He dug his blade deeper into the assassin's neck, drawing blood. He hoped the gesture would make his intention quite clear.

"Surrender," Gregory growled.

The Saracen only smiled back at him.

"I said surrender." He pressed the sword's point deeper into his neck.

"Gregory," William croaked behind him. "No."

"Don't give me your sermons now, brother. I'm in no mood to hear how the heathen deserves to live as much as you and I."

A rustle of cloth moved behind Gregory. The fool was attempting to get up again.

"Stay down," he said to his brother, keeping his eye closely fixed on his captive. "You're too injured to move. Wait there until your servant Tufic can tend to you."

More movement from behind. The idiot never could listen to good advice.

"In the name of all that's holy, I said…" Gregory turned slightly to scold his brother's stupidity only to find himself looking at the sneering grin of Al-Dula. A long knife flashed across his throat and Gregory felt his own blood gush from the open wound.

Collapsing to his knees, the baron could hear William's

desperate screams barely above the pounding drum of his own heartbeat in his ears. He searched the room, his brother struggling to his feet and reaching down unnoticed for a single torch that lay on the ground.

What are you doing, brother? He couldn't actually speak the words as his own blood poured down his windpipe, effectively choking the life from him. Black spots danced before his eyes. Lightheaded, he looked back over to the grinning face of his murderer.

"I believe you have something of mine," the Saracen warlord said, reaching down and pulling the satchel from around Gregory's shoulder. "Now, Emir, leave them both. They'll both be dead by morning."

The sound of someone clearing his throat sounded behind the two Saracens. "Gentlemen," came a raspy voice from behind them.

Both Al-Dula and Emir turned to see the Djinn, slouching over with one arm clamped desperately at his abdomen. Blood poured from between his fingers as he glared at the two men. The lit torch clutched tight in his hand hovered precariously over one of the wooden barrels with Asian lettering.

William, what are you doing? Gregory's eyes were growing dim. He was dying. But he'd hoped that he had distracted Al-Dula and Emir long enough to allow his brother to escape.

"You should leave," he growled, lowering the torch ever so slightly. If Gregory didn't know better, he would have sworn he could see a smile underneath his brother's shroud. "This barrel contains nearly a hundred pounds of a black powder my father, Samir, discovered on his travels through Asia. It is highly flammable. With the lid off, all it will do is flare up in a quick burst of flame." He paused as he sucked in a lungful of air. "But the heat...the heat will be so intense that the other barrels... closed and compressed...will burn as well. The entire cavern will go up in a ball of flame. You want to live? Do so now before

I forget that I am not a murderer and take the two of you with us."

Do it, brother! Drop the torch! Gregory wished that his vocal cords still worked. He wished he had strength enough to light the powder himself.

But the would-be Caliph seemed unconcerned. "Fine by me," he laughed as he arrogantly strode toward the door. His hashshashin, not nearly as confident, hung back. "We have what we've come here for. We'll allow you and your infidel brother to die however you see fit."

It was the Djinn's turn to laugh now—a deep-throated, wet chuckle as he pulled his hand away from his abdomen, reached into his cloak, and pulled out a round, shiny object. It looked to Gregory like a ring. But that made no sense. Solomon's ring had been inside the chest. He'd seen it with his own eyes.

Al-Dula's eyes expanded at the sight. "What is that?" he asked, digging into Gregory's pouch, pulling out the gold chest and opening it. A gasp hissed from his open lips. "It's not here!"

"I do not understand," Emir said. "I watched you from the shadows. I saw the ring when you opened the chest myself. It was still watching when you gave it to the baron."

The Djinn's laughter increased to near hysterical proportions. It was the insane, almost manic laughter of a man who knew he was about to die—but would be victorious, nonetheless.

"Have you not heard, assassin?" the Djinn cackled. "I'm a thing of magic. It is mere child's play to conjure an item from a box." Then suddenly, his glee shifted to a somber silence. "You shall not have this evil ring. I will take it with me to the grave." He paused a final time, then spoke again. "Now. Run."

He then dropped the torch into the opened barrel, which immediately erupted in great swell of flame. Al-Dula, who was closest to the door, bolted toward freedom. His servant, Emir, lunged toward the Djinn in a last-ditch effort to wrest the arcane artifact from his enemy's grasp.

Gregory watched all this with quiet detachment. His time was nearing its end.

Of course, he knew this had been his brother's plan the entire time. It was the only way to destroy his precious golems. To bury them forever in the cavern below his homestead. He also knew that William had given him the empty box in hopes that he would escape the fate that he'd set for himself. In the end, the Djinn had tried to save even him.

Yes, he thought. *Father would be proud...as am I.*

And Gregory De L'Ombre, closing his eyes to the sound of battle and the crackling of fire, thought about his beautiful daughter...remembered his loving wife...and prayed to a God he'd abandoned years before until he was no more.

EPILOGUE

A.D. 1190 – Cairo, Five years later

Al-Dula ibn Abdul's lungs heaved violently against his chest as his bleeding bare feet pounded against the cobblestone street. He wasn't sure how much further he could go. He'd already been running since sunset and now it was nearly midnight. The Saracen warlord knew he had to find shelter, fast, from the demon.

The demon. He'd believed the creature had died...nothing more than a mere leper dressed as an ancient spirit. He'd even watched, from the safety of a desert dune, as the subterranean explosion had shaken the entire encampment. He'd seen the man's friends set the remains of his estate ablaze, in hopes that even without a body, his spirit would be lifted to the heavens. He was certain the man was dead. But two years ago, shortly after Saladin conquered Jerusalem, liberating it from the infidels, stories of the Djinn and its demonic army resurfaced.

Since that time, the creature and its Knightshades, as its army was called, seemed bent on finding Al-Dula. No matter where he settled, the demon would soon follow, as if some invisible force guided the Djinn on its quest. The skill and way it had hunted him, Al-Dula was beginning to believe it truly was a spirit sent from Allah as punishment for his sins.

A piercing, unearthly howl erupted from somewhere behind him, snapping him out of his reverie and urging him forward. The cry that sailed through the winds of the autumn Cairo evening could not possibly be human. A sliver of ice slid down the back of his neck, his body shaken by uncontrollable spasms.

Coming to the corner of a house built from desert sand and hardened by years of the blistering sun, Al-Dula peered around, looking for signs of his pursuer. A plan was forming in his brain. He had to rest first. Just a few minutes was all he would need. Then, he would make his way to Shefara's Pub and hide away in one of the rooms on the second floor. Al-Nafani's men would be there. They would keep him safe. Secure. Nothing—not even a spirit of vengeance sent by Allah himself—would be able to slip past those nomadic warriors.

Catching one more breath, the Saracen sprinted across the street, moving onto a horse trail of dirt and droppings. The pub was only two more blocks away. He craned his head, listening. Nothing. No more inhuman howling. Not even the sound of feet padding the rooftops above, as he had heard only a half a mile before. Perhaps the creature had given up. He might have actually lost the Djinn in the maze-like streets of Cairo.

He darted in and out of the shadows without incident until he came to Shefara's Pub. He slipped quietly through the oak doors and up to the bar where Shefara scrubbed away at the filth clinging to the bottom of one of her mugs. She gave him a curt glance of acknowledgment and continued at her task.

"Shefara, is Al-Nafani here?" he demanded, breathing heavily, and wiping away the perspiration that dotted his forehead. His tunic and robes were soaked with sweat, filth, and not a little blood. His portly frame was not meant for such a run. His eyes searched the room nervously.

Shefara looked up at the warlord and smiled. The few teeth remaining in her head were blackened and stained with disease.

"He's here, all right," she said as she chipped away at some hardened mass on the edge of a wooden goblet. "But I expect he's in no mood to be seeing you tonight, Al-Dula."

Al-Dula understood what she meant. After Saladin's victory of the westerners, men such as Al-Nafani and Al-Dula were now wanted for treason against the great warrior who'd liberated the Holy City in the name of Allah and unified the people. For the two of them to be seen together, would be the same as screaming their intentions of overthrowing their new Sultan.

But the Saracen had more immediate concerns now. The Djinn would track him down sooner or later. He needed a place to hide...to think about his next move and he needed protection to do it. His own men had been slaughtered by the creature and his demon army earlier that night. Only he had survived to fight another day. But it would mean little if he could not procure the protection he needed. Thankfully, Al-Nafani was as mercenary as anyone could be. For the right price, he would offer up his men no matter what the Sultan thought.

"I do not care of your opinion, woman!" he said, tossing a silver coin on the bar. "Get him. Bring him to my room."

Without waiting for a response, Al-Dula darted up the rickety staircase and plowed into the bedchamber he'd hired on retainer. He slammed the door shut, barred the door, and dropped to the thin mat on the floor used for sleeping.

Finally, with some modicum of safety, he reached into a pouch underneath his robes and removed the metal cylinder containing the *Sefer Yetzirah*, the Book of Creation. In the five years since coming into possession of the scroll, he'd only recently managed to find someone capable of translating the ancient Hebraic text. But he'd never been able to get the book to the old man long enough for a full translation to be conducted. Every time he came close, the Djinn would appear and force him on the run once more. It was maddening.

He attempted to stifle a chuckle at the irony—the two objects that would have given him an invincible army strong enough to overthrow that pompous braggart Saladin, and one was buried in a collapsed cavern under tons of rock and the other was, well, unreadable to him. His fingers mindlessly traced the intricately carved relief along the side of the scroll's container in his hands.

He stashed the Book away in his robes when footsteps scrambled in front of his door. His heart raced as he drew his dagger carefully from the sheath tucked into his belt. Strong fists pounded against the door.

"Let me in, you traitorous dog!" commanded the bark-like voice of Al-Nafani. "I haven't got all night. There's still ale to drink and women to see to."

The Saracen scrambled to his feet and rushed to open the door. Ushering his guest in, he scanned the corridor outside and secured his room once again. Taking a deep breath, he turned to face the man he was about to trust his life with...a man who had always hated and despised him.

"I need your help," he said, staring his one-time enemy in the face. "And I'll pay handsomely for it."

AL-DULA FELT secure for the first time that night, nestled in his bedchamber with four armed guards just outside the doorway. His window was now barred from the outside with iron grating. Al-Nafani's best men lay in bunks downstairs in the tavern area. And nearly one hundred other mercenaries kept watch outside in the city streets. Al-Nafani's services did not come cheap, but the fee was well deserved.

The Saracen peered through the bars of his windows at the

street. The sun would be up in three hours, and he praised Allah for that. Spirits such as the Djinn tended to avoid direct daylight and he would once again be able to slip away safely. Only a few more hours and he'd be free.

His thumb absently caressed the etched contours of the scroll container as he watched one of the mercenaries scampering for the cover of shadow across the stone paved street. *If only I'd recovered the ring,* he thought. *I'd be able create my own army of golems and the demon would never be able to come near me again.*

Al-Dula crouched down and found his place on the bed mat in the complete darkness of the room. He knew he shouldn't sleep. Though he faced a long day ahead and would need some rest, sleep was simply out of the question. His eyes closed only a few seconds before he felt the siren song of sleep creeping up on him. He knew it was a mistake, but he'd been awake for so long now. The mercenaries were on watch. What harm could there be in just a few minutes slumber? His thoughts trailed off as the oblivion of dreams engulfed him.

His eyes snapped open with a start. A warm, red glow broke through the barred windows, casting a symphony of shadows that danced to the rhythm of Al-Dula's beating heart. He became even more alert from the sounds of many feet running from the public house. *What was going on? What was happening?*

Al-Dula clambered to his knees and peeked over the sill of his window. His widened eyes stared in horror as Al-Nafani's men fled from the flames that were now consuming the building. The mercenaries were abandoning him, not even looking back to see Shefara's public house going up in flames. The cowards were running away.

"Allah preserve me," the Saracen muttered to himself as he reached for his cloak, threw it around his shoulders and unsheathed his sword. His chest heaved, but Al-Dula could not seem to gather enough air into his lungs. He looked down at the crack under the door. Black smoke ebbed its way through into his room. The fire had reached the second floor of the pub. Al-Dula had no choice. He could either stay and die in the flames or flee and hope to escape the Djinn's trap.

There really was no choice.

Throwing open the door, a wave of heat and smoke pushed the Saracen back momentarily. *Like the flames of hell itself*, he thought as he pushed forward into the blinding darkness of smoke and fire. He staggered through debris, inching his way toward the staircase and hopefully to freedom. His hand reached out, gripping the banister and he leaped three creaking steps at a time until he reached the landing.

The bar room wasn't as bad as the floor above, with only scattered fires torching a few of the tables and chairs. Across the room lay the oak door of the exit and survival. Only a few more feet. He pushed forward only to stop abruptly as the pub's door opened to reveal the solemn face of Al-Nafani, sword in hand.

"I'm sorry, old friend," the mercenary said, as he blocked the exit. "You paid well. But the Djinn paid better."

With the last comment, he nodded his head toward the back of the bar room. Al-Dula turned slowly around to see the black clad visage of the demonic spirit that had ruined the lives of so many. The creature stood stock still, neither speaking nor moving. Its taloned hands gripped two large scimitars, which whirled in tandem with one another. The creature was demonstrating its skill with the blade.

The door slammed shut behind the Saracen. The thieving mercenary had locked him in here with the beast. The creature that now walked casually toward Al-Dula with menacing grace. Its long, black flowing cloak, hood, and shroud seemed to meld themselves with the fire, smoke, and shadows...giving off a completely eldritch appearance.

"What do you want from me?" Al-Dula screamed, backing his

way toward the door. On instinct, he drew his sword from his belt and held it out toward the Djinn. He couldn't stop his arm from shaking. He lost his grip and the blade crashed helplessly to the ground.

"Please. What do you want?"

The creature, not saying a word, glided freely through the film of smoke that now filled the air. It was as if the Djinn was born of the flames themselves.

"Answer me!" he screamed as his knees buckled and he collapsed to the doorstep with nowhere else to run. His lungs burned as tears of both fear and smoke filled his eyes.

The creature stopped, just short of the Saracen. From all around them, movement caught Al-Dula's attention. From the shadows, black armored warriors materialized, surrounding the once powerful warlord. The Knightshade.

He was beaten. *I will die here this night,* he thought to himself as he scanned the room at the silent sentries that watched mercilessly.

The Djinn moved forward, bent down, and reached its hand inside Al-Dula's tunic. When the hand was withdrawn, it opened to reveal the Book of Creation.

"This does not belong to you," the creature said quietly. The voice was strange. Not at all what the Saracen had expected. It was melodious, not course and fearful. "Its rightful guardian is here now...to take it from you."

The scroll dropped back into Al-Dula's lap.

"As for you, murderer of good and noble men," the Djinn continued. "If you make it out alive tonight, see to it that you never return to the *Outremer* again."

That voice. So strange. So beautiful. Beyond what he had ever expected...what was it the creature had just said? He would live? His heart beat heavily against his breast. This was too much to believe. He would live. But the creature continued.

"Behold, your spirit of vengeance."

Sheathing both swords in its belt, the Djinn pulled its hood back.

That face.

He knew that face. Al-Dula's eyes widened in confusion and terror. It was that infidel baron's own daughter! Isabella. But what had happened to her? Her once beautiful and pristine face was now scarred and mottled with puss-filled sores. Her right eye drooped at an unnatural angle. Leprosy! She was now a leper.

"Hear me, beast," she said. "You and your treachery destroyed the lives of the two men that meant more to me than all the world. You deserve death. But today, I am able to show you mercy. Not because of me, but for the memory of the one who came before me. The one who gave his life to save others. I will not tarnish that memory with your blood."

The woman turned to her men and nodded some unspoken command. They moved silently back into the shadows of smoke and were seen no more. Looking back at Al-Dula, she drew her one of her swords again and placed it at his throat. A flick of her wrist and a small trickle of blood poured out of a tiny cut.

"That, murderer, is for my father. Let it be a reminder to you," she said. "Now, the one who protects the Book is here. It is he who has constantly led me to your path. The scroll calls to him. The bad news for you is...I don't believe he will be as forgiving as I."

And with that, Isabella stood up and looked toward the back of the tavern. In the shadows, a hulking mass emerged. A clay giant unlike any of Gregory's golems. This one had the head of a man, though no face, and was etched with strange symbols over its entire hide. Its size dwarfed those created by Rakeesha and the cold, stare of its eyeless face filled Al-Dula with dread.

"No, wait!" the Saracen screamed at Isabella. "Here, take the Book. Give it to him! I don't want it anymore!"

"I fear it's much too late for that," she said, staring in awe at the golem as it lumbered toward Al-Dula. "Much too late for that."

As the golem strode toward him, Isabella bowed slightly to it, walked around Al-Dula's trembling form, and walked out into the rising sun.